Debts of Dishonour

JILL PATON WALSH

Debts of Dishonour

An Imogen Quy Mystery

HODDER &
STOUGHTON

First published in Great Britain in 2006 by Hodder & Stoughton
A division of Hodder Headline

A Hodder & Stoughton book

1

A CIP catalogue record for this title is available from the British Library

Hardback ISBN 0340 83919 8
TPB ISBN 0340 83945 7

Typeset in Plantin by Hewer Text UK Ltd, Edinburgh
Printed and bound by Clays Ltd, St Ives plc

Hodder Headline's policy is to use papers that are natural, renewable
and recyclable products and made from wood grown in sustainable
forests. The logging and manufacturing processes are expected to
conform to the environmental regulations of the country of origin.

Hodder & Stoughton Ltd
A division of Hodder Headline
338 Euston Road
London NW1 3BH

ACKNOWLEDGEMENTS

Even a fictional college like St. Agatha's should have a plausible resemblance to a real one. My thanks are due to many Cambridge friends who have briefed me about the ins and outs of college governance. I owe a debt of thanks to Carolyn Caughey, my editor at Hodder & Stoughton for unfailing help and support, and my debt to John Rowe Townsend, now my husband, is even greater than usual.

JPW

I

'Ah, Miss Quy!' said the Master of St Agatha's College, Cambridge. 'Imogen! I'm glad I've caught you. I want to ask a favour of you.'

Imogen Quy, closing behind her the door of the room in Fountain Court which served as her office, went across the court towards him, smiling. She liked Sir William; between Master and college nurse there was long-standing affection.

'Whatever it is, the answer's yes,' she said.

'I'd be grateful if you would dine at High Table next Thursday.'

Imogen didn't often dine at High Table, though as a fellow of the college she was entitled to do so. Usually she had supper at home with her lodgers Fran and Josh.

'I'm afraid there's an ulterior motive,' Sir William said. 'It will be particularly helpful that evening to have with us a good conversationalist who is also a pretty woman.'

'Flattery, flattery,' said Imogen. She was thirty-five and didn't regard herself as a beauty, though more than one man had been attracted to her in his day. 'And isn't High Table conversation supposed to be noted for wit and brilliance rather than feminine charm?'

'It's an unusual occasion. We have a rich and important man dining with us, who may be heavy going. He doesn't have much in the way of cultural interests, or so I'm told, and he wouldn't be entertained by college gossip. I'm sure a female face and voice will cheer things up.'

'Won't Dr Longland-Smith be there? Or Mrs Mayhew?'

'Sue Longland-Smith is away on her sabbatical, and Belinda Mayhew will be giving a lecture at Bristol.'

'So I'm a fallback. I'm inclined to think I should feel insulted.'

Sir William was embarrassed. 'I'm sorry,' he said. 'I do seem to put my foot in it these days.'

'Don't worry,' Imogen said. 'I shall look forward to being there. It sounds intriguing. Who is this very rich man whose presence seems to be a problem?'

'He's actually an alumnus of the college. You must have heard of him. Sir Julius Farran. He heads the Farran Group. It's a big financial conglomerate which he built from scratch. Somebody called him the Takeover King. He buys and sells whole companies, and is massively wealthy – although, to tell you the truth, it makes me feel a little uneasy to think of concerns that are making real things, using real skills, employing real people and providing livelihoods, being bought and sold over the heads of the people who work for them.'

'It doesn't sound as if you approve of Sir Julius.'

'Well, perhaps I should be careful about jumping to conclusions. I don't really know a great deal about the world of business. The new bursar, Peter Wetherby – have you met him yet? – says that Farran is a genius in his way, and often does a company a power of good. Shakes it up and makes it perform.'

'And he's coming to dine in college.'

'Yes, at Wetherby's suggestion. It's the first time Farran has been here since I became Master, and I believe the first time since he went down, all those years ago. Actually he has a right to dine in college. Any of our MAs can do so twice a year if they care to arrange it. I understand Farran didn't distinguish himself as a student and only scraped a third. He was busying away outside, though, and I gather had made quite a lot of money by the time he went down. In due course he paid the fee and took his MA. He hasn't shown any interest in the college since then, so far as I know. But anyway, he's coming next Thursday, and bringing young Andrew Duncombe with him. You remember Andrew, of course. The most brilliant economist we've had in years. He left us; threw up his fellowship to join the Farran outfit. You're looking startled, Imogen.'

'Yes, I am, a little. I remember Andrew Duncombe well. Very well. But I wasn't expecting to see him.'

'Perhaps you thought, as many of us did, that Andrew wouldn't show his face here again, having left us so suddenly, without warning. But we shouldn't bear malice, should we? I believe he's become Farran's right-hand man. He rang me the other day to warn me that the great man would be coming and to give me a few tips on how to deal with him. The tips, he said, were off the record. Ply him with plenty of wine, keep the conversation general and lively, don't let him get on his high horse, don't argue with him, because he can be difficult if crossed . . .'

'And make sure you have a resident pretty woman.'

'Oh, really!' said Sir William. 'I've apologised once. Once is enough.'

'It sounds like an irresistible occasion,' Imogen said. 'Thank you very much. I'll look forward to Thursday. And it will be – er – interesting to see Andrew again. I liked him rather a lot.'

'You manage to like most people, don't you, Imogen? An endearing characteristic. Most of the fellows don't like him at all; they say he sold out. But there, you were just on your way home, weren't you? Ride that bike of yours safely, my dear. We can't afford to lose you.'

Imogen left the college by the Chesterton Lane gate and pedalled home to Newnham. Her way was along the Backs, beautiful even now on a bleak day of late winter, but all her attention was needed to preserve her life in the heavy traffic. She entered the relative peace of Newnham Croft with relief. Her own house, on one of the streets that led off Grantchester Street, was a welcome refuge from a job that she loved but that could be demanding. It was just a week into the Lent term, the peak time for sporting injuries. Undergraduates were notably remiss in protecting their own persons. And there was always somebody needing relief from a minor ailment, or a shoulder to weep on. In addition, she'd allowed her off-duty hours to become a little too fully occupied with voluntary activities. Today she had to feed somebody's cat, visit an old lady who was in good health but low spirits, and telephone friends to arrange a meeting of the Quilters' Club. It was pleasant to get home and find that Fran, a research student at St Agatha's and by now a close friend, was in the house and fixing herself a scratch lunch out of the fridge.

Fran cut a rough cheese sandwich and a large tomato in two, and passed half across to Imogen.

'What's the news from college?' she inquired.

'Fascinating, as a matter of fact. I have to help to entertain a tycoon, Sir Julius Farran. Know who he is?'

'I've heard of him. Isn't he supposed to be a bit of a crook?'

'I wouldn't know about that. He's incredibly rich, and he's a St Agatha's man.'

'And potential benefactors are always welcome?'

'Come now, Fran,' said Imogen sternly, 'how could you harbour such unworthy thoughts?' That particular unworthy thought had in fact occurred to her during her conversation with the Master. But it was not Sir Julius who was uppermost in her mind.

'And would you believe it, Andrew Duncombe is coming over, too.'

Fran sat up, interested. 'Andrew Duncombe! I went to his lectures at one time, as an undergraduate. We all thought he was brilliant. And . . . have I got it wrong? Isn't he the Andrew you used to talk about a lot? The one who was . . . close to you?'

'Yes, he was close to me,' Imogen said. 'Perhaps too close.'

'But it ended when he left the college?'

'How do you know there was any "it" about it? He was a friend.'

'There are friends and friends,' observed Fran sagely. 'And there are "just good friends". I've always supposed he was one of those. You were fond of him, weren't you?'

Yes, I was fond of him, thought Imogen. And that was the right phrase for it. She'd been fond of Andrew; she hadn't been in love with him. Yet he'd been her lover for more than a year.

It hadn't been the tempestuous passion of her youth, the passion that had cost her such devastating agony, to say nothing of a medical career, when she had given all for love and been brutally abandoned. That passion had seared her, left her wretched for years, still made her wretched when she thought about it. She had known she couldn't go through all that again, felt she would never again trust any man. Maybe, she'd felt then, she would be celibate for the rest of her life.

She'd taken the job at St Agatha's. Then Andrew had arrived, a young lecturer of her own age, married but in process of divorce. Andrew had confided in her; people always did. His experiences had paralleled hers. For him, too, there had been a passionate and prolonged affair, but for him it had ended in marriage. And the marriage had been disastrous; a few months later his wife had contemptuously left him for a man who had lots of charisma but was, in Andrew's opinion, intellectually null.

He and Imogen had comforted each other, and the comfort had led, before very long, to bed. It hadn't been a passionate relationship, but it had been quite a satisfactory one. There was attraction enough to make it work on the physical plane. Andrew had turned out to be a deft and considerate lover. They hadn't lived together and hadn't seen any need to tell the world about themselves; if whispers got around the college or the neighbourhood, they didn't get to Imogen's ears. They had made a point of not being committed to each other; if they weren't committed neither of them could be let down.

When, after a year, Andrew told Imogen he was joining the Farran Group and would be leaving Cambridge, he'd made it clear that this would end the affair; he'd offered a somewhat muted apology and she'd told him there was nothing to apologise for. After he went, she missed him more than she'd expected, but it was nothing like a replay of the earlier disaster. She had settled down to being on her own again and been tolerably content, though well aware that for a childless woman in her mid-thirties the clock was ticking. They sent each other Christmas cards.

'I heard something about him a few weeks ago,' she told Fran. 'I was told that he had a glamorous girlfriend. Maybe he's going to marry again.'

'And you wish him happiness?'

'Why not? He hasn't done me any harm.'

After Fran had gone, she went on thinking about Andrew. So now he was rising rapidly in the Farran empire. Making lots of money, probably. And with a girlfriend who was no doubt beautiful and fashionable.

She'd heard it said that Andrew had sold his soul. Had he really? It would be interesting to see him again. And to meet the man who'd bought it.

2

With help from Fran, Imogen applied unaccustomed make-up to her face and wriggled into her one and only long dress, a rather slinky green silk. This wasn't suitable attire for cycling to college, and her car was currently on loan to a friend two counties away, but Fran's boyfriend Josh gave her a lift in his decrepit Skoda. Her return time being uncertain, she would go home by taxi. Josh, who held mildly left-wing views, was a little shocked at the thought of Imogen hobnobbing with capitalism, but at the same time he and Fran were eager to hear what Julius Farran was like at close quarters.

It seemed that someone had got wind of the great man's visit, for a small demonstration with a couple of placards denouncing global capitalism was forming up at the main gate. Josh threatened, not too seriously, to abandon the car and join the demonstration, but relented and drove Imogen round to the side gate in Chesterton Lane, from which she could enter the college without having to run a gauntlet. She arrived early for sherry, traditionally served in the Parlour from seven to seven thirty, to find the Master already there, with two or three of the senior fellows and the new bursar.

'I'm still having pangs of conscience,' said Sir William, 'at getting you into this. But I'm sure you will improve the occasion and if necessary have a civilising effect. And if I may say so, how charming you look!'

Imogen was aware of Sir William's generosity with his

compliments and regarded it as an amiable weakness. But it had its effect; from being a little nervous she was suddenly confident, feeling that she looked good and was equal to this or any other occasion.

'You know Dr Barton and Professor Sunderland, of course,' Sir William said. 'But I don't think you've met Peter Wetherby. Peter, this is Miss Quy, whom we are lucky enough to have as our college nurse.'

'Imogen,' said Imogen.

She looked at the new bursar with interest. His predecessor, though kind and considerate, was generally thought to have been insufficiently worldly for the appointment, and to have let the college finances slide. There had been relief when he retired. Wetherby looked to be made of sterner stuff. He was a man of a little over average height, fiftyish, trim, immaculately turned out. He had a clipped, decisive voice, a small moustache, and a faintly military air. He had, she thought, a cold eye; and he didn't seem impressed by Imogen.

'I shall hope not to trouble you,' he said to her with a little smile, and turned back to the Master.

The room was filling up, but, to the expert eyes of those present, rather slowly.

'It looks like being a low turnout,' said Dr Barton. 'Some of the younger fellows are conspicuously absent.'

'They don't want to break bread with Julius Farran,' said Professor Sunderland. 'But,' – as two new figures appeared in the doorway – 'the Terrible Twins are here.'

The Master looked round. 'So they are,' he said. 'Conspicuously present. Damn. I hoped they'd be among the absentees.'

'I'm afraid they're here in disgust,' said Dr Barton. 'I have forebodings.'

Imogen knew the Terrible Twins well. They were junior

fellows, and were the college's resident extremists. They were a contrasting pair. Carl Janner was smooth in speech and manner, and dressed with a touch of dandyism. Imogen suspected that under the misleading exterior was a sharp and focused mind. Clive Horrocks was slight, pale, with thin, carroty hair, reedy voice, and a tendency to sarcasm. Both were probably in their late twenties.

'But where is our distinguished guest?' asked Barton. 'Are we sure he's going to turn up?'

'Frankly, it would be a relief if he didn't,' said the Master.

Sir Julius, mindful perhaps of the rigours of college accommodation as it had been in his youth, was not staying in college but at the Garden House hotel. He arrived in the Parlour five minutes before the summons to hall. Andrew Duncombe, the fellow who'd defected, was with him, a tactful step behind. It was undoubtedly an entrance. The people nearest the door fell back; the Master advanced with hand outstretched.

Julius Farran was in his later sixties: a large, bulky man. He wore a new-looking MA gown, which obviously wasn't his natural garb. Academic gowns, Imogen had long suspected, were designed for the lean, impoverished scholars of long ago, and always seemed slightly absurd on the corpulent. But Farran had presence and looked what he was: a man of power, accustomed to dominate the company he was in. A bit past his best, though, she thought. A big, heavy face, a dangerously high colour, bags under the eyes; but the eyes themselves were small and shrewd.

He was not, at first, in a good mood.

'I suppose the show of force at the main gate is in my honour,' he said. 'Not quite the welcome one would have chosen.'

'We can't stop a peaceful demo,' the Master said, 'and I

don't suppose we'd try to if we could. They're entitled to let off steam. I'm sure there won't be any violence.'

'I should hope not,' said Sir Julius. But he was thawing. 'Thank you, Master,' he said, accepting a glass of sherry, 'for not showing me the cold shoulder, reappearing in the college after all these years.'

'A pleasure for all of us,' said the Master, courteous even if on this occasion untruthful.

'It was Wetherby here who suggested I should come,' said Farran. 'And young Duncombe as well. An excellent idea. I should have thought of it long ago.'

The Master introduced two or three senior fellows and Imogen, on whom Sir Julius's eye rested appraisingly for a moment or two. And after brief courtesies had been exchanged, Sir William led the way in to dinner, signalling to Farran to take the seat on his right, and to Imogen to sit on his left. The senior fellows and the bursar were also at the top of the table; a rather small number of their juniors, including the Terrible Twins, were lower down, and with them Andrew Duncombe.

At the head of the table, conversation went reasonably well, though a little stiffly at first. Farran asked the Master questions which the Master had answered many times and was quite willing to answer again, on perennial academic issues: the threatened independence of the university and of its colleges; the sources of its funding; the criteria for appointment of fellows and the admission of undergraduates. Farran pro-pounded the view, commonplace but always acceptable at high tables, that Britain's top universities needed their freedom if they were to stay in the world's premier league and that they must contrive to admit as students the brightest and most promising young people, wherever they could be found. He didn't, as Imogen had half expected, set a cat among the pigeons by claiming that universities would be more successful if run as commercial enterprises by captains of industry.

Imogen noticed, however, that he was pushing his glass forward rather frequently to be refilled with the college's good claret, and as the meal went on he relaxed into informality and reminiscence. He recalled his own undergraduate days, which seemed to have been enjoyable if undistinguished. He gave it to be understood that he had been fined for a couple of minor misdemeanours, had rowed in the college's third boat, and had enjoyed the favours of more than one young woman from Newnham or Girton. He hadn't gone to many lectures or done much work, he admitted, which no doubt was why he'd got a poor degree, but it hadn't done him any harm in life.

Over pudding and a fine dessert wine, he turned to Imogen, looking at her with some interest. He inquired about her life and duties, and expressed the view that the college must feel itself fortunate to have her.

'Indeed we do,' said the Master. 'Continually.'

Further down the table, the talk was less harmonious. From where she sat, Imogen could hear little of what was being said, but it sounded first disapproving, then angry. Much of the anger seemed to be directed at Andrew. The rounded baritone of Janner and jarring reedy tenor of Horrocks stood out. Andrew was being accused by his former colleagues of treachery, of prostituting his talents, and of pushing his snout into the capitalist trough. He was defending himself quietly and steadily, but clearly not enjoying the experience.

At the end of dinner the Master said grace and led the way into the senior common room, where port, Madeira and fruit were laid out. Seating in the room was arranged, as was the custom at St Agatha's, so that the party could break into three or four conversational groups. This was where the Terrible Twins carried out their coup. By a neat and swift manoeuvre they guided Sir Julius into a group consisting of themselves and like-minded colleagues.

Carl went straight in to the attack. 'Sir Julius,' he began, 'I believe you made your first million while you were still an undergraduate.'

Sir Julius, not knowing what he was in for, smiled wearily and said, 'Yes. Everyone knows that. It's brought out whenever I'm mentioned in the newspapers.'

'And may I ask how you did it?'

'That's common knowledge, too. I was a poor boy from industrial Yorkshire, here on a scholarship. I saved a hundred pounds from my first year's grant and bought a big old house on a mortgage to rent out to other students. It made a profit; I branched out into other ventures and gradually they got bigger. It wasn't difficult. That's what I say when people ask me the secret of success. A little talent and a lot of application, I tell them. The rest will follow . . .'

'You had a state scholarship, I believe, and they came with generous grants in those days. Do you think that using the university as a launching pad for a business career was a proper use of the public money that financed it?'

'There were no strings to the grant,' said Sir Julius. 'I think I used it rather well.'

A junior fellow came round offering port or Madeira. Sir Julius took the Madeira. Carl Janner leaned forward with the air of an inquisitor.

'So you went down already rich,' he said. 'Soon after that, didn't you bring off your first takeover of a company?'

'Yes, I did,' said Sir Julius. 'Why are you asking me? All of this is on the record. Could we not talk about something else?'

'The first company you acquired was a finance company, Loan-Easy or some such name. It lent money to poor people at high interest, didn't it?'

'At a rate appropriate to the market,' Sir Julius said.

'Moneylending!' put in Clive Horrocks.

Sir Julius made no response, but was now looking irritated.

Carl Janner went on: 'Then you took over West Midlands Engineering, and within weeks you sacked four thousand employees.'

'It was that or liquidation.'

'And you sold the company at a profit of nearly five million!'

Carl's tone was moving from questioning to assertion. Obviously he had prepared his brief. He went on to speak of property deals, of donations to political parties, of competitors either bought up or driven out of the market. The Madeira came round again, and Sir Julius accepted a refill. By now he was growing angry.

'This has gone on long enough!' he declared. 'I didn't come here to be interrogated!'

Andrew Duncombe said to Carl, 'Why don't you put your questions in writing? Sir Julius will gladly answer them. This is not the time or place.'

Carl took no notice. 'Companies that you own are importing cheap goods at the expense of our jobs and our economy. And outsourcing their call centres to Asian countries that pay Third World staff at a fraction of what you would have to pay them in this country.'

Sir Julius, furious now, rose to his feet. 'They are well paid by the standards of their own countries!' he declared. 'We are giving them a livelihood. And now, once and for all, will you please let this subject drop!'

He had raised his voice. Other conversations in the room died, and everyone listened. Out of the silence came the thin, abrasive voice of Clive Horrocks.

'The subject,' he announced, 'is racist exploitation!'

Sir Julius, face redder than ever, struggled to speak.

Peter Wetherby said, loudly and angrily, 'This is a disgrace! How dare you treat a guest like this?'

'Sir Julius is not a guest,' said Carl Janner. 'He is a member of the college.'

'Master!' Sir Julius appealed across the room. 'Can you not put a stop to it?'

Sir William had risen to his feet, but was clearly at a loss. The Master of a college is not like the chief executive of a company. Essentially he is a first among equals, with little power to give orders and less to see them carried out. He hesitated.

Imogen had already been alarmed by Sir Julius's florid complexion. Now he was breathing hard and obviously under stress. Without stopping to think, she plunged in. She had once been a ward sister, and knew what an air of authority could achieve. She marched across to the Terrible Twins.

'Just pack it in, you two!' she told them. 'Do you want to give the man a heart attack?'

There was a brief, startled silence.

Then, 'Piss off, Imogen!' said Clive.

But Carl, quite relaxed, leaned back. 'OK,' he said. 'We've made our point. There's no need to go on with this. Come on, Clive, let's not waste any more time!'

The two of them stalked out. The Master went across to Sir Julius.

'I am so sorry,' he said. 'Please don't think that display was typical in any way. I doubt whether anything like it has happened before in the history of the college, and I hope it never will again. Perhaps Miss Quy and I could take the empty seats and we could turn to more pleasant matters.'

Sir Julius was not to be mollified. 'No, thank you,' he said. 'Enough is enough. Andrew, will you call the Garden House and get my car and driver sent round? And, Master, I suppose there's a loo somewhere at hand? I'm afraid I'm not feeling too well.'

'There's one close by, in Fountain Court. Just through that door and down the steps. But do be careful.'

Sir Julius lumbered across the room. Imogen realised that he was slightly drunk. There were only three steps down, but they were too many. He stumbled, there was a cry of alarm, and he was sprawling at the foot of them. The Master and Dr Barton went to him and lifted him up, but he couldn't put his right foot to the ground and seemed unable to move on his own.

'Oh, my God!' groaned the Master. 'What a night of disasters! And thank Him once more for Imogen! Where is she?'

'Here I am,' Imogen said.

Five minutes later, Sir Julius Farran was in a chair in Imogen's little surgery; she had given him painkillers and was attending to a sprained and already swelling ankle.

'I'm putting this cold compress on it,' she said, having stripped off shoe and sock and rested Sir Julius's foot in her lap. 'We'll give it half an hour or so and then I'll bandage it up. I'm pretty sure there isn't a fracture, but you ought to have it seen by a doctor.'

'It isn't going to be,' said Sir Julius. He seemed to have been more physically than mentally affected by what he'd drunk, and was certainly sober by now. 'I've had enough trouble without that. It was bad enough having to be attacked by those two young slobs, and now this . . . Those steps are a menace. I've half a mind to sue the college. Serve it right if I did.' He laughed, then winced. 'You're a good girl,' he said. 'I like you. I'd give you a job any day. Why don't you follow Andrew and join me at Farran Group?'

As if on cue, there was a tap at the door and Andrew, who

was familiar with Fountain Court and knew Imogen's surgery well, came in.

'How are you now, Julius?' he inquired.

'Surviving. Do you know this young lady?'

'I do indeed,' said Andrew.

'I've just offered her a job.'

'I have a job already,' said Imogen. 'Please don't try to get up, Sir Julius. I want you to rest a bit longer.'

'The car's outside, when he's ready,' said Andrew. 'It's roomy. It won't be any trouble getting him into it. And the demo has melted away.'

Imogen found another chair, and the three of them sat in silence for a few minutes. Sir Julius looked as if, relieved by the painkillers, he might be nodding off. Imogen studied Andrew. It was only a year since she'd last seen him, but he'd changed. The thick black hair was tinged with grey, which suited him. The thin, clever face had filled out a little. He'd obviously left his gown in the car; his collar and tie were immaculate and his suit was of a cut and material not commonly seen in St Agatha's. Subtly he seemed to have modulated from academic to businessman. But when he cast a glance at her and half smiled, there was a sudden glimpse of the Andrew she'd known so intimately. She smiled in response without thinking, then reminded herself sternly that he belonged in her past, not in her present life.

Sir Julius had not gone to sleep after all. He was looking at both of them through sharp, heavy-lidded eyes. Though sober now, he seemed shaken.

'I'm not worried about those two idiots,' he said. 'They're not going to assassinate me; they can't even damage me. But there are those around who can, you know, and would if they got the chance. You don't have a life history like mine without making enemies, real enemies. There are some who'd blow my brains out, or more likely stick a dagger in my back. And some of them aren't far away. I have to be on the alert all the time.'

'I'm not going to take that seriously,' said Imogen. 'You're upset.'

'I'm perfectly serious,' Sir Julius said. 'Andrew could tell you. Luckily, I've managed to gather a few people around me whom I can trust. But if I were an insurance company I wouldn't insure the life of Julius Farran.'

'Perhaps we should drop this subject,' said Andrew. His tone of voice made it sound like a polite 'Shut up.'

Sir Julius wasn't shutting up. 'I'm sure Miss Quy – I shall call her Imogen – is the soul of discretion,' he said. 'You have to be discreet in your profession, haven't you, Imogen? I'm a judge of character, I know I can trust you. And,' he added with emphasis, 'my life is not secure. My enemies are cunning. If one of these days you read that I have fallen under a bus, remember these words!'

'I'll try to forget them,' said Imogen. 'You're not yourself tonight, Sir Julius. And now I'm going to bind up that ankle. I'll give you some more paracetamol; you should get home and to bed. And tomorrow morning I really do think you should see your doctor, to make sure it's nothing serious.'

Later, in the taxi going home, Imogen recalled the fierce intensity with which Sir Julius had made his last remark. She'd said she would try to forget it, but she knew she couldn't. She would have a lot to tell Fran and Josh about the events of the evening, but the discretion he had imposed on her would prevent her from telling them that.

3

Next morning, Sir Julius telephoned Imogen, without the intermediacy of any secretary, to thank her in terms at once apologetic and cordial for her attention to his ankle. It transpired that he had already telephoned Sir William Buckmote, and their apologies had been mutual. They had agreed, said Sir Julius, that the events of the evening were to be put out of mind. It was to be as though they had never happened. The relationship between Sir Julius and St Agatha's was valued on both sides and would continue in happier circumstances.

Sir Julius then surprised Imogen by inviting her to the boardroom lunch that took place on the first Thursday of each month at his offices in the City. It was just a get-together of his top management, he said, not an occasion for talking shop, and they liked to have a guest. She might find it interesting, and his colleagues would be sure to enjoy her company. The next occasion was in the following week.

Imogen thanked him politely. She didn't decline the invitation, but pleaded pressure of work and put it on hold. And she had hardly hung up when Andrew rang, to add his apologies for the previous night's embarrassment.

'I can't help feeling,' he said, 'that if it hadn't been for my suggesting it Julius wouldn't have been there and it wouldn't have happened.'

'A bright guy like you should be able to spot an elementary

fallacy,' Imogen said. 'If all sorts of things hadn't happened, this wouldn't have happened. If the Terrible Twins hadn't set on him, and he hadn't got upset, he wouldn't have fallen down those steps. Or he might have fallen down them anyway. Or he might have been run over as he left his office. You're not to blame, Andrew.'

'Of course you're right, I'm not culpable. It's just that "if-only" feeling. Never mind. The truth is, Imogen, I'm ringing because I want to talk to you.'

'You're doing so now. Go ahead.'

'I'd like it to be more than a phone call. There are things I'd like to discuss with you face to face. Why don't we have lunch together some time soon?'

'Well . . . what are the headings for discussion?' Imogen asked cautiously.

'Some are to do with my working for the Farran Group. I don't know whether I can go on doing so or not. It all depends on Julius, and I'm worried about him, for reasons I'll explain to you. And I have personal difficulties that I'd find easier to discuss with you than with anyone else.'

'Easier with me than with your girlfriend?'

'That's part of the problem. She and I are in process of breaking up. I have to talk to somebody who'll understand. And that's you. So perhaps for old times' sake . . .'

'You know we can't go back, Andrew. That affair's over. But if you need a shoulder to weep on, mine's always available.'

'As many an undergraduate can testify,' said Andrew. 'I'd still like to talk things over with you. It's that gift of yours.'

Imogen was touched. She'd been fond of him, after all. A recollection of the old intimacy moved like a shadow across her consciousness.

'Of course,' she said. 'As for lunch, did Sir Julius tell you he'd invited me to the boardroom lunch?'

'I didn't know that. Julius acts on impulse. But I'm glad. I hope you accepted.'

'Actually I played for time.'

'Well, do say yes. You'll find it interesting and you'll get an idea of the way things are at Farran. I shall be there, and we can get together for tea afterwards. Pencil it in your diary now.'

'So I let him fix it,' Imogen told Fran.

'Really!' said Fran. 'Sometimes I think you aren't fit to be allowed out by yourself. You just can't see a stile without wanting to help a lame dog over it. What's in this for you?'

'Well, nothing much,' Imogen admitted. 'But Andrew seems to be in trouble, and I can't just behave as if it had nothing to do with me.'

'I don't see why not. You don't owe him anything. Men! Just you watch out. Don't let him start things up with you again.'

'I've made that clear to him. I don't suppose he'll want to, anyway.'

'His marriage failed. You restored him to sanity. So then he walked out on you . . .'

'He didn't walk out on me. He walked out on the college.'

'Same thing, in effect. Then off he went and leaped into another relationship, and that's failing too. You know, once might be a misfortune, but twice looks like incompetence.'

'A misquote from Oscar Wilde,' said Imogen. 'Don't be so heartless, Fran.'

'You bring out the cynic in me,' said Fran.

'And I'm a bit worried about Sir Julius,' Imogen said. 'He seemed last night like a man getting to the end of his tether.

He shows all the signs of stress and high blood pressure, and I'm sure he drinks too much.'

'I despair,' said Fran. 'Incurable and indiscriminate helpfulness, that's what you suffer from. Probably terminal.'

There were always things to be done in London, and it was a fine day. Imogen's programme included coffee with an old friend, an art exhibition, and a little window-shopping for things she couldn't afford. At half past twelve she turned up at the premises of the Farran Group, in a street in the City that bore an ancient name but was now a narrow canyon between monuments to unimaginative modernity. The Farran building had branches of three or four banks among its companions, and seemed to have done its best to look like one. The lettering over its doorway was in discreet Roman capitals; the lower part of its façade was in a granite the colour of pale cheese, flecked with spots of marmalade. The lobby was of heel-clicking dark green marble, the reception desk of solid mahogany.

Imogen gave her name, waited for five minutes, and was greeted by a fashionably dressed young woman who announced herself as Fiona and led her to the lift. She was attractive, indeed stunning: convincingly blonde, with expertly styled hair, grey-blue eyes, a perfect complexion and an air of friendly superiority. She explained as she escorted Imogen to the floor above and along a short carpeted landing that she was Sir Julius's personal assistant. Imogen, trained by experience to pick up minor indications from expression or gesture, noted almost unconsciously the perfunctoriness of Fiona's tap on Sir Julius's door and the hint of familiarity in her address to her employer.

Sir Julius's room was more like a spacious and comfortable study than an office, equipped with a sofa and two armchairs and lined with bookshelves. A massive desk, singularly free of paperwork, occupied only a corner of it. Sir Julius lumbered across to greet her, guided her to a seat, and thanked her gravely for coming.

He looked a different man from the one who had stumbled into her surgery, flushed, distressed and breathing hard, a few nights earlier. He was on his own ground here, dominating the room, wearing a suit that did all a suit could do to disguise his embonpoint. And he seemed pleased to see her.

'I'm glad to see you're not limping,' Imogen said.

'No, the sprain went away, thanks to your ministration.'

'And I don't suppose you saw your doctor.'

'No, I didn't. I don't believe in calling in the medics if I can help it. We're programmed to recover naturally from most things, aren't we? I like to leave it to nature.'

Imogen, noting afresh his high colour, suppressed a momentary impulse to ask him whether he'd had his blood pressure checked lately. He was undoubtedly sober, but his eyes were slightly bloodshot and there was just the faintest suggestion of an aroma around him, perhaps of whisky.

He went on, 'It was rather an unhappy evening at St Agatha's, I'm afraid. However, I hope I've mended fences with Sir William. It's an association I'd like to develop.'

Imogen let that pass.

'Apart from meeting the Master,' Sir Julius said, 'the one thing that redeemed the evening, to tell you the truth, was making your acquaintance.'

Imogen let that one pass, too.

'So it's a personal pleasure to see you here today. But it may have occurred to you, as an intelligent woman, that I could have an ulterior motive. It wasn't a passing whim when I talked of offering you a job. I would very much like to have you with me here. In the Farran Group, I mean.'

Imogen was startled. She hadn't taken the remark about a job seriously. 'I'm very happy with the college,' she said.

'We need a bit of beefing up in the personnel department,' said Sir Julius. 'We're supposed to call it Human Resources these days. Employee health and happiness and all that. And you showed just the qualities I would look for. Decisiveness, as when you dealt with those two young men. Obvious competence in your profession, a sympathetic way of dealing with people, a gift, I would surmise, of intuition, and under it all just a touch of steel, a toughness that would be there if really needed. Am I right?'

'It's not for me to say,' said Imogen.

'How much does the college pay you?' Sir Julius asked.

Caught on the wrong foot by the suddenness of the demand, she told him.

'I can offer you three times that,' he said. 'With prospects, if you do well.'

'I'm afraid . . .' Imogen began, but Sir Julius stopped her.

'I don't need an answer this minute,' he said. 'Think about it. I asked you to this lunch partly so you can meet the head office team. That will help you decide.'

And in the sparsely elegant boardroom a little later, over a pre-lunch glass of champagne, Imogen met a group of people who might be thought of, she realised, as potential colleagues.

They were, she noted, six men and only one woman. The woman and all but one of the men were middle-aged; all seven wore suits. Sir Julius introduced her first to an older-looking man, Lord Robinswood.

Lord Robinswood was tall, slim, handsome in a sixty-plus way, with crisp, slightly wavy silver hair. He bent courteously towards Imogen, expressed polite interest in her work at St Agatha's and informed her that he was an old acquaintance of

Lady Buckmote, the Master's wife. A few casually dropped remarks let her know that he moved in distinguished circles; he was a former ambassador to important countries and now applied his talents to counselling important companies. But the conversation didn't have much time to develop before Sir Julius moved her along to the person next to him. This was a tall, massively built but not overweight man, probably in his mid-forties, with thick dark hair, heavy brows, deep-set eyes and a slightly swarthy complexion. His physique contributed to an air of power and authority which if anything exceeded that of Sir Julius. As a pair they were impressive.

'This is Max,' Sir Julius said. 'Max Holwood. He is our chief executive. He's also my son-in-law, although that has nothing to do with his appointment.'

'The appointment came first, you see,' said Max. His voice was rich and deep.

'This is Miss Quy, Max, whom I've told you about.'

'Yes, of course.' Max looked searchingly at Imogen; she felt momentarily uneasy under his scrutiny. 'You're at St Agatha's, Miss Quy, aren't you? Now, let's see, what ought I to call you? Is it Professor or Doctor?'

His tone of voice was genial, but Imogen could recognise a put-down when she met one. Max must know perfectly well who and what she was. He was not so much placing her as putting her in her place.

'My name is Imogen,' she said. 'You're welcome to call me by it. I am the college nurse.'

'An important personage, I'm sure,' said Max. Again his voice was friendly, but the tone was patronising, a shade derogatory. He looked away from her towards the door. 'And I see that St Agatha's is well represented here today. Julius seems to be creating quite an enclave.'

Imogen had already noticed that Andrew was in the room,

though he had not yet spoken to her. But the new arrival was a surprise.

'It's Mr Wetherby,' she said. 'Our new bursar.'

'Yes. He's a non-executive director here. It doesn't take a great deal of his time. We're quite happy for him to be a college bursar as his main vocation. We're rather pleased with the link. And now you must meet Helen.' Max led Imogen across to the only other woman in the room. 'Helen Alderton. Helen is our head of personnel.'

Imogen started. She had just been offered a job in Helen Alderton's department. Julius had made no mention of consulting anyone about it. Would Helen see her as a potential rival? Imogen smiled, a little uncertainly, as Max moved away. Helen – dark, thin, with broad high brow, narrow chin, and visible lines of disapproval in her face – didn't respond.

'You come from academia,' she said.

'Yes, I suppose so. I'm not really an academic, though.' Imogen declared her profession once more.

'I'm glad to hear it,' Helen said. 'Academics don't really cut the mustard with me. I've known and worked with a good many of them, and found more noses in the air than feet on the ground.' Helen looked around her; for the moment there was no one within earshot. She went on, 'Well, at least as a nurse you're in the real world. Welcome to this male-dominated corner of it. And to think I married into it. That's my husband, Bill McNair, over there. Bill is useful to Julius, or Julius would have had me out. He went off me long ago.'

Somewhat startled by this bitterness, Imogen said brightly, 'You must have an interesting job. And very responsible.'

'I'll allow you to say that. But it's responsibility without power. Too much high-level interference.' A pause. Then, 'Look, I don't have to be told why you're here. Julius is trying you on for size. He probably knows I'll leave before long anyway.'

'I haven't any intention . . .' Imogen began; but Sir Julius was returning and she left the sentence unfinished.

She was introduced briefly to Helen's husband, Bill McNair, the finance director, a small wiry Scot, sharp-faced, fast-talking and probably fast-thinking. Lastly, she met Lester Hancock, head of marketing, who interrupted the telling of a long, involved joke to ask her how she was doing, but went back to it without waiting for a reply. By the time the somewhat feeble point of the joke had been reached, Sir Julius had moved over to the table and people were taking their seats.

She hadn't known what to expect of the boardroom lunch. Actually it was rather lavish. Smoked pheasant breast for a starter was followed by baked sea bass on a bed of green lentils, poire belle Hélène and an extensive array of cheeses. The wines were a Châteauneuf-du-Pape with the starter, a Pouilly-Fuissé with the fish, a Sauternes with the dessert and a Taylor '86 port for those who still had capacity. Seated in the place of honour beside Sir Julius, Imogen had the agreeable consciousness of being liked by her host, and was inclined to think that Helen Alderton's sourness was either intrinsic to her character or connected with resentment at a potential rival. She had to remind herself of Sir Julius's reputation as an aggressive and predatory businessman.

Sir Julius wasn't playing that part at present. He told her of his country house in Suffolk, to which he retired for relaxation at the weekend when he could, although that was not as often as he would wish; of the garden which was his pride and joy although he didn't have much time to tend it himself; of his wife of twenty-five years, who didn't care for London, and of his daughter Rowena.

'Who of course is married to Max,' he said. 'And lives in the next village to ours with her two boys. I'm afraid neither Max nor I can spend as much time with our families as we might wish. Some might describe us as workaholics.'

'You speak for yourself, Julius,' said Max from across the table, 'not for me. I work hard while I'm here and forget about it when I'm not.' To Imogen he added, 'Julius really is a workaholic. I tell him from time to time that he should ease off. But he takes no notice.'

His tone was humorous, but Imogen detected an edge to it. She turned the conversation aside by asking Julius about his grandsons. It appeared that he felt affectionately towards them and gave them handsome presents at birthdays and for Christmas, but didn't actually know them very well. From further along the table, the voice of Helen Alderton was momentarily heard in apparent disputation with another board member. Lord Robinswood entered the conversation and smoothed things down with the effortless suavity of one who had survived a diplomatic lifetime; and increasing attention to the meal was accompanied by a growing sense of calm and relaxation. Imogen sensed that under the surface of harmony there were tensions and cross-currents, but Sir Julius didn't seem to be aware of them. She noted with disapproval that he was drinking more wine than she would have thought wise, and Max was not far behind him.

The lunch did not drag on. It was not intended to. The executive directors – the two McNairs and Hancock – had their jobs to go to. Max had an appointment in his office. The two non-executive directers, Lord Robinswood and Wetherby, disappeared together, intending to share a taxi to the West End. Sir Julius shook Imogen's hand, thanked her warmly for coming and said he hoped to hear from her, then stumped off towards his room.

Andrew, who hadn't talked to Imogen at the lunch, now appeared at her shoulder. 'I'm not going back to work today,' he said. 'And it's still fine. Let me walk you down to Covent Garden, and we'll have some tea.'

4

'S o,' Andrew said. 'You've now had a glimpse of Farran Group. Of course, the board is only the tip of the iceberg. But those are the people I have to work with, and that you'd work with if you accepted Julius's offer.'

'It was only a glimpse,' Imogen said. 'There must be a lot going on that I don't know about.'

'There is indeed. Let me fill you in. First, Julius and Max. You must have seen this for yourself. Julius is the old lion. He's led the pack for years, and he's always been a brilliant operator. If it was a matter of picking up a dying company and bringing it round, or putting together a spectacular deal, or carrying out a coup from which he walked away with a huge immediate profit, Julius was your man. And he had time and energy to be quite a womaniser as well.'

'He's been married for a long time, hasn't he?'

'Oh, yes. To Lucia. She always knew what he was like. They have separate lives, but they still get on well together. In fact she's on the board, though she doesn't often go to board meetings and you won't see her at the boardroom lunch. I think they're fond of each other, in their way.'

'He mentioned a daughter, Rowena. I suppose she's some-thing they have in common?'

'Well, no. Lucia's his second wife. Rowena's mother is the first wife, Anne, who's still alive and lives with her. As Julius got his knighthood after the divorce, it's Lucia who is Lady

Farran. Julius is devoted to Rowena, and I suppose to the grandsons, though he doesn't quite know what to make of them. He was never one of nature's dads. Kicking a ball around and that kind of thing are not for Julius.'

'And Max?'

Andrew frowned. 'Yes, Max. Max is the young lion, though he's not all that young. Forty-six next year. Max was Julius's discovery, fifteen years or so ago. Julius saw Max as a kind of second self: tough, quick-thinking, determined, never letting go. And physically powerful, too; not the kind of man you'd want to get into a fight with. Mind you, Julius himself wasn't any kind of softie. There was a spell in his early years when he seems to have got himself involved with some racketeers in Naples. It's said that he stabbed a man in a street brawl and spent months in an Italian jail. You won't find anything about that in the bio we put out on the Farran website.

'Anyway, Julius hired Max with an eye to the future and moved him quickly up the firm. And when Max and Rowena met and seemed to like the look of each other, he encouraged them heavily into marriage. He liked the idea of keeping power in the family; so did Max, so long as the family included him. There was some kind of tacit agreement that when Julius retired Max would take over.'

'And is that still going to happen?' Imogen asked.

'That's the key question. Julius is sixty-eight now, and I think he still has faith in Max, but now the time has come he's not so sure he wants to retire. At least, that's my interpretation. How the group would get along with Max at the helm is another matter. Julius thinks himself a brilliant judge of character and ability, but he may have got it wrong in picking Max. For one thing, Max is a gambler. A gambler in business, I mean, not in casinos. He'll take a big risk in the hope of a big success. Julius was never a gambler; he wouldn't bet unless he knew he'd win. I'm afraid that if Max was in charge he'd bet the shop on some enormous project and ruin the business. Meanwhile, Max is aching to get Julius out of the way and his own hands on the levers.'

'Can he do that, if Julius doesn't want to go?'

'Not easily. Julius founded the company and controls a lot of the shares: about forty per cent. He's put them in trust for Rowena, but as senior trustee he still calls the shots. Big outfits like banks and investment companies have most of the rest, plus a lot of small shareholders who don't really count. In extremity, the big boys could probably get together and vote Julius down, but they won't do that if they can help it. So long as he's sober and compos mentis, he's safe.'

'You said sober,' Imogen said. 'Does that mean . . . ?'

'I'm afraid it does. You'll have seen the signs. Julius has been drinking more and more over the last two or three years, and the drink's getting the better of him. He's under stress, getting paranoid, probably losing confidence a little, though he won't admit it. And feeling his age. He hasn't looked after himself.'

'I must say, he doesn't seem healthy to me. Who is his doctor?'

'Oh, that's Tim Random. A friend of Julius's for many years. I've never met him myself, but of course I've heard about him. He and Lucia would like Julius to go and take what they call a holiday but would really be a cure. Tim knows all about that; in fact it's his business. He runs a place on the coast that looks like a hotel but is really there to dry out rich people. Julius is dragging his heels; doesn't believe he's addicted, is far too busy and so on. His general policy is to keep away from doctors. But he takes notice of Lucia and Tim, and they're two to one. I wouldn't be surprised if he went.'

'And where do you come into this picture, Andrew?'

'Rather on the edge of it, Imo, to tell you the truth. The fact is, I'm Julius's man. He brought me into the company over a bit of resistance from Max, who couldn't see that the Farran Group needed an economist. Julius took a fancy to me, as he seems to have done to you. He offered me three times the salary I was getting . . .'

'Snap!' said Imogen. 'That's what he offered me.'

'Also, plenty of time to work on my book, and loads of research assistance. And I was rather out of love with academia just then. I didn't seem to be obviously in line for a chair, or the mastership of a college. Julius tempted me, and I fell.'

'Are you regretting it now?'

'I'm heading that way.'

'On moral grounds?'

'Not really. Julius doesn't ask me to do anything I object to. If I put out a report from time to time that gets mentioned in the financial pages, he's quite happy. He's rather changed his style since he made his money and got his knighthood. He aims to be respectable. But Max is gunning hard for the succession, and he doesn't give a damn for respectability. I can live with Julius but I wouldn't be so keen to work for Max. There are personal reasons, too, why I might need to jump ship.'

'You mentioned the relationship with your girlfriend, Andrew. And you rather invited me to ask about it, by what you said on the phone.'

'Yes, I did and I'm glad you have. And you may not know it, but you've almost certainly met her already.'

Imogen stared. 'Have I, indeed?' she said.

'She's Julius's PA. I expect she took you up to his room.'

'Fiona?'

Andrew nodded.

'She's lovely, Andrew. Roses pale by comparison. Though perhaps she's not the English rose type.'

'Lovely is as lovely does,' said Andrew. 'She's not being lovely to me. I may as well tell you the dreadful truth.'

'Which is?'

'She's started an affair with Julius.'

'Andrew, this is ridiculous. He's twice her age.'

'Nearer three times, as a matter of fact. He's nearly seventy. She's twenty-five.'

'But with Julius! He's gross!' Imogen shuddered. 'Imagine being made love to by him!'

'Disgusting, isn't it? The trouble is, I can imagine her being pawed by him. It rather sickens me with both of them, to tell you the truth.'

'It sounds so improbable. I mean, even if I have to say it to your face, you're a good-looking man. You're bright, and you're kind as men go, and if you haven't lost the knack you're quite a good lover. So what has Julius got that you haven't?'

'Money,' said Andrew. 'Lots and lots of money. I'm well paid, but I'm only an employee, not an owner. Julius has money on a scale that you and I can't even imagine.'

'Andrew, are you sure you're not jumping to conclusions? A personal assistant must have some kind of intimacy with her boss, from working together.'

'Not this kind of intimacy,' Andrew said.

'Is it in the open? And have you and Fiona actually broken up?'

'It's not in the open, and Fee and I haven't broken up exactly, but we're more than somewhat fractured. I know what's going on, and she knows I know, and Julius knows she knows I know, and nobody says anything. She has a flat of her own here in London, two or three streets away from mine, and she doesn't mean to part with it. She and Julius both have past form, lots of it. I can't believe she cares two pins for him, but I think he's besotted with her. Of course, it's always possible that Lucia might put her foot down or Julius have a heart attack or something.'

'He doesn't look in good shape to me,' said Imogen. 'But I can't approve of wishing him a heart attack. Incidentally, you were in my room at St Agatha's when he talked about having enemies, and about being pushed under a bus. How seriously do we take that? Are there really people who would do him in if they got the chance? He didn't sound as if he was joking.'

'Julius does have enemies,' said Andrew. 'Serious enemies. Like Robert Dacre, whose business he closed down by what Dacre thought were dirty tactics. Dacre took it badly and actually threatened Julius on one occasion. And there's Bill McNair, whom you've met; Bill joined Julius years ago, when Sub-Prime Financiers were taken over. He thinks he's made a big contribution to the group's success, but that Julius has grabbed the lion's share of the swag. They smile sweetly at each other, but we all know that Bill is seething underneath. He's a smart money man and he's also a crook; I'd trust him about as far as I can throw a grand piano. And Helen Alderton, his wife, the woman scorned. She was Julius's mistress for a while, till he got tired of her. She hates him now, venomously.'

'Well, I don't know!' said Imogen, round-eyed. 'I never knew business was such a jungle.'

'It is, and Julius is a predator. As a matter of fact, if there was a queue to push him under that bus, I might be at the head of it.'

'Andrew,' said Imogen, 'don't say silly things. Shouldn't you either have it out with Fiona or accept that you've lost her?

A pretty face is all very well, but there are plenty of other attractive women in the world.'

'Fiona is more than a pretty face. I know her well, all too well. She's as bright, and as hard, as a diamond. In a way that's part of her attraction. But there's another woman I could be fond of, in a different way from the way I feel about Fee.'

'Oh. You have the knack of surprising me. Would it mean anything if you told me who it is?'

'It's Rowena. Julius's daughter. Rowena's lovely, and she's wonderfully musical, and you can tell just by looking at her that she's all the things Fiona isn't. I've only met her three or four times, but I think she could be the real thing for me. You wouldn't believe a man like Julius could beget anyone like her. Unfortunately she's about as unavailable as anyone could be. She's married to Max. And Max is as jealous as hell.'

'Oh, Andrew, Andrew. I always knew you were susceptible. If that's how you feel about Rowena, I have to wish you luck. Only, don't fall on your face again and come to me to be rescued.'

Back in Cambridge, Imogen penned a polite note to Sir Julius, thanking him for his hospitality and regretting that she couldn't accept his job offer. Life in St Agatha's went on. It was the Lent term. Several rugby players, an oarsman and a hockey player suffered minor injuries, bringing cuts, sprains and bruises to be attended to. There were colds and digestive upsets, for which she dispensed remedies and sympathy, and occasionally the consequences of excessive revelling, for which she had remedies but less sympathy. An elderly don collapsed in his rooms and was whisked into hospital; Imogen accompanied him in the ambulance and listened patiently to his complaints when he quickly came round, asserting that there was nothing whatever wrong with him, and demanding to be taken straight back to college as he had work to do. A woman undergraduate who had incautiously contracted a quasi-marriage with a research student, providing meals, laundry and conjugal comfort, was distraught when he broke with her to concentrate on his dissertation. Imogen, who had seen this happen before and took a very poor view of the young man in question, would have given him a piece of her mind if he'd been at St Agatha's, but didn't feel she could go round and make a scene at Sidney Sussex. She offered wise advice, while knowing there was only one sure and simple cure: time.

There was excitement for St Agatha's on the river. In the Lent races the college's first boat, lying halfway down the top division and brilliantly stroked by Colin Rampage, made four bumps and correspondingly went up by four places. In the next term's May races, which were a separate series at the culmination of the academic year, St Agatha's was already fifth, the highest position reached since 1923. Achievement of a similar four bumps in the four days of the Mays would make it Head of the River. Hopes were high; members of the college from the Master down were showing unprecedented enthusiasm and even trekking to the towpath to see the heroes in action.

Imogen, busy as ever, had not much time to think about the affairs of the Farran Group. She wondered, with a mixture of affection and impatience, what, if anything, Andrew was doing about his love life, but she didn't hear from him and felt it would be intrusive to inquire. She was surprised to find that although she was sure she didn't want Andrew any more as a partner for herself she still felt a little jealous of the unknown Rowena. She thought from time to time about Sir Julius: about his troubled face on the evening of his humiliation, about his fears, then about his improbable-sounding affair with the beautiful Fiona. She wasn't sure whether he was monstrous or pathetic or both.

She still hadn't made up her mind when she picked up her newspaper one morning and read that he was dead.

5

The story was on the front page, although brief and not in a prominent position. It read:

FINANCIER DIES IN FALL FROM CLIFF

It was disclosed last night that a body found at the foot of a 100-foot cliff near Eastham-on-Sea on Tuesday was that of Sir Julius Farran, founder and chairman of the Farran Financial Group. Police said that Sir Julius, who was staying with his wife at a nearby hotel, appeared to have fallen to his death while taking a late night walk by himself on the headland. Foul play is not suspected.

Local residents said that a similar death had occurred in the same spot three years earlier, and that requests that the stretch of coast should be fenced off had been ignored.

'They didn't so much as put up a warning notice,' said Mr Reg Smithers of Eastham. 'This was an accident waiting to happen.'

Sir Julius (68) had a chequered career in the world of finance and figured in several controversies. A cabinet minister on one occasion referred to him as a piranha in the money pool, but on being challenged amended the description to 'a very big fish'. In later years he was a noted donor to charity.

(*Obituary, page 17. Business implications, page 23.*)

Imogen was deeply shaken. The sudden death of a known person is shocking in any case, and now the troubled thoughts about Sir Julius and about Andrew's problems that had been lurking at the back of her mind came surging forward. She reached for the telephone and dialled the Farran Group number, to hear a recorded message saying that on account of Sir Julius's death the switchboard would be closed for the day. Calls to Andrew's home and mobile numbers were equally unproductive. Imogen left a message on his voice mail and returned to the newspaper, her coffee cooling as she turned the pages.

The obituary of Sir Julius was at the head of its page, ran to a column and a half, and was accompanied by a picture of its subject as he might have looked twenty years before. It began with an anecdote, admitted to be possibly apocryphal, about the early revelation of his talents in primary school, when he bought a pound of wrapped sweets and sold them in ones and twos to double his money. At secondary school, until authority stepped in, he had allegedly made small loans for short periods to impecunious schoolmates, at rates of interest which on an annual basis ran to a thousand per cent or thereabouts. Being a bright boy, he got a state scholarship to Cambridge, but, as the obituary drily observed, 'he distinguished himself by a consistent absence from lectures and college activities and, had it been possible to fail his degree examinations, would undoubtedly have done so.' On graduating he went to Italy, where he made large amounts of money which were never fully explained.

From then on, the obituary continued, his career featured a series of financial coups on an ever-increasing scale until in middle age he was a millionaire many times over. At this stage he incurred widespread odium and clashed several times with worker or student demonstrators, on one occasion being seriously injured while fighting his way out of a corner. Later, however, he moved towards respectability, selling the less reputable of his enterprises, making generous donations to charities and political parties, and achieving his knighthood. He became an accepted figure in the City, although he was never entirely able to put his former reputation behind him.

He was survived, the notice concluded, by his second wife, Lucia, and by one daughter from an earlier marriage.

The business pages reported that the Farran Financial Group share price had fallen at first on the news, but had more than recovered by the end of the day. It was expected that Lord Robinswood would become chairman but that Max Holwood, continuing as chief executive, would wield the real power. The paper's financial editor speculated that Max would pursue an aggressive policy in the former Farran tradition and the profits of the group might well increase.

In the evening Andrew rang, rather breathlessly returning Imogen's call.

'We've been at sixes and sevens all day,' he told her. 'An emergency board meeting. Robinswood in the chair, but Max given full powers to run the group until the smoke clears away. There are a lot of things I'm not happy about, and it doesn't look too good for me personally. But tomorrow Max and I are going to Eastham for the inquest. We may have to give evidence on Julius's state of mind.'

'What on earth was he doing at Eastham, all those miles away?'

'I'll tell you everything after the inquest, Imo. Just for now, I need to get some rest and prepare myself for tomorrow.'

The next day happened to be a busy one for Imogen. Besides the usual aches, pains and minuscule injuries, there was the aftermath of a nasty incident in which an undergraduate had fallen foul of a pair of troublemakers coming out of a pub. He'd been beaten badly enough to be taken to Addenbrooke's, and was now discharged into Imogen's care with a fearful black eye and multiple bruises. He was lucky it wasn't worse.

On the day after that, Andrew rang with the full story. The verdict, he said, was as expected. It was death by misadventure.

'You asked what he was doing at Eastham,' Andrew said. 'The short answer is that he was drying out, or supposed to be, at Headlands, the place I told you about where they treat rich alcoholics. Julius was there, reluctantly, with Tim Random and Lucia keeping an eye on him. Tim is running Headlands pretty well full-time these days; he's retired from doctoring except for a handful of rich old patients. Lucia was being the dutiful wife. And Julius was staying under a false name, because there could have been bad publicity if the news got out.'

'I get the picture, I think. Julius got off the lead?'

'Yes. He went out after they'd all gone to bed, wandered along the cliff path and walked over the edge. We saw the place. It was easily done. In fact, it gave me a turn just to look over. It's an eroded surface, very sheer, with a layer of rock below. The autopsy showed the kind of injuries you'd expect; it must have been nasty for Lucia and Tim, having to identify the body. No marks of any other violence. And this is the point, Imo. The autopsy also showed recent consumption of quite a lot of alcohol: possibly not enough to make him drunk but certainly enough to impair his judgment. With that evidence, the verdict was a foregone conclusion.'

'But, Andrew, how would he get at the drink? A place like that wouldn't have a bar.'

'Of course not. All alcohol strictly forbidden. In fact, guests have to agree that their rooms can be inspected at any time without notice. But the world is full of wicked ingenuity. We learned that there's a kind of bootleg trade, and that locals find ways of smuggling bottles in, at a price. We even heard tales of baskets being lowered from windows.'

'That doesn't sound like Julius.'

'Anyway, whatever the explanation, he'd got hold of enough alcohol to send him to his death. You could say drink was his downfall, literally. And you know, Imo, in spite of his past and all I've said about him, I've realised since his death that in a way I rather liked the old rogue.'

'I thought you did. So, in a way, did I. I suppose he'd mellowed, though I haven't heard that he gave his ill-gotten gains back.'

'I shall miss him,' Andrew said. 'In fact, without him I don't think I can stay with Farran Group for long. Max doesn't like me, and I don't like Max. Or trust him. Did I say I wouldn't trust him as far as I could throw a grand piano?'

'No, that was Bill McNair,' Imogen said.

'I wouldn't trust either of them as far as I could throw a grand piano. And I should have added "with one hand". Then there's your bursar, Peter Wetherby. A spooky character if ever there was one. He flits in and out like a shadow; gives me the creeps. Incidentally, he and Max and McNair spent a good deal of time yesterday in Julius's room, going through his papers. I was definitely not invited. I suppose now he's in charge Max can do as he thinks fit, and it may just have been prudent housekeeping, but I can't help wondering. Were there documents he'd prefer not to see the light of day?'

'What's spooky to me,' said Imogen, 'is the similarity between falling under a bus and falling off a cliff. They're almost by-words for a simple and undetectable crime – one smart shove and the deed is done. No weapon, no poison, can't go wrong.'

'Unless the victim is smarter than you are. He might turn the tables and stop you. Or even push you under the bus or over the cliff yourself.'

'Not very likely, I'd think, if you were reasonably fit. You'd have the benefit of surprise. And if the victim was drunk at the time . . . ?'

'No, Imogen, no. Too far-fetched. It would have had to be

Lucia or Tim, or some passing vagrant, and none of these would have any motive. Now if Max had been on the scene, I'd have been tempted by your theory. He's a vicious bastard, and capable of anything. But we're talking fantasy now. Imo dear, you've given me good advice at one time and another. Now let me give some to you.

'Julius is dead. It's the end of the matter. Put it out of your mind.'

Actually it wasn't the end of the matter. There was the question of the college flag. This was the subject of High Table debate at St Agatha's. It was the custom of the college to fly the flag at half mast to mark the death of a distinguished member or a major benefactor. Sir Julius, like it or not, was a member of the college, but was he distinguished or merely notorious? He was not known to be a benefactor, and hadn't had much time in which to arrange benefactions even if, after his unhappy visit, he was minded to do so.

The debate was brief and the outcome unanimous. St Agatha's was not going to fly the flag for Julius Farran. But perhaps someone should represent it at his funeral? There was a marked lack of enthusiasm for this duty. The bursar, Peter Wetherby, being an associate of Sir Julius, was the obvious choice, but had said that as a member of the Farran board he didn't think it proper to represent the college as well. Several other fellows were approached, but contrived to excuse themselves. In the end, Lady Buckmote, the Master's wife, known to all as Lady B., stepped into the breach, as she had done on more than one such occasion. She had met Lucia Farran in the course of some charitable work, and offered to go. And, also as she had done more than once, she invited Imogen to go with her and share the driving.

The word 'No' did not have a prominent place in Imogen's

vocabulary. On a fine Wednesday, she and Lady B. set out for Welbourne St Mary, the village in rural Suffolk where Sir Julius and Lady Farran had twenty years earlier moved into the spacious and beautiful Old Rectory. The Farrans were not frequent worshippers, but Sir Julius's generosity had saved, almost single-handedly, the structure of the fine fifteenth-century church, and the Rector, who himself lived in a three-bedroomed house on the edge of a new development, was grateful and ungrudging. All was to be done traditionally, with burial in the churchyard and a headstone already on order recording Sir Julius's beneficence.

The church was crowded, and the parking space alongside it was full of large cars, three or four of them chauffeur-driven. Sir Julius might have had enemies, but he clearly had a large number of friends and acquaintances who felt it appropriate for them to pay their last respects. The readings, by Lord Robinswood in a finely tuned tenor voice and by Max Holwood in his strong, down-to-earth baritone, were, respectively, the passage beginning 'Let us now praise famous men' from Ecclesiasticus and the parable of the talents from St Matthew: the story of the man who doubled his master's money, whereupon 'his lord said unto him, Well done, thou good and faithful servant: thou hast been faithful over a few things, I will make thee ruler of many things: enter thou into the joy of thy lord.'

The parable of the sweeties writ large, thought Imogen, recalling the obituary. She and Lady B. had slipped quietly into the body of the church and could see little of the principal mourners; but when the coffin emerged and a little procession made its way to the graveside Lucia Farran signalled to Lady B. and Imogen to join it. This gave Imogen an opportunity to study Sir Julius's widow and, with great interest, her step-daughter Rowena. Lucia was tall, upright, and stood unmoving, dignified and expressionless, as the traditional words were spoken. She was not weeping, but a sense of the weight of the occasion hung about her. Rowena was pale, with an oval face, wide eyes, and an open expression, her hair – what could be seen of it – dark and curling a little. Imogen liked the look of her. Tears fell unchecked from her eyes as those around threw earth on the coffin and the Rector spoke the closing words of the service: 'We commend to Almighty God our brother Julius, and we commit his body to the ground; earth to earth, ashes to ashes, dust to dust. The Lord bless him and keep him . . .'

At this point, a wild figure burst through the little group around the grave. A young man, dishevelled, with unruly red hair, shoved the Rector aside and was at the brink, looking for a moment as if he would jump down on the coffin. Instead he bawled down at it: 'Filthy bastard, God damn you to hell!'

There was a moment of horror. The young man, having apparently shot his bolt, stood gasping, his chest heaving. Then Max Holwood leaped at him and grabbed him. He resisted and there was a brief tussle. But Max was far too strong for him, and manhandled him away from the graveside. Some yards away, they stopped; Max bore him to the ground and held him hard down.

Three or four of the mourners moved uncertainly towards them, but turned back as the Rector recovered himself and spoke. He said, in clear tones, 'I have never seen, or heard of, anything like this before. But the holy act of committal to the ground, by its nature, rises above such gross intrusion and cannot be affected by it. I shall therefore continue. The Lord bless our brother Julius and keep him, the Lord make his face to shine upon him and be gracious unto him, the Lord lift up his countenance upon him and give him peace. Amen.'

The service was not quite over, but Imogen slipped silently

away and hurried across to where Max was still pinning the intruder down. He looked about twenty years old, and the fight had gone out of him. Max said, 'Don't even think of running away,' and relinquished his grip.

The young man stood up, as if with difficulty, and complained, 'He's hurt me!'

Imogen stepped forward, saying, 'I'm a nurse. Show me.'

He showed her red marks on his wrists and pulled up his shirt to display marks of bruising on the ribs. There was nothing serious, and she didn't feel inclined to offer sympathy.

'You'll live,' she said crisply, and to Max, 'He's not really hurt, but you did hit him quite hard.'

The young man was now staring at Max.

'I know you,' he said. 'I've seen you with Bastard Farran before. Seen you at his house. Seen you with the other two. I wish you'd all gone over together, the lot of you. I hope you rot in hell along with him!'

'He's deranged,' said Max contemptuously. 'The question is, what do we do with him now?'

'We ask the Rector,' Imogen said.

'In the meantime,' Max said, 'here he stays.'

The young man spat in his face. Max seemed about to deliver a blow that would have felled him, but Imogen interposed herself with an urgent 'Don't!' and he drew back.

The service ended, and the Rector seemed to be urging the mourners to move across to the Old Rectory, where there would be refreshments. As they drifted away, talking in little shocked groups, he came across to where Max, Imogen and the prisoner waited. And it was immediately plain that he knew the young man well.

'Derek!' he said. 'How could you? That was an act of desecration, a vile thing to do! May heaven forgive you, which is more than I can do at the moment.' To Max he said simply, 'I'm sorry.'

Derek said defensively, 'I had to do it. People praising that bastard after all he's done!' Then, with a sudden access of bravado, 'I did it, didn't I? I did it! I took the shine off their faces! There was a reporter there, I saw him. It'll be in the papers.'

'Were there any reporters here?' asked Max.

'There was a junior from the local weekly here earlier on,' the Rector said. 'But when he'd taken the names at the church door he vanished. Didn't want to sit through the service, I suppose. So he missed the story.'

Derek's face fell.

The Rector, still speaking to Max, went on, 'So with a bit of luck it won't get out. And I don't suppose you want it to.'

'You suppose correctly,' said Max.

'Right now,' the Rector said, 'I should prefer it if you'd let him go.'

Max said, 'If that's your wish, Rector, then yes, of course. But obviously you know more than I do. He says he knows me, but I don't know him.'

The Rector said, 'Derek, get away out of my sight. Don't let me see you again until you're ready to apologise on your knees, to the memory of a dead man, and to all the people you have offended. And don't harass Lady Farran any more, or it will be a police matter.'

'And get out fast,' Max added, 'if you don't want a boot in your backside!'

Derek went, like a cork from a bottle.

The Rector said, 'Derek's behaviour is outrageous, I know, and can't be tolerated. His grievance has obviously become more than he can handle. I must try to get some help for him. Mind you, the grievance is real enough. He believes that

Julius Farran wrecked his father's life and destroyed his own prospects.'

'And who might his father be?' Max asked.

'Robert Dacre.'

'Oh,' said Max. 'That explains it. Dacre hated Julius. But what happened to Dacre had to happen. He lost out, that's all. He's one of life's losers. Incidentally I didn't know the Dacres lived around here.'

'They don't, they're fifty miles away. But Derek got on the internet and tracked Sir Julius to the Old Rectory, and every so often he's been coming over here and making a scene. It's got worse in recent months. The Farrans could have applied for an injunction against him, but Julius didn't want to. However, with Julius dead and buried, and after today's events, I hope most fervently that Derek will see reason and give up.'

'He'd better,' said Max. 'Julius had gone soft. There won't be any tolerating of nonsense now.'

'I'm afraid there'll be talk all over the village about this episode,' said the Rector. 'We'd better go and join the others. I shall do what I can to calm it down.'

Imogen had her share of human curiosity. 'What's the bitterness about?' she inquired when the Rector had left them.

'Oh, just an imagined grievance,' said Max, in a tone of finality. 'We'd better join the party too.'

If it hadn't been for the graveside incident, it would have been a pleasant gathering, as receptions after funerals often are. However much the departed person is missed, there is a lightening of spirits, a fresh and revivifying awareness that life is valuable and goes on. And although there were some present who regretted the death of Julius Farran, there were many who were not much attached to him. There were acquaintanceships to be renewed. Lord Robinswood and Lady B. had met before;

Lady B. knew Andrew well from his time at the college; most of the Farran board members remembered and greeted Imogen, though Peter Wetherby walked past her twice without seeming to see her. Around the big drawing-room of the Old Rectory the shadow gradually lifted, conversations became animated, and most of those present began to enjoy themselves.

But Imogen's curiosity remained. Some instinct made her still uneasy when she remembered Julius's remarks about his enemies. Finding herself in a corner with Andrew, she told him what the Rector had said and asked him, 'Just what is it about the Dacres?'

Andrew didn't share Max's reluctance to tell her.

'Let's go into the garden for a minute,' he said. 'This isn't for public consumption.'

They stepped through a French window on to the immaculate Old Rectory lawn.

'The Dacres are part of Julius's pre-reformation past,' Andrew went on. 'Robert Dacre owned a family business, in a town called, if I remember, Tuesday Market, somewhere in East Anglia. He was the third generation. A small local department store, the kind of thing that hardly exists any more. It wasn't all that profitable, but it had fine high-street premises and other buildings around the town. Julius bought it as a going concern. But he wasn't interested in running it. For him it was a property deal. He closed it down, paid off the price he'd paid for it by selling its own assets, and had a million or two left over. A classic Julius coup, but Robert Dacre had failed to see it coming. He felt he'd ratted on his employees, who all lost their jobs, and he himself was left with quite a lot of money but no occupation. He's been fuelled by resentment ever since.'

'He was one of the mysterious enemies that Julius was talking about, the night of the ankle, wasn't he?'

'He was. He once burst into the Farran offices and threatened him. Shouted abuse, in fact. And I know he fired off libellous letters about Julius to all kinds of people. Julius wouldn't sue; he didn't want his linen washed in public, especially since he became respectable. But latterly he was getting nervous, as you know.'

'And what about Derek?'

'I'd never set eyes on Derek until today. But it looks as if he's inherited his father's grievances. A chip off the old block, apparently. Obsessive. Has a personality problem.'

'I've known quite a few young men with personality problems,' Imogen said thoughtfully. 'I wouldn't have thought Derek was a dangerous type. Weak, I'd have said. But obviously he'd screwed himself up to sticking point in order to make that gesture at the grave. He could just possibly have screwed himself up to do something even more dramatic.'

'Imo, dear,' said Andrew, 'I can read your tiny mind. You're still asking yourself, Did Julius fall or was he pushed? I don't think that's a realistic line to pursue.'

'It's just a hunch I have,' said Imogen. 'And hunch is funny stuff. The word can be shorthand for quite a complex coming together of thought processes, not always conscious. I've done fairly well with hunches in the past.'

'If you think it's murder,' said Andrew, 'I can offer you some suspects. Tim Random and Lucia, for instance. They were there at Headlands, more or less on the spot. They might be in cahoots together. Lucia must have stood to inherit a lot of money.'

'Is Dr Random here today?'

'I can't say for sure, because I don't know him by sight. But I don't think so. If he'd been here I suppose he'd have been at the graveside with the family. But with that place to run and still some patients to care for, there are all sorts of reasons why he might not have been able to come.'

'I haven't seen Fiona,' Imogen remarked.

'No, she's back at base. Somebody had to mind the store. And as Lucia was well aware of what went on between her and Julius, it might not have been tactful anyway. But, reverting to suspects, my favoured one would be Max. He's ruthless. He wanted control of the group and now he's got it. How's that for motive? The only snag is that we've no reason to think he was anywhere near Eastham at the time.'

'You told me not to speculate,' Imogen said. 'Now you're doing it.'

'Touché. The obvious summary of the event in question is that Julius got out, got drunk, and wandered over the edge. End of story. But actually I'm beginning to convince myself. I know Max; he's a shit and a ruthless shit. He could be a murderer. And he's married to Rowena; I could murder him for that. And look, she's drifted away from Lucia. I want to go and talk to her.'

In the next quarter-hour Imogen looked across at intervals to where Andrew and Rowena stood in a bay window. Their conversation was a lasting one. She didn't hear a word of what was said, but wondered if their expressions indicated affectionate interest in one another. Perhaps not; Rowena, fresh from her father's funeral, would hardly be in a mood for dalliance. But when Lady B. came up to Imogen to say it was time to set off for Cambridge the two were still talking. Max was not in the room.

Next day, Imogen telephoned her old friend in the police, Mike Parsons. Mike owed her some consideration, having scored professional successes with her help and been promoted from sergeant to inspector. As a good policeman, he had a widespread network of colleagues, friends and enemies.

'I'll always break a rule for you, Imogen,' he said cheerfully. 'Yes, I remember reading about the guy who fell down the cliff at Eastham, and as it happens I've an old mate at the station there. I'll ask if there's anything dicey in the background. Though I must say it doesn't seem likely to me.'

An hour later he rang her back. 'All clear, plain and above board,' he said. 'No mysteries, no grounds for suspicion; all done and dusted, file put away. Does that put your mind at rest?'

'Oh, yes, it does. It's a relief, Mike. Thank you enormously. Now I can stop thinking about it.'

But she couldn't. Not quite.

6

Belinda Mayhew was a strong, clever, overworked woman of about Imogen's age. She was Fellow and Tutor in Classics at St Agatha's. She had three young children, and her husband, an archaeologist, was often away from home. Her life was a nonstop struggle with professional and family exigencies and against the clock. She coped and was cheerful, but chat was a luxury denied her, and as she could never afford to be off colour she had few chances of talking to Imogen.

The day came, however, when Belinda wanted to discuss with Imogen in her little surgery the personal problems of a student she was worried about. She had time, when the matter was resolved, to stay for a mug of coffee; but for once she was not cheerful.

'My fellowship comes up for renewal this year,' she said, 'and it looks as though it won't be renewed.'

Imogen was shocked. She had a shrewd idea of the academic reputations of the fellows, and knew that Belinda was a distinguished scholar in her field. She also had well-informed and up-to-date knowledge of what the students thought of those who taught them. Belinda was liked and admired by fellows and undergraduates alike.

'Why ever . . . ?' she began.

'Oh, it's the financial crisis. You know that St Ag's is one of the poorer colleges. And we hadn't realised how badly dear old

Dr Honeywell had been managing things. He made the wrong investments at the wrong times, and he came up with accounts that made things look better than they were. It wasn't dishonesty; just incompetence and over-optimism.'

'I knew Dr Honeywell wasn't thought to be the most brilliant of bursars. But I didn't know things were as bad as that.'

'I'm afraid they were and still are,' said Belinda. 'But now we've got the new man in. Peter Wetherby. He came with the reputation of being a toughie, and he's living up to it. He's been given what amounts to full financial control – it was a condition of getting him – and he's practically running the college. The days of ruthlessness are upon us.'

'I hardly know Mr Wetherby,' said Imogen. 'I see him occasionally crossing the court, or on his way in or out of college. Sometimes he says "Good morning" and sometimes he just nods. He knows who I am, but he doesn't talk to me.'

'He's the same with me,' said Belinda. 'He's away in London a lot, and always busy when he's here. I don't think he has time to be a human being. Somebody the other day called him the smiler with the knife. That seems apt to me, except that he doesn't smile much. He's certainly wielding the knife. I'm told he called in the steward and the head chef, and told them to cut the cost of catering by twenty per cent.'

'That won't make him popular,' Imogen said; and then, 'If you did lose your fellowship, would you get one in another college?'

'Doubtful. Looking around, I don't see a vacancy at present. I might try for another university. But with all the children at school and Hugh away so much, it would be awful to have to move. You know, Imogen, this is hitting me hard. I love my subject, I love St Ag's, I love my students. Doing what I do is what I'm for, and here is where

I want to be. But don't let me get too sorry for myself. Millions of women have it worse.'

'I hope there'll be a change of mind and you'll stay,' said Imogen.

'I don't think so,' Belinda said, drinking up her coffee. 'And there may be other casualties. Several people have the jitters. Alarm and despondency all round.'

'I suppose I might get the sack,' Imogen said, struck by a new and unwelcome thought. 'They could get a nurse from some other college to double up.'

'No, no. Yours is the safest job in St Ag's. They won't part with you whatever happens. They love you too much. Quite right, too. Oh well, now I must dash. Time to collect Joanna from school, and make some lunch, and take James to the dentist's.'

Morale among the fellows of St Agatha's was low. Among the undergraduates, a few became aware by a kind of osmosis of the anxieties of their seniors, but most had other things on their mind. Examinations loomed, and even those not yet due to go down worried about what degrees they would get, what jobs they would find afterwards, and the alarming debts they would some time have to repay. Yet for most the natural exuberance of youth broke through.

Hopes that St Agatha's would go Head of the River in the May races were still high. The pundits who watched the leading crews in action were nodding sagely, noting the style and power of the St Agatha's eight. Colin Rampage, who had stroked St Agatha's to victory in the Lents, was confidently expected to do so again in the Mays.

But three weeks into term, the experts at St Agatha's began to worry. Colin Rampage was cutting training. Worse, and unforgivably, he was failing without explanation to turn up or even to apologise. This was unprecedented; serious rowing men simply did not behave in such a way. Fellow undergraduates reading Colin's subject reported that he was equally neglecting his studies, missing supervision, failing to turn in papers. His tutor had remonstrated with him, and had been treated off-handedly.

Somebody had seen him, on a morning when he should have been training, getting on a London train. Somebody else had suggested that he should be trailed, to see what he was up to; but this was dismissed by some as unethical and by others as impracticable. Josh, who with Fran formed Imogen's current household, was not a St Agatha's man, but out of loyalty to Fran had transferred his affections and was one of the affronted enthusiasts. He had graduated over a period of three years from the status of shivering novice, shouted at by bossy coaches, to being himself one of the domineering figures who tear perilously along the towpath on bicycles, yelling instructions to the rowers and threatening disaster to themselves and to anyone who gets in their way. He was declaiming furiously on Colin's iniquity after supper in Imogen's kitchen when the phone rang. It was Andrew.

'I'm on my way to Cambridge,' he said. 'Can you give me a bed for the night?'

'Andrew! This is sudden. What's happened?'

'All sorts of things have happened. I'll tell you later.'

'Well, yes, I can give you a bed . . .'

'Good. I'll be with you shortly. I can park in the fellows' car park, can't I?'

'Officially, certainly not. But you'll get away with it. The porters will remember you.'

Fran said, 'So Andrew's coming. Sounds interesting. Josh and I are going round to the pub. We won't get in your way.'

'Don't give me that meaningful look,' Imogen said. 'I don't

know what it's all about, but it isn't what you think. Actually he sounded worried.'

And Andrew's first words when he arrived were, 'Imo, dear, I hope your shoulder is ready to be wept on.'

'It's always at the ready,' Imogen said. 'Weep on.'

'I have news for you, and it's serious. In fact, you might say disastrous. But also interesting. I'll give you the disaster first. I've been fired by Max.'

'Oh, Andrew, I'm so sorry. Why?'

'Well, the reason is rather a shaming one. Max caught me looking at his diary.'

Imogen was shocked. 'I'm not surprised at anybody not liking to find someone looking at his diary,' she said. 'But how did it happen? Why were you looking into Max's diary? What did you expect to find?'

'Give me a chance. I can't answer three questions in a single breath. Maybe you remember that I told you that the day after Julius died Max and Bill McNair and Peter Wetherby were all in his room going through his papers. I didn't like that, not just because I wasn't invited but because I wondered if there might be nasties coming to light that I hadn't known about. And then, I kept thinking about your suspicions.'

'You more or less laughed them out of court,' said Imogen.

'I know I did. But the more I saw of Max enjoying his triumph, the more I wondered whether your suggestion was as far-fetched as I'd thought. Max wanted control so much, he'd have done anything to get it, I thought, perhaps even murder. And now he's revelling in it, throwing his weight about, giving orders right and left. To add to it all, he's inherited Fiona.'

'Inherited Fiona? What do you mean?'

'To put it politely, Fiona has switched over to him. It didn't take long. Julius was no good to her, dead. It's Max now who's rich and powerful. Follow the money is Fiona's motto. She followed it from me to Julius, and now she's moving on. Max is happy; it adds to his euphoria to have a delectable piece of arm-candy. He'll be showing her off in fashionable haunts, which is more than Julius can ever have done.'

'But Max is married, isn't he? To Rowena?'

'Yes. That's not likely to stop him. He's two-timed Rowena before. And Rowena is lovely. She doesn't deserve to be stuck to a thug like Max.'

'It's an odd coincidence,' Imogen said, 'that only today I've been hearing about somebody else who's got his hands on the levers of power and is making the most of it. That's our new bursar, and you know who he is.'

'Of course. Wetherby. And when he came out of Julius's room with Max he was smiling, a kind of satisfied, cat-that's-swallowed-the-cream smile, if you know what I mean. Imogen, what if that pair are in cahoots? I can feel my suspicions growing as I speak.'

'You haven't told me about the diary.'

'No more I have. Well, the other day I was finishing the paper I've been writing on trade with eastern Europe, and I went on working when everyone else had gone home. I happened to wander into Max's room, and there was his diary lying open on his desk. And the thought came to me: what if there was something in it that would tell me where Max was the day Julius died? I remembered what day that was, because it happened to be my wedding anniversary. Without thinking about it, I turned the diary back to that date, and bingo, there was an entry that said simply, in the space for "evening", "See J.F." Which of course would mean Julius Farran.'

'That doesn't sound much like evidence,' Imogen said.

'No. But just a moment. Max must have know that Julius was at Headlands. So either he'd arranged to see Julius there, or just possibly Julius was going to slip out and see him. Either way, it looks as though he was on the scene around the time the supposed accident happened. However, I didn't have time to look for anything else. Max suddenly appeared. He'd come back for something he'd forgotten and saw what I was doing. He was furious.'

'Not surprisingly. And?'

'I thought for a moment he was going to hit me. Then I could sense that he was bringing himself under control. He said, quite quietly, "Get out of here. I'll see you in the morning." And next day he sent for me – *sent* for me; he wouldn't have done that in Julius's day – and said, "How long has your contract to run?" I told him it was about a year. He said, "I don't want you here. Write out your resignation and clear your desk. I'll pay you the full amount up to your expiry date." So I went. And actually I've done quite nicely, because I was thinking I'd rather leave anyway than work under Max. So here I am, without a job, but I'm about to have a hundred thousand pounds in the bank.'

'Congratulations!' said Imogen. But the touch of irony was lost on Andrew.

'And I'm free to go gunning for Max!' he added. 'I want you to help me.'

'Andrew, we need to understand each other. I'm not interested in gunning for Max or anybody else. I was concerned about Julius, and I would dearly like to know how he came to his end, that's all. I don't care where the chips fall.'

'I'm not proud of what I've done,' Andrew said. 'But I've done it and I'm going to follow it up. I want to go and see Rowena soon, and find out if I can what Max was doing that day. And I've been thinking that now I'm through with the Farran Group I might come back to the college. I want to talk to Sir William about it.'

Privately Imogen thought that coming back to the college might be more easily said than done, but it wasn't for her to disillusion him. 'Just for now,' she said, 'pick up your bag. I'll sort out some towels for you, and show you where you're going to sleep.'

'I wondered,' said Andrew hopefully, 'whether for old times' sake . . .'

Imogen had wondered, too, as she waited for him to arrive. But now she was not in doubt.

'You're in the spare room,' she said.

Andrew and Imogen were drinking coffee together the following morning when Fran appeared in her dressing-gown.

'Had a good night, Andrew?' she inquired with some interest.

'Very,' said Andrew, not letting on that he had been assigned to the spare room.

'What will you be doing today?'

'I'm hoping to see the Master this morning. Who knows, I might be rejoining you all.'

But half an hour later he returned from the lodge disappointed.

'Sir William was very amiable,' he said. 'And very forgiving about my desertion. But when I told him what was in my mind he was a bit cautious. I suppose he had to be. He said he had to go out in a few minutes' time and we needed to have a proper talk; could I come back tomorrow morning?' Andrew pulled a face. 'So it looks as if I'll be with you for another night, if you can bear it.'

Imogen expressed regret at the hitch and willingness to provide accommodation for as long as it was needed.

'Oh, it will only be for one more day,' Andrew said. 'Then I'll leave you in peace for the time being. Perhaps I'll be coming back to St Ag's for good before long. You know, I've really quite missed the old place. Julius's money never quite compensated for what we have here.'

The day was fine, and in spite of the setback Andrew was soon in good spirits. He made a call on his mobile and then said to Imogen, 'Drop everything. We're going for a drive in the country, to see someone special.'

'Rowena?'

'Got it in one.'

'Of course I'd like to meet Rowena. But I can't really drop everything. I have a surgery at eleven.'

'Ask your pal Bridget to do it. What's the college-nurse mafia for, if not to help out in an emergency, such as a sunny day?'

'You remember all about my life, don't you? But yes, Bridget owes me a favour or two. I'll see if she can.'

Bridget could, and by mid-morning they were driving out of Cambridge.

'This is the way we went to the funeral,' Imogen said after a while.

'Yes. Rowena lives in Welbourne All Saints, the next village to Lucia and Julius. She was Julius's ewe lamb, you know. The only person in the world that Julius really cared about. She'll give us coffee. And then I thought we'd go to the coast and take a look at the scene of the crime.'

'Or accident,' Imogen said.

'Crime or accident, as the case may be. But the more I think about it the more I think it was crime.'

'I remember seeing Rowena at the funeral. I thought she looked nice. She seemed the only person there who was really upset.'

'She may well have been. She was the darling of Julius's heart. And probably the only person who really loved *him*.'

'I suppose she knows you're bringing somebody with you?'

'I told her I might, and who you were. She said she'd be delighted. Rowena is a sweetie. In fact' – with a sideways look – 'I think I could go in deep with her, given the chance. Pity she's married to that thug.'

'Your affections are readily bestowed, Andrew. You were looking somewhat affectionately at me last night.'

'Of course I was. My affection for you is lasting . . .'

'If intermittent.'

'Not so. I have been faithful to you, Cynara, in my fashion.'

'Oh, stop quoting. It won't get you anywhere. Now tell me why Rowena lives in a village three miles away from her mother.'

'Lucia isn't her mother, she's her stepmother. More step than mother, in my observation. Lucia's a chilly person. They get on well enough together, but that's about all.'

'You mentioned Welbourne All Saints. The funeral was at Welbourne St Mary, wasn't it?'

'It was. The villages both take their names from their churches. I'm told that on a clear day you can see the spire of one village church from the other. Julius wanted to bring his daughter and his new wife closer, but perhaps not too close. He'd bought the Old Rectory when he married Lucia, and he bought Stonegates for Rowena as a wedding present. Max has been quite happy, immuring Rowena at Stonegates to raise his children while he goes on with his business life in London and his sexual recreation at Lilac Cottage. That's his cottage in Hertfordshire. He spends the weekend with his wife, sometimes.'

'Does she have to put up with it?'

'Max is very dominant. Brutally dominant, you might say. And Julius was no less dominant in his own way. Emotionally dominant where Rowena was concerned. Between the two of them she never stood a chance. Over-protected childhood, two or three years at a classy boarding school, a year in Switzerland, married at nineteen to her father's nominee.'

'Couldn't she divorce him?'

'Rowena won't go for a divorce. She has the boys to think of, and her mother, who lives with her. Julius's first wife, Anne, superseded by Lucia.'

They drove on in silence, out past Cambridge suburbs and surrounding villages, along fast dual carriageway and then into narrow lanes and deep, peaceful countryside. Welbourne St Mary came first, with church and Old Rectory on their left; and Imogen, out of idle interest, measured the time it took to drive on to All Saints. It was only some five or six minutes, and she noted the sign for a footpath leading away across fields, which might well have been a short cut.

Stonegates was stockbroker Tudor, built probably between the two world wars: attractive and handsome enough, it exuded an air of affluence. A broad gravel drive curved its way to a parking area in front of the house. Stepping from their car, Andrew and Imogen heard piano music, soft and plangent, from within.

'That'll be Rowena,' Andrew said. 'She plays rather well, doesn't she?'

'Very well. And what a lovely piece. Mozart, isn't it?'

'No, no. Schubert. One of his impromptus, I think. Like to bet?'

'I'm not a betting person. I expect you're right.'

'I'm sure I'm right. Let's hear it through.' They waited in the porch until there was a pause in the sound; then Andrew rang a bell that jangled somewhere in the house.

In a minute Rowena Holwood came to the door. Imogen had had only a glimpse of Rowena at the funeral, and was glad to get a closer look. She was probably close to thirty, but looked younger; slight and not tall. Her face was pale, eyes dark, hair falling in curly disorder on her shoulders. She wore a white shirt and fawn slacks. Not actually frail for all her slightness, Imogen thought, scanning her with an experienced eye. She might be wiry and quite strong. But there was an air of vulnerability about her that, in Imogen's experience, often appealed strongly to the protective instinct in men. Indeed, she sensed vibrations suggesting that the instinct was at work in Andrew.

'Hello, Andrew,' Rowena said, 'come in,' and offered a cheek to be kissed.

Andrew introduced Imogen.

'Hello, Imogen,' Rowena said. 'I've heard about you. It's lovely to meet you.'

'It's nice of you to welcome me.'

'A friend of Andrew is a friend of mine. That sounds like an awful cliché, but it's true. Anyone who came with Andrew would be sure to be nice. Come through into the drawing-room.'

It was a room some thirty feet long, lightly furnished but with what were obviously fine period pieces. And in the corner was the piano, a Broadwood. Rowena walked over to it and closed the lid.

'We heard you playing,' Imogen said. 'I thought it was Mozart, but Andrew says it was Schubert.'

'Andrew's right, it was Schubert. The A minor impromptu.'

Andrew said, 'I hadn't realised, Rowena, how good you are. You ought to have been a professional.'

'Oh no. If you heard a professional play that, you'd notice the difference.' She sounded embarrassed. 'I'll go and make the coffee,' she said.

'She really is good,' Andrew said when Rowena had left the room. 'And I think getting better. Of course, with the boys away at school she has time on her hands. I believe when they first came here she spent a lot of time getting the house as she wanted it. She made a lovely job of that, too. We might be able to look around it before we go. But now it's done, she's short of occupation.'

'With the boys away she could get a job, couldn't she?'

'Max wouldn't stand for that. For him, she's part of the display. Lovely wife in lovely house. They do have weekend guests or give dinner parties occasionally, and he needs Rowena for that.'

'She could do voluntary work.'

'I think she's got a bit of the cold shoulder from the village. It's the Julius effect. Julius is – was – a controversial figure, to say the least. Plenty of people in both villages didn't like having him around. They may feel differently now he's gone.'

Over coffee, Andrew, unable to conceal his dislike of Max, made several remarks that seemed to Imogen a little too pointed. Rowena countered them in neutral tones, neither leaping to Max's defence nor indicating discontent with her lot. Eventually she rebuked Andrew by saying mildly, 'Max is my husband, you know.'

Changing the subject, Andrew inquired after her mother.

'She's in her room,' Rowena said. 'I'm afraid she doesn't often come out of it. She isn't well at all.'

'It's a heart condition, isn't it?'

'Yes. It's degenerative and disabling, but seems to be fairly stable. Dr Random doesn't want her operated on at present. She takes a lot of medication which seems to keep her going, but she can't move around much.'

'Dr Random?' Imogen said with interest. 'He was your father's doctor, wasn't he?'

'Yes. A family friend for many years. He's more or less retired, but he still treats Mother for old times' sake. My mother trusts him implicitly. He comes in often, and that helps to keep her happy. She worries whenever he's away. Now, I have a suggestion. Perhaps Imogen would like to see around the house and garden, and then both of you to stay to lunch? It won't be anything special, just whatever I can find in the fridge.'

'That would be lovely,' Andrew said. 'Wouldn't it, Imogen?'

But the tour of the house didn't happen. Five minutes later there was a crunch of wheels on the gravel outside.

'It's Max!' Rowena exclaimed. 'Without warning. I had no idea!'

The expression on her face told Imogen what her words had tried to conceal. It was a look of alarm. She hurried to the door. Andrew and Imogen looked at each other, Imogen somewhat baffled.

'This means trouble!' Andrew said.

'Whose car is that in the drive?' Max was asking.

Andrew stood as Max strode into the room. 'It's mine,' he said.

'Andrew! What the devil are you doing here? And Miss Quy?'

'It's just a friendly visit,' Andrew said.

Max confronted him. He was three inches taller than Andrew, and more powerfully built. His mood was unpleasant.

'Just a friendly visit to my wife in my absence and without my knowledge? And just after I dismissed you? What the hell are you up to?'

'I'm sorry if you feel I should have mentioned it to you,' Andrew said. 'It was rather spur-of-the-moment.'

'You came to tell her how beastly I'd been to you?' Max said contemptuously. 'Or am I being naïve? Is there more to it than that?'

Andrew said, in a sturdier tone, 'Max, I don't have to account to you for my movements. I'm a free agent, and so for that matter is Rowena.'

Imogen sensed danger and thought it time to intervene. She said, bending the truth slightly, 'We're on our way to a day at the seaside. Andrew thought it would be nice for me to meet Rowena and so it is.'

'And I asked them in for coffee,' Rowena said.

Max waved his wife aside, but Imogen could feel that he was slowly bringing himself under control. After a heavy pause, he said with studied politeness, 'Quite so, Miss Quy. I understand. You'll realise that it seems a little strange that he should choose to bring you here at such a moment. I recommend that he doesn't do so again. I don't expect the hospitality of my house to be extended to sacked employees.'

'I think we should go, Andrew,' Imogen said.

As Max calmed down, Andrew in turn was becoming angry.

'I don't like the way you behave, Max,' he said. 'Surely Rowena is free to invite somebody in for coffee without all this fuss.'

Imogen said sharply, 'Andrew, come on!'

Max said, 'Enough said. But I have some important business to discuss with my wife, and not much time. I think Miss Quy is giving you good advice.'

Andrew said, 'Good-bye, Rowena. I shall be seeing you.'

He walked out at a deliberate pace. Imogen followed. Outside, Andrew said, 'God, I feel humiliated. And to tell you the truth, I didn't feel sure as I came out that I wouldn't feel his boot in my backside.'

Imogen said, 'He's a bully. Try not to feel like that. And think of Rowena's situation. You shouldn't have told her you'll be seeing her again. I dare say you will, but it won't be going down well with Max.'

'God, I'm a fool!' Andrew said, agreeing with her. He hesitated before getting into the car. 'Do you think he'll beat her up? Should I go back in and face him again?'

'No,' said Imogen. 'He won't beat her up. He sees her as his property, and he won't damage his own property. He's violent, but it will take other forms. I can't tell what they are, but he's making her suffer.'

'She ought to be got away from him,' said Andrew.

7

'A worrying start to the day,' Imogen said. 'That gives me a lot to think about. And not quite what I thought we were thinking about.'

'It's exactly what I'm thinking about,' Andrew said. 'You've just seen what Max really is. A murderous bastard. Capable of anything. He wouldn't turn a hair at eliminating Julius if he decided Julius was getting in his way. I'm sure now he killed the poor old soak. One push from a great hulk like him and Julius wouldn't stand a chance.'

'Hold on!' Imogen said. 'There's a big gap between being a violent bully and murdering somebody.'

'It doesn't seem such a big gap when you've seen Max in action. As we have twice, at the funeral and just now. I have no trouble at all in jumping the gap. I've a hunch as big as a house. You say you believe in hunches, Imo. Try believing in this one.'

'Sorry, Andrew. I have a hunch that there's something wrong, but I can't put it any stronger than that. That's why we're driving to Eastham, isn't it?'

There was a pause.

'Andrew, you really are serious about Rowena, aren't you?'

'Of course I am. I'm surprised you ask, Imo. I've always felt you know me better than I know myself.'

'No comment on that. But she's not a first love, or a second.'

'Or a third or a fourth for that matter. But I don't love by numbers. This is different. With Jenny it was passion, and with Fiona it was sex pure and simple. Well, not so pure or simple. But sex, for sure, with a capital X.'

'And what was it with me? Affection? Comfort? Force of habit?'

'Don't be like that, Imo. You know I love you, always have, always will.'

'In a way.'

'In a good way, I think.'

'Not everyone would think so, though I don't mind. It may have been the right way for us. But Rowena is different?'

'Well, yes.'

Another pause.

'How long have you known her, Andrew?'

'Since soon after I joined Farran. Julius and Lucia gave a garden party at the Old Rectory. Rowena was there, of course. We got talking and liked each other. I walked her home to Stonegates by the field path, and walked back an hour later with my head full of her. It was like being an adolescent again, with the advantage of not being an adolescent. And from that it grew. I haven't been with her much, we're not lovers, not yet, maybe not ever, but I know and so I think does she. You know how sometimes if you're lucky you meet someone and you can feel that your minds fit together like pieces of jigsaw clicking into place and it's very satisfying? Well, with Rowena it's like that but it's something more, it's kind of organic, like being intended by nature and ready to grow into each other, like grafting. And it's wonderful of course that she's so musical, because I care a lot about that too.'

'Dear Andrew. I believe you're the last of the romantics. But it won't be easy to prise her away from Max.'

'Max!' Andrew stiffened at the wheel. 'Max!' She could

sense the anger boiling up in him afresh. 'The rotten fucking bastard! Talk about murder, I could murder *him* given half a chance!'

'Andrew!' Imogen was alarmed. 'There's a stopping place just along there. Pull into it! I'm going to drive for a while. Move over and calm down. You heard me: C-A-L-M down. Just think about having a nice day at the seaside.'

Eastham had known better days. The only resort for miles in either direction, it had been a Victorian watering place, and a few hotels had clustered at the northern end of its bay. The railway had brought an inflow of holidaymakers of modest means, and encouraged the building of a promenade, a pier and a public park, to which were added a bowling green and miniature golf. A couple of amusement arcades, a cinema and some scores of boarding-houses had followed. But the motor-car and cheap air travel had hit it hard; its chilly pleasures couldn't compete with the beaches of the Mediterranean. Though there were some for whom it had nostalgic appeal, it was by now decidedly down at heel.

The main street was almost deserted when Andrew and Imogen arrived. They parked without difficulty and asked along the street about Headlands, meeting only blank looks until they reached the one genuine-looking pub, the Fisher-men's Arms. Here a single elderly customer, sitting huddled over the remainder of a pint, seemed willing to talk to them.

'Headlands?' he said. 'Oh aye, everybody knows Headlands.'

'Nobody seemed to be telling us,' Andrew remarked.

'Folk around here don't like to talk about it. They wish it was somewhere else.' He eyed them with some interest. 'Headlands has what you might call rather special customers. Mind you, I reckon there's no sense in objecting to it. It brings a bit of money into the town. And business for a few, though it's not a kind of business they talk about.'

'Yes, but how do we find the place?' Andrew asked.

Wrong priority, thought Imogen. If the old man was inclined to talk, he should be encouraged.

'Can we buy you a drink?' she asked.

'That's very kind of you,' he said, draining his glass and passing it across.

Andrew, with a look of heavy patience, went to the bar and bought him a pint.

Imogen said brightly, 'Tell us your name.'

'It's Ben. You don't need no more. Everyone knows me around here. What's your name?'

'Imogen.'

'That's a fancy one.'

'It's the name I was given. And this is Andrew.'

'Andy, did you say?'

'No, Andrew, not Andy,' said Andrew stuffily.

Imogen dug him in the ribs and went on, 'Now we know each other, don't we, Ben? Tell me, why do people not like to talk about Headlands?'

'Well, there's stories that go around, and folk think they don't reflect well on the town. You know what they call that place locally? They call it Dryout Towers.' He paused to let it sink in. 'I expect you know why, if that's where you're going.'

Andrew said, with even heavier patience, 'Perhaps you'll kindly tell us how to get there.'

'If you're going to drive, you'll have to go back out of town and look for a little road on your right. That goes to Headlands cross-country, so to speak. Or if you were so minded you could park at the end of the promenade, near here, and walk along the cliff. Headlands is where you might expect it to be: on the headland. It's a mile or so further along.'

'Thank you,' Andrew said, and made to move on. Imogen stayed him.

'Those cliffs are very steep, aren't they?' she said.

'They're famous for it. None else like them in this part of England.'

'And dangerous, I suppose?'

'It's not cliffs that's dangerous,' the old man said. 'It's people that's stupid.'

'I seem to remember reading about a fatal accident here a few weeks ago.'

'Yes, there was. It was at a spot they call Hell's Elbow. Some famous fellow, I can't remember his name. But he was drunk, of course. They shouldn't have let him out.'

'I suppose it was something of a scandal?'

'Yes, it was. Doesn't do the town any good. The folk up there say their patients – well, they call them patients, I call them drunks, and none the better for being rich – they say they stay in the grounds, but I've seen more than one of them wandering around outside and so have others. Local people don't walk on the cliffs no more because they don't like meeting them. Call it prejudice if you like. Me and my mate Charlie didn't mind; we used to go up there on fine days; we had a neat little sheltered place in a hollow where we could have a smoke and a chat. We'd come down here and have a drink, too.' He had downed his pint at remarkable speed. 'But Charlie's gone now; got a bit of money and lit it out of town. And the youngsters all go; there's nothing for them here.'

Andrew weighed in. 'Was there any suspicion locally about that death?' he asked. 'Anybody wondering if it really was an accident?'

'I don't know anything about that,' the old man said. 'They've fenced the spot where it happened.' Then, suspiciously, 'Why are you asking? What do you have in mind? You're not police or something, are you?'

Imogen was mildly irritated. She felt she could have kept the old man talking and might have charmed her way to further information. But once the thought of the police had occurred to him, the chance had gone. His readiness to talk had dried up, as it would have done in the actual presence of a policeman. She thanked him, smiling, for his help, and they returned to the car. Looking round, she saw that he was staring after them.

'I think we'll walk, don't you?' Imogen said. 'It's a beautiful day.'

'But we're going to make inquiries at the hotel, or whatever it calls itself. Don't you think we need to arrive by car? I mean, just turning up on foot, dressed as we are, looking like passing hikers or something . . .'

'Don't worry, Andrew,' Imogen said, with just a touch of malice. 'Your Oxbridge accent will make up for the absence of a Mercedes. Come on.'

The promenade ended in a turning area, from which a footpath wound away up a slope to the cliff top. From there Andrew and Imogen could see Headlands, commanding the landscape. It had clearly in earlier days been the most prestigious of Eastham's hotels, and the furthest out of town. Beyond it, a further headland was visible through slight ultra-violet haze, some further two or three miles distant.

It was a perfect day, with slight cotton-wool puffs of white cloud drifting in reflection across the water, and a sea that displayed a thousand colours, ranging from pale eau-de-nil to deep, intense blue. Imogen couldn't take her eyes from it. She walked in a happy daze along the cliff path.

'You'll be over the edge yourself if you don't watch out,' Andrew warned her. 'And we've a job to do. We have to find the spot where it happened.'

'You weren't listening, were you? The old chap we were talking to said they've fenced it off. There couldn't be a bigger clue than that. And if you can bear to take your eyes off the ground, just look at that sea. It changes from second to second. And the clouds that "all the summer through the water saunter". Quote.'

'Auden?'

'The very same.'

'Disallowed. It isn't summer yet.'

'Objection overruled on grounds of pedantry. Anyway, if it isn't summer now it will be. Somer is i-comen in. Quote.'

'Disallowed, on grounds of unbearable smugness of quoter.'

'You're getting back to normal, Andrew. That's good. But now do me a favour and just look at that sea.'

They stopped, looked and moved on, along slightly rising ground with two or three indentations where the sea had taken a bite out of the cliff. They saw the fence from a distance. There was no mistaking it. It was still new, about three feet high and easily climbable: designed to deter rather than to exclude. At its seaward side was a sheer and obviously perilous drop. The path now skirted safely round it.

On a nail was the torn remnant of a notice; the rest of the notice lay, ripped in half and trodden, on the path. Andrew picked it up with idle curiosity, expecting a warning to keep clear. The actual wording was a shock. It was printed in large type, such as these days could be produced on a computer, and it said:

REJOICE!
Here Julius Farran,
King of crooks,
Met his deserved end,
Bound for hell!

Imogen, startled and shaken, said, 'Heaven help us! Andrew, I'm spooked. What do you make of that?'

Andrew said, 'Somebody's torn it down. But it's fairly clean. It can't have been here long. A few days, I should have thought, at most.'

'And it's weeks since Julius died. This is a form of hate mail, and the hate's still alive. Pursuing him beyond the grave!'

They could see dawning in each other's eyes the same thought.

'I'll bet it was that wretched lad who broke into the funeral,' Andrew said. 'And got beaten up by Max.'

'He wasn't beaten up. Roughed up a bit, maybe. Derek was his name, wasn't it?'

'Yes, Derek Dacre.'

'Whose father had a grievance.'

'Yes, indeed. I knew Robert Dacre, remember. He was furious about what Julius did to him, but he wasn't crazy. This will be Derek's doing, off his own bat. His old man should tell him to stop it.'

'Maybe we should see Mr Dacre senior,' said Imogen thoughtfully. 'I expect you could find him.'

Andrew nodded. 'I can indeed. He's not all that far away.'

'But this doesn't really tell us much. We know how Julius died, by falling, but this doesn't give any clues as to why: whether he fell or was pushed, or for that matter committed suicide.'

'Julius didn't do that,' said Andrew with confidence. 'I knew him pretty well, you know. He wasn't the kind of man to kill himself. But now we're here, let's have a look.'

He climbed over the fence. Imogen hesitated.

'Come on,' he said. 'It's quite safe. We're both sober, and no murderers in sight. Max is miles away.'

Gingerly she stepped over the fence and stood beside him.

Though the edge had been eroded in the past, the ground seemed firm under their feet. The cliff fell away, sharp and sheer, for perhaps a hundred feet, and below was a shelf of rock from which an irregular litter of boulders stretched out to sea. Beyond them was a narrow beach of wet sand, clear of any footprint; further out a line of seaweed and a quiescent sea. Imogen had never had a good head for heights, and when she looked down the steep fall she felt an alarming touch of vertigo. Instinctively she stepped back. Andrew, beside her, sensed how she felt, put an arm through hers and steered her away. She was slightly shocked.

'It didn't need a push from behind, did it?' she said wanly when she'd recovered. 'Have we come on a wild-goose chase? Couldn't it have been an accident after all?'

Andrew said, 'No. I knew Julius well. He was self-preserving in the highest degree. He drank too much, but he was never drunk in his head, if you know what I mean, and I don't believe he'd have gone over that brink of his own accord in any circumstances. All I'm convinced of as a result of seeing this place is that it was an ideal spot for such a murder. And Imogen, I know in my bones it was Max. We know from the diary entry that he was around that night, and we know what stakes he was playing for. It may take some proving, but we're going to try. For now, we need to see inside Headlands and talk to Dr Random. Then we'll see what Lucia can tell us. And as you suggested, we'll go and see Mr Dacre. He lives at Tuesday Market. Hardly out of our way.'

8

Headlands was solid and handsome. It had presence. It was late Victorian, and had been adventurously modern in its own day: rosy red brickwork with decorated gables, horizontal layers of white brick and generous white-framed windows. The parking area, well concealed from the rest of the grounds, held half a dozen expensive cars. A broad, weed-free gravelled drive led through immaculate lawns to a porticoed front porch and a white-painted front door with elegant fan-light. Its name was discreetly displayed, without any descrip-tion; it might have been the private house of a prosperous family.

Inside, all was deep carpet, cream walls and restful pictures. A button pressed at the reception desk brought an attractive and well-dressed woman in early middle age. Andrew had prepared his mission statement, and explained that he and his sister were looking for a safe and comfortable setting in which their Aunt Laura might, with help, recover from the addiction into which she had fallen since the death of Uncle Herbert the previous year.

Imogen, herself a straightforward soul, heard him with a mixture of admiration and unease; she'd never before been party to an imposture and wasn't quite sure that a desirable end justified such a means.

'I'll find out if Dr Random is free,' the receptionist said. They were asked to wait for a few minutes in a parlour with easy chairs and copies of *Country Life, Good Housekeeping, Investors Chronicle* and *Fortune*. A maid, young and with a homely accent, put her head round the door to offer them a cup of coffee; they declined with thanks, and after an interval that seemed discreetly timed neither to imply over-eagerness on the one hand nor lack of consideration on the other were shown into the comfortable study of the director, Dr Timothy Random.

Dr Random, a well-preserved man of perhaps sixty with a small, neatly trimmed beard, was friendly. For a moment his face seemed familiar to Imogen, but she couldn't place him. He introduced himself, hoped he could be of service, and invited them to tell him about Aunt Laura.

Andrew embroidered his story with what seemed to Imogen to be a good deal of relish. Aunt Laura had been kind, sweet-natured and loved by all; she and Uncle Herbert had been Darby and Joan, devoted and inseparable. Unfortunately she had gone to pieces when he died, and although friends and relatives had rallied round her as best they could she had sought comfort at the bottom of a glass. Sherry had been her downfall. She had increasingly often been found helpless, unable even to undress and go to bed, not getting proper nourishment. Neighbours had been shocked by the number of empties found in her house; it seemed she had been drinking two or more bottles of sherry a day.

Dr Random nodded sympathetically. Unfortunately, such cases were not as rare as one could wish. He was sure they could do something for Aunt Laura; a course of four or possibly six weeks would work wonders, and Headlands had something approaching an eighty per cent success rate in relieving clients of their dependency. He had better make it clear at once that treatment was not cheap: the standard charge was nearly three thousand pounds a week.

That was no problem, said Andrew; Uncle Herbert had been a successful stockbroker and had left his widow very well provided for. Imogen listened with interest as further details unrolled; she was almost beginning to believe that Aunt Laura and the late Uncle Herbert really existed.

Dr Random had questions to ask. This was not a hospital or a mental institution, he pointed out. Could he be assured that Aunt Laura was not violent, was not mentally ill or suffering from clinical depression?

Andrew assured him that Aunt Laura was of an even temperament, amenable and also highly intelligent. She could do *The Times* crossword in ten minutes flat, he added proudly, 'or at least she can in her better days'.

Imogen thought it time to ask about the qualifications of the staff.

Dr Random was a little vague. 'I am of course medically qualified myself, and I have specialised in the treatment of addictions,' he said. 'Most of our staff are not, strictly speaking, qualified, but all are experienced in the sympathetic management of dependency.'

'And are your patients allowed out?'

'It's understood that they don't go out unaccompanied. We have daily walks or car excursions accompanied by staff. Of course they can leave altogether if they wish, but I'm pleased to say that hardly ever happens.'

Imogen asked two or three practical questions, of a kind that would probably not have occurred to Andrew, and then asked, 'Might we possibly look around?'

'Of course. We shall be delighted. Mrs Frodsham will accompany you and show you our facilities.'

He picked up the telephone and the well-dressed lady reappeared.

With her they made a tour of Headlands. It was all spotlessly clean, well furnished, tastefully decorated and quiet. In a dining-room the tables were being laid for lunch by the young maid they had previously seen and an older one. Four patients sat separately in a vast drawing-room which had a proportionately large bay window with spectacular views out to sea. Instinctively, Imogen moved over towards the nearest of the patients, meaning to make some friendly remark, but Mrs Frodsham intervened.

'We would rather you didn't go too near to our guests,' she said. 'They're sensitive about their reasons for being here, and we don't want them to feel they're being looked at like animals in a zoo.'

In a smaller adjoining room four people were playing bridge, oblivious to visitors; in another room two patients were listening to Bach on excellent hi-fi equipment, while two more had a Scrabble board placed between them. There was a library which would have seemed well stocked on a cruise liner, and at the top of the house was a gymnasium with rowing machine and treadmill. A heavy gentleman was pedalling an exercise bicycle at a stately pace. Everything seemed peaceful and orderly.

Dr Random was waiting for them at the end of the tour.

'I'm sure Aunt Laura would be very happy here,' said Andrew brightly.

'May I take down some details?' Dr Random asked. 'There'll be a little paperwork, I'm afraid. And of course, we would like to have a letter from her own doctor. Not a referral exactly, since as I said we are not a medical hospital, but a report on her condition and needs. He will know what's expected.'

Andrew said, 'I believe you had a tragedy here a few weeks ago. The death of Sir Julius Farran.'

Dr Random's tone of voice turned chilly. 'Yes,' he said.

'The accident occurred quite close to here. He fell from the cliff.'

'It must have been very unpleasant for you.'

'It was indeed. But I would prefer not to talk about that. Everything about it that needed to be said was said at the inquest. No criticism was made of Headlands. It was a sad affair, but it is in the past.'

'I had hoped to discuss it with you.'

'May I ask what is your interest in the matter?' the doctor inquired.

'I worked for Sir Julius until his death.'

Dr Random's tone became icy. 'And now you have come here to inquire about a place for your aunt. That is rather a coincidence, isn't it?'

'Well, coincidences do happen!' said Andrew limply; but even to Imogen it didn't sound convincing.

'Look here, who and what are you? A journalist, an undercover policeman, a private detective?'

'I'm none of these things,' Andrew said. 'I'm a friend and former employee of Julius Farran, that's all. Until the other day I was a director of the Farran Group. I have a natural interest in the matter.'

'Then why didn't you tell me that in the first place?' Dr Random demanded. 'Not that I would have told you anything if you had.'

'That's why I didn't.'

'Because there is nothing more to tell that is not already known. As for your Aunt Laura, if she exists, you'll have to look elsewhere for accommodation for her. I have no vacancies. Good-bye.'

'Well, you blew that!' said Imogen crossly when they were outside. 'All we've done is act out a silly charade. If you'd left it to me, I believe I could have found out how Julius managed to be outside and at large in the middle of the night. As it is, we're no further forward.'

'Sorry, Imo,' said Andrew, crestfallen. 'Another time . . .'

'I don't suppose there'll be one,' said Imogen.

As they walked away down the drive, the maid they'd seen in the house came running up to them.

' 'Scuse me,' she said, breathless, 'would you be going into town?'

'Into Eastham?' said Andrew. 'Yes, I suppose so.'

'It's cheeky, I know,' the girl said, 'but if you are, could you maybe give me a lift? I'm going off duty and my bike's got a flat tyre. And I'm due at the dentist's in half an hour.'

'I'm afraid you're out of luck,' said Andrew. 'We've come here on foot.'

The girl's face fell. Then she said, 'Oh well, I guess I've time to walk.'

'Come with us,' Imogen invited her.

'Oh, thank you,' the girl said, 'if I won't be in the way.'

'Of course you won't,' said Imogen. 'It's nice to have company. Tell us your name.'

'Lisa,' the girl said. 'Elizabeth really. Old-fashioned, isn't it, but there, I'm stuck with it.'

'And you work at Headlands. Have you been there long?'

'Too long. About six months, I reckon. I'm looking around, but jobs are scarce in these parts. Otherwise I'd have left by now.'

'You don't like it, then?'

'No, I don't,' the girl said emphatically.

'What's wrong with it? Do they work you too hard?'

'Not really. No harder than you'd expect. I don't mind hard work. Keeps your mind occupied. But I don't like the atmosphere.'

'I can understand that,' Imogen said sympathetically. 'I'm a nurse and I know what nursing's like. It asks a lot of you, but in the end it's rewarding.'

'I'm not a nurse, and it's not rewarding to me. It's not that I mind working with alcoholics. They're pretty harmless really. Here they're mostly recovering from their withdrawal symptoms or being psychologised or just getting used to life on mineral water. But it's so quiet it's uncanny. You can hear the silence. Like a morgue, almost. I mean, nobody's happy or talkative or enjoying themselves. I feel if ever I raise my voice I get hushed. And the management don't welcome questions from lower grade staff like me. Mrs Frodsham, she always speaks quite softly but it's as if she had ice in her vocal chords; she puts me down so quietly I feel like I don't really exist. As for Dr Random, well, he's the spookiest person I ever knew.'

Andrew said, 'You're not exactly making a sales pitch for the place, are you?'

'No, I'm not. I wouldn't put anybody I cared about in here. Not that I know of anything they've done wrong, it's just the feel of the place. And there's been three deaths while I've been here.'

Lisa hesitated before going on. 'I mean, I don't want to give you the wrong idea, there wasn't neglect or suspicious circumstances or anything. There was one man that got his hands on the whisky and binged in his room all night and died of acute alcoholic poisoning, and how did he get hold of it, that's what me and Kate in the kitchen wondered. Then there was an old lady found dead sitting in her chair, heart failure they said, natural causes, but it was a shock, she was as lively as a cricket the day before. And then of course there was Sir Jules Whatnot, that there was quite a to-do about, you might have heard of it. Got out at night and walked over the cliff at Hell's Elbow. Seems to me Dr Random should have been in trouble over that, letting him get out unsupervised, but no, he's Teflon-coated he is, he could say black was white and the bigwigs in town would take his word for it.'

Lisa's tone was warming up from disaffection to indignation as she spoke.

'I wasn't that happy about Sir Jules Thingummy,' she said. 'He always seemed a bit reluctant, like he didn't want to be here. His wife was with him, of course; they were quite affectionate, well, kiss-on-the-cheek affectionate if you know what I mean, but no more than that. Dr Random often had his lunch with them. And when he did, he had a glass of wine with his meal, and you should have seen the patients all looking at it, because they weren't allowed any drinks, but of course there was no reason why he shouldn't. The night Sir Jules died, I was on duty, and there was actually an argument going on among the three of them – Sir Jules and his wife and Dr R. – and a couple of visitors they had.'

'Did you know these visitors?' Imogen asked.

'No, I hadn't seen them before, but I took a good look at them. One was a big hefty fellow, quite good-looking but I wouldn't fancy him, and the other was a tall, thinnish man with a little moustache. They was all in the small parlour, a sort of private room where the patients don't go, and I heard raised voices. In fact there was a bit of shouting. I was quite curious, tell you the truth, but I couldn't hear what it was about. Anyway, it had died down and they'd broke up by the time I went off duty, and I suppose Sir Jules and his lady had gone to bed. And I never saw Sir Jules again. He was found next morning dead.'

'You weren't asked to give evidence at the inquest?' Imogen said.

'No. No reason why I should have been. And I wasn't going to volunteer, I can tell you. Keep your head down, that's what

I always say. There wouldn't have been any point in it. It wouldn't have made any difference anyway. We all know what happened. Poor old Jules, they say he was a bit of a crook but I really felt quite sorry for him.'

Andrew said, 'There are two things that puzzle me. How he got hold of the drink and how he got out of the house.'

'There's always ways of getting liquor if you want it badly enough. Somehow or other it's smuggled in, never mind the rules, never mind that it makes nonsense of being cured. It's said there are characters in the town that'll supply it, at a price. Dr Random didn't know about that business, or so he said, and told the inquest he'd put a stop to it. As for getting out, well, Headlands isn't a prison. People who come here have to sign an undertaking not to go out without permission, but that's all that prevents them. It's no secret where the side-door keys are kept, and there was a set in Sir Jules's pocket when they found him. He'd have been able to get back in, if he'd lived to do so.'

'And why was he wandering around in the middle of the night?'

'Nobody knows for sure. But he liked to walk on the cliff in the daytime, with his wife, and she said at the inquest she supposed he just took a fancy to it that night. He often didn't sleep well, she said. She was fast asleep herself. They had separate bedrooms joined by a dressing-room between them, and she didn't know until morning that he was missing.'

'You're very well informed, Lisa,' said Imogen.

'Well, it's interesting, isn't it, specially if you work at the place where it happened. And there isn't much excitement in Eastham. A bit of it goes a long way . . . Well, here we are in town already. It hasn't taken much longer than it would've done by road. I'm still in nice time for the dentist.'

'And we're still in time for lunch,' said Andrew when she'd gone.

9

They drove along the front at Eastham, and in the absence of anything that looked like a serious restaurant returned to the Fishermen's Arms. Ben was no longer there. The lunch menu was uninspiring: a choice of prefabricated lasagne, production-line steak pies, and battered scampi that were all too obviously reheated from the freezer. Andrew and Imogen negotiated for ham sandwiches – available in white bread only – and drank their beer in the public bar, now inhabited only by a bored landlord and a couple of local males who leaned on the counter and engaged him in intermittent desultory conversation. Occasional glances of mild curiosity were directed at the incomers, and Imogen and Andrew thought it wise not to talk about their visit to Headlands; walls might have ears. They drank their beer and left.

'We learned a lot from Lisa, didn't we?' Imogen said. 'But we need to know more about the inquest. And there has to be a local paper.'

There was; it was the *Eastham and District Advertiser*, and it was easy to find. Its premises were a little shop in the main street; it was clearly not printed there, and a sign in the window said that advertisements were accepted for the series of eight local papers to which it belonged. There was a resident reporter, but he was new and very young and was just going out on a story. The girl left in charge of the shop made no difficulty about allowing them to see the back number for the week in which the inquest on Julius Farran was held.

It had made the front page, and was fairly detailed. A local resident, walking early on the beach with his dog, had seen the body of a well-dressed man lying below the cliff. He hadn't touched it, but was sure it was dead. He had hurried to the police station, where PC Eaton was on duty.

PC Eaton said that in view of the nearness of Headlands the possibility that the dead man might be a resident there had immediately occurred to him, and he had telephoned to inquire whether anyone was missing. The immediate response had been negative, and as there was no road access at Hell's Elbow he had set out on foot along the beach to investigate. He had found the body and had noted its position and its injuries as far as visible, and hadn't touched it. On his way back he had received on his mobile a call from the hotel to say that Sir Julius was not in his room, that his wife had been woken up and was in a state of distress, and that Dr Random was driving her into town. He had telephoned Sergeant Davis, who was now on duty and had taken over the inquiry. The body was in danger of being covered by the incoming tide. Sergeant Davis gave evidence of its recovery and removal to the mortuary, and of its identification as that of Julius Farran by his widow and the doctor.

There was extensive and somewhat gruesome evidence by the police pathologist, who described the injuries suffered and confirmed that they were consistent with a fall from the cliff. There was nothing to suggest any other cause. The time of death would have been somewhere between midnight and 4 a.m.; the amount of alcohol in the body would suggest that Farran was likely to have been not incapable but sufficiently affected to have wandered accidentally over a cliff. The night had been dark and cloudy but dry, and there were no signs of a struggle or of the involvement of any other person:

Dr Random confirmed the police account so far as it concerned Headlands and said that while inmates were not locked in they had to agree that they would not go outside without the knowledge and permission of the staff. Alcohol was strictly forbidden, and Sir Julius had shown no sign of breaching these conditions.

The coroner questioned Dr Random about Sir Julius's medical history and state of mind. Dr Random said he had known Julius for many years; he had no depressive tendency, but after years of overwork, and with his increasing age, the habit of drinking too much had grown alarmingly. He had at last been persuaded to agree to treatment at Headlands. The treatment appeared to be succeeding. On the night of Sir Julius's death he and Lady Farran had sat with Sir Julius watching the late-night news on television, after which they had all gone to bed. Sir Julius was then sober and had appeared calm and untroubled.

Finally the coroner called Lady Farran. Lucia confirmed having sat with Sir Julius and Dr Random in her husband's room until about 11 p.m. Sir Julius was then sober and there was nothing obviously amiss. Like the doctor, she had believed that he was adapting well to his treatment and that it was succeeding. She had gone straight to sleep and had not seen him again alive. She described in quiet, stoic tones the telephone call from hotel reception the next morning and her discovery that his bed was empty.

Eventually, becoming irritated by the coroner's line of questioning, Lucia said to the coroner, 'I think you are implying that this may have been suicide. I can tell you that Julius was the last person in the world to take his own life, and that if he had meant to do so he would have found a less messy way than this.'

The coroner said at once, 'I make no such implication.' His finding, accompanied by suitable expressions of sympathy, was of accidental death. He recommended that Headlands should make it impossible for inmates to get out at night and should inquire urgently into how it had been possible for one of them to get access to alcohol, with a view to preventing it. Dr Random, who was still present in court, readily assured him that these things would be taken care of. The coroner also recommended that the borough council should turn its attention to safety precautions on a dangerous stretch of coast.

'Has anything transpired since then?' Imogen asked, thanking the girl as she closed the newspaper file.

'Not that I know of,' the girl said, turning away to deal with an inquiry about an advertisement for a sofa, in excellent condition, for sale at thirty-five pounds or near offer.

'Well,' said Imogen as they returned to the car, 'what did you make of that?'

'I was surprised how lightly the coroner let Dr Random off on the question of how Julius had access to drink in a place where for obvious reasons it's barred.'

'No doubt Dr Random's a distinguished figure locally. I dare say the coroner was very respectful of him. That wouldn't emerge in the newspaper report. And there are some rather odd omissions, aren't there? Nothing said, apparently, about the bootlegging of liquor. And nobody mentioned the little party or conference or whatever it was that went on in the small parlour that night.'

'Maybe it wasn't thought relevant.'

'Or maybe it was all too relevant for somebody.'

Andrew burst out laughing. 'I wonder if we're a pair of egghead Keystone cops,' he said. 'One minute you're accusing me of letting my imagination run away with me in the matter of Max. Now I wonder if it's your imagination that's on the rampage and you're building up a great conspiracy theory. Perhaps Julius was murdered by a committee?'

Imogen said, 'Be serious, Andrew. I'm sure Lisa didn't invent that gathering. It took place, and it can't be an accident that Julius died so soon afterwards. Now, can we do a bit of constructive guessing about who was there? Dr Random, Julius and Lucia to begin with. A hefty man, handsome but tough-looking . . .'

'Max, of course. We know from the diary he was there.'

'Actually, what we know is that the initials J. F. were pencilled in.'

'Same thing.'

'Not quite. Don't jump to conclusions, Andrew.'

'You're a fine one to talk. Go on.'

'And a man with a little moustache.'

'Your precious bursar,' Andrew said. 'What a collection! Can we be right, Imo? Are we jumping to conclusions again?'

'I think we must be right,' Imogen said slowly. 'They were there. The key people of Farran Group, or most of them, all in the small parlour at Headlands. A kind of parliament. But why, Andrew, why?'

'An unofficial board meeting? Or even an official one? Boards aren't obliged to meet in a boardroom. And an obvious reason for meeting at Headlands would be that Julius was there. He was the chairman, after all. However, remember that I was a board member at the time, and I didn't get notice of any meeting.'

'That could be significant in itself. Was there an in-group and an out-group?'

'Well, there were Julius appointees that Max didn't like and who didn't like him. Notably me and Helen Alderton.'

'But there'd be a – what do you call it? – a quorum?'

'There certainly would.'

'Supposing,' Imogen said, 'supposing it was a meeting called to sack Julius?'

'Well, there's a scenario. The board tells Julius he's fired. He can't bear it. The company was his life. In agony of soul, he gets out the bottle of bourbon he's hidden at the bottom of his luggage and swigs the lot. Then he wanders out. Goes to the brink, looks down, tells himself it's all over with him, and on impulse he jumps.'

'It brings us back to the suicide theory,' Imogen said. 'And perhaps it's the most likely one. But somehow I don't believe it.'

'Nor do I!' said Andrew. 'I just know it was murder and Max did it. And that theory lets out Max.'

For a moment Andrew looked downcast. Then he said, 'Half a minute, this won't wash. The board could vote Julius out, that's true. But it wouldn't stick, so to speak. In the last resort, he held the winning cards. He could have sacked the board.'

'I thought you said the controlling shares were in trust for Rowena.'

'Yes. But Julius still had control really.'

'He doesn't now he's dead, Andrew.'

'No, of course not. It's . . .' Anger boiled up afresh in Andrew. 'It's Max. It's fucking Max! With Julius dead, Rowena holds the shares but Max wields them. The say-so is still his! He may have got her to make them over to him by now, for all I know, but in any case he's totally dominant. Look, it's as clear as daylight. Max was playing for the jackpot! With Julius out of the way, he was made. Who says Julius went out that night on his own? Max could have invited him out to talk things over, got him to the edge, and then quick as a flash, the sudden shove! I know it as well as if I'd seen it!'

Imogen said, 'You could be right, Andrew. But how on earth could we prove it? Max isn't going to admit anything. Lucia and Dr Random gave evidence, and they didn't mention anything suspicious. And to be blunt, you blew it with Dr Random. We'll not get anything out of him.'

'We can do better with Lucia,' said Andrew. 'I've known her ever since I first joined the Farran Group. Julius asked me to the Old Rectory for the weekend, to exhibit me. I was his handsome, brilliant, etcetera etcetera young discovery. And, to tell you the truth, Imo, she rather fancied me.'

'Of course, she would,' said Imogen. 'Who could resist you?'

'Don't be sarcastic. It might be useful.'

'I take it nothing actually came of this fancy.'

'Indeed it didn't. She's twice my age.'

'That isn't always a hindrance.'

'I suspect you of jealousy,' said Andrew smugly.

'And I suspect you of vanity,' said Imogen. 'Fifty fifty. Let's get back to business.'

'We could visit Lucia now,' Andrew suggested. 'It wouldn't be much of a detour.'

'She may be out, of course.'

'I'll call her number anyway.'

'You know it by heart?'

'Of course. It is – was – Julius's number when he was in the country.'

But Lucia's telephone was on voice mail.

'We'll drive there regardless,' Andrew said. 'And whether we find her or not, we can go on and see Mr Dacre.'

In fact, however, by the time they arrived at the Old Rectory, Lucia Farran was at home. As on the day of the funeral, Imogen found her impressive: tall, upright, strong-looking, well-made, with an accent that was decidedly 'county'. She would have been taller than Julius Farran and no doubt in much better health. Imogen guessed that Julius had married above his social station. Lucia's greeting to

Imogen was cool but friendly; her manner to Andrew was affectionate, but in a way that suggested a favourite nephew rather than a potential lover.

She had heard on the grapevine of Andrew's dismissal by Max.

'Whatever had you done,' she inquired, 'or not done, to get on the wrong side of Max?'

Tactfully if not truthfully, Andrew said the trouble was basically an incompatibility of approaches to the business. 'Naturally Max wants things to be done his way. It's only to be expected. I don't have any grievance.'

Imogen looked to see whether his fingers were crossed, and thought that if they weren't they ought to have been.

Lucia was sympathetic. 'A new broom,' she said. 'I suppose it's a common phenomenon, making a clean sweep. I must say, if it were Max doing the sweeping I wouldn't care to be in the way.'

She doesn't like Max, Imogen decided, and can't be bothered to conceal it.

Lucia went on, 'I hope you knew, Andrew, how appreciative Julius was of what you did.'

'I think I did,' Andrew admitted modestly.

'It may all be for the best that you've got away from Max.'

It was plain from Andrew's expression that he realised he had a licence to say what he thought. He took the opportunity and said, with his engaging grin, 'Let's be honest about it. Max is a shit and I hate his guts.'

Lucia made no pretence of being shocked. She smiled in return and said, 'Oh, Andrew, it's so good to see you. I do hope we're going to stay in touch.'

'I hope so.'

'You must miss Julius a lot,' Imogen said to Lucia.

'I do, of course. This house feels empty without him, even though he spent most of his time in London. Julius filled whatever space he was in.'

'Until Max came along,' said Andrew grimly.

'Until Max came along, indeed. But until recently Julius could cope with Max. He held the whip hand, after all. It was when he began to slide that Max really pushed his way in. And although heaven knows Julius was a controversial figure, he was always a changed man when he got down here. He was very good to the village and the church. It's a pity his last weeks were so sad and the end so disastrous.'

'We were all shocked,' Andrew said.

'At least the verdict was a relief.'

Andrew was startled. 'Could it have been anything else?' he inquired.

'We were a bit afraid of a suicide finding. It depended rather on who was called to give evidence. Of course, Tim and I told the truth, but we know there were some who might have suggested otherwise. The coroner was merciful. I think coroners often are; they'll avoid a suicide verdict if they reasonably can.'

'You mean you really think he might . . . ?' Andrew began. But Lucia backed away.

'It was death by misadventure,' she said firmly. 'So far as I'm concerned, that's it. And I miss him and shall go on doing so, even after I've remarried.'

There was half a minute of silence, almost audible.

Lucia went on: 'Yes, I may as well tell you, Tim Random and I intend to marry as soon as possible – within a few weeks, we hope. Julius would have wished it. His widow and the old friend of both of them: what objection could there be? The world won't have anything to say about it, and neither of us would care if it did. Have you met Tim?'

'Only once,' Andrew said, neglecting to add that it was earlier in the same day and hadn't been a happy occasion.

'I'm sure you'll meet him again. He's a good doctor and a good friend. Though he is a little elusive, being so busy.'

As they drove on the way to see Mr Dacre at Tuesday Market, Andrew said, 'I'll bet she and Random are lovers, and may have been for some time. I wouldn't blame her for having somebody on the side. Julius was away most of the time, and she must have known that he played around a bit.'

'How well do you think Julius will have provided for her?' Imogen asked.

'I understand – unofficially, because probate hasn't been granted yet – that he's provided for her very handsomely. They were on good terms, you know, and Julius was rich beyond the imaginings of people like us.'

'Then the thick plottens,' said Imogen. 'Lucia and Dr Random had lots of motivation to get rid of Julius. His death brings them freedom to marry and lots of money with it.'

'We're not living in the 1880s. She could have divorced Julius and married Random any time, if she'd wanted.'

'And given up a splendid house and a way of life and a position in local society?'

'Well, that's a point. Julius would have hated it; he enjoyed those things himself and wouldn't have moved out to make it easier for her. And if she'd insisted on a divorce she wouldn't have had the financial claim on him that she has as his widow. But anyway, Imo, I don't really believe in that pair as suspects. Max is still my man.'

IO

It wasn't difficult to work out how Tuesday Market got its name. It was an ancient if undistinguished small town at the centre of a broad agricultural area, and the market in question had been held in its central square since the thirteenth century. Indeed, the standard local history, the work of an imaginative antiquarian, alleged that it had first received a charter to hold this market from King Stephen, himself a somewhat improbable monarch, though he undoubtedly existed.

Unfortunately the charter had been mislaid somewhere along the line, but the market was still in existence. The town came to life every Tuesday morning, and until lately had slept through the rest of the week. But Sir Julius Farran had seen development possibilities in it. It was a pleasant enough place to live in, and there was scope for a comfortably traditional retirement complex, attracting people who could trade profitably down from their expensive homes in the cities and enjoy rural peace and prosperity. This was what had taken the place of the long-established department store of Dacre and Son, established in 1854. To satisfy the planners, the complex had included half a dozen fancy shops and a recreation centre, and in a gesture to its origins the whole development was known as Dacres.

This was a hollow joke to Mr Robert Dacre, great-grandson of the firm's founder. Among other omissions, he had failed to protect the use of his name. Moreover, a further coup by the

Farran Group had made it possible for Mr Dacre's own commodious Victorian house, built by his great-grandfather at a conveniently short distance from the business premises, to be surrounded by affordable housing, much despised by those who could afford better.

The present Mr Dacre was a melancholy widower, rich but with little to do. He had no sporting or cultural interests; he did not play bridge or enjoy travel. His life had been devoted to the welfare of his business and its employees. He had expected to continue running it after the takeover, with the added resources of a large company behind him. He had been devastated when, within months, it had been abruptly closed down.

It was in fact market day when Andrew and Imogen drove into Tuesday Market, but it was mid-afternoon and by now the traders were dismantling their stalls. Andrew had admitted to nervousness about the reception they would receive, but Robert Dacre, a balding man in late middle age with a vestigial fringe of reddish hair that reminded them of Derek, was polite though cautious.

'Of course I remember you,' he said to Andrew. 'The brilliant young man who popped in and out of Julius's office from time to time. I don't blame you for what happened to Dacres. The whole affair was a hundred per cent Julius, and he never consulted anybody. However, it's a surprise to get a visit from you. Could it possibly be that some of Julius's misdeeds have been found out? My son would be delighted even now if they were. For myself, frankly, it's too late. I was furious at first, but I had to come to terms with it. The damage is done, and it can't be undone.'

'Your son is Derek, isn't he?'

'He is. He's taken it all very hard, poor lad. He'd supposed all through his teens that he'd be taking charge of Dacres. Couldn't be bothered with exams or university, because he thought his future was all mapped out. I'm afraid I led him to think he'd be safe with the new owners. I should have known better, of course. It's one of the things I blame myself for.'

'Derek's been expressing his views rather forcibly, hasn't he?' Andrew said.

'Oh dear. You mean the business in the churchyard? I had a call from the Rector of Welbourne St Mary's about that. I apologised humbly, of course, and I gave the boy a thorough ticking-off. I call him a boy, but the truth is, he's over twenty and I can't control him. He hasn't been up to anything else, I hope.'

Andrew and Imogen had agreed that it wasn't up to them to tax Robert Dacre with his son's behaviour. They let the last remark pass.

Dacre went on, 'So please tell me what brings you here. You haven't by any chance been talking to young Janner, have you?'

Andrew looked puzzled.

Imogen said to him, 'That's the very articulate young don who was slagging off Julius the night of the incident at St Agatha's.'

'I remember now, only too well. Apart from that occasion I've never met him,' Andrew said. 'He did seem to be remarkably well informed.'

'So he ought to be,' said Dacre. A faint hint of satisfaction lightened the melancholy of his expression. 'He got the information from me. But of course Julius was still alive and there was some point in exposing him. Now he's gone, it doesn't matter. At least, it doesn't matter to me any more, though I'm afraid it does to poor Derek. Tell you the truth, he's got obsessed, and it worries me a lot. I do all I can to keep him out of mischief. He's a good boy at heart, you know, but headstrong. It's a good job he hasn't seen my dossier, or there's no telling what he might do.'

'Your dossier?'

'Yes. That's why I mentioned Carl Janner. I had a whole dossier of information on Julius, and he borrowed it for the dinner in Cambridge. I gather from Carl that he made good use of it and really got Julius on the run.'

'I'm not sure I would put it like that,' Andrew said. 'But it did result in a disastrous evening.'

'It could have been worse, in fact positively explosive. But I warned Janner not to use the really damning stuff. That could have blown Farran out of the water. But the downside risk was frightening. Julius was a crack shot with a libel writ, and most of what we knew couldn't be proved. He might have ruined us with nothing achieved. Janner took my advice; I think he had a high regard for his own skin.'

'Where's the dossier now?'

'Janner still has it. He asked if he could keep it for a while. I knew he was working on an anti-Farran project of his own – writing a book, I think – and I didn't want to discourage him, so I told him he could do as he likes with it.'

Imogen said, 'I think you told us Derek hasn't seen it.'

'No, he hasn't. And I don't want him to. He's furious enough without that. It's better if he doesn't know it exists.'

'I wonder if you're right,' Imogen said thoughtfully.

But Mr Dacre didn't seem to be listening. 'I just wish he'd calm down. And now, can I offer you a cup of tea? I'm afraid I don't have any cake or biscuits or the things that people offer at teatime. These days I don't entertain.'

Afterwards, in the car, Andrew said, 'I'm surer than ever it was Derek who put up that notice at the cliff edge.'

'We don't absolutely know it was Derek,' Imogen said, 'and even if it was, I don't think it's up to us to punish his father for it. Poor Mr Dacre, he's sad enough already.'

Andrew said, 'I've made up my mind what I'm going to do next. I'm going to confront Max in his own office.'

'Max won't want to see you.'

'He'll have to see me. I shan't go away until he does. But first of all tomorrow morning, of course, I have to see the Master again and talk about coming back to St Ag's. The more I think about it, the more I'm sure that's what I want to do. Maybe getting sacked by Max was a blessing in disguise.'

'I wouldn't count your chickens,' Imogen said cautiously.

'Well, if Sir William meant one half of what he said when he was trying to persuade me not to go, he'll welcome me with open arms. Now, what about tonight? Where am I sleeping?'

'I'm shocked that you even ask,' said Imogen. 'You'll be in the spare room again. Close your eyes and think of Rowena.'

Andrew drove across from Newnham to St Agatha's next morning. Imogen went with him, meaning to catch up on some chores and telephone Bridget to find out whether anything alarming had happened during her absence (it hadn't) before her morning surgery.

Andrew was in high spirits; Imogen doubtful, wondering whether he would be back in her surgery crestfallen or whether – perhaps even worse – Sir William, who never liked to disappoint anybody, would have offered him misleading hopes. It was the first of these surmises that proved right.

'Nothing doing,' he told her an hour later, in a tone more of surprise than anger. Sir William had been cordially forgiving about his earlier desertion; had quite understood his feeling the need to move on and had realised that academic salaries were far too low for a young man of his brilliance. He was sure the Governing Body would be delighted to have Andrew back, but alas, the college was in the worst financial straits for many years and there was no hope whatever of an appointment being approved. Andrew had wondered about a university appointment as distinct from a college one, but the Master was just as discouraging. A Harvard economist of worldwide reputation had recently been persuaded to come over to Cambridge, in a rare triumph of counterflow, and had brought a team with him. There wouldn't be any vacancy in the foreseeable future.

'So I'm sorry, Andrew, but it doesn't look as though we can offer you anything at the moment,' Sir William had said. 'But of course, things may improve. Peter Wetherby is working hard for us, and we're very impressed by him. He's working at present on a brilliant investment which he says may pull us round, and enable us to open our arms again. In the meantime, we're having to take some rather stiff financial medicine. In fact, later today I have to receive a deputation from the junior common room. We're having to cut off some financial support that we give to poorer undergraduates, and as you can imagine this causes great indignation – taking it out on the poor and so on. However, don't give up hope. And in the meantime, you know you'll be very welcome to dine at High Table from time to time and keep in touch. Though I'm afraid High Table isn't what it used to be. You wouldn't believe the kind of wine we're bringing ourselves to drink these days.'

'Peter Wetherby!' said Andrew with disgust, recounting the interview to Imogen. 'I know him better than the Master does. Essentially a nobody. No drive, no personality. Nothing.'

'But clever?' Imogen said.

'Sly and crafty, maybe. Not all that bright, compared with other accountants I know. In fact, I think he's just a bean-counter!'

'We might have been better off if Dr Honeywell had counted his beans more carefully,' Imogen remarked mildly.

'I suppose so. Let's hope the wonderful Wetherby justifies

his build-up. This is the golden age of accountancy, after all. The heyday of the unproductive. The baggage train runs the regiment.'

'Try not to be so sour,' Imogen advised him.

'Don't spoil it. I'm enjoying being sour. It helps me get into the mood for dealing with Max.'

'Andrew! Do be careful what you say and do. I won't be there to pick up the pieces, you know.'

'You won't come with me?'

'I can't. I was away all day yesterday. I can't decently ask Bridget to give me another day off.'

'What will you do today, then?'

'Well, in a minute I have my surgery. Then I think I might try to have a word with Carl Janner. I'm intrigued by that dossier that Mr Dacre mentioned.'

Out of the corner of her eye as she crossed Fountain Court, Imogen glimpsed Peter Wetherby, going out through the main gate. He was a strange figure, she thought, not for the first time: moving swiftly and silently, seeming hardly to make an impression on the air as he went. What was the word for him? Catlike? Shadowy? Even a little sinister? No, that was nonsense, she told herself. True, he walked alone; she had never seen him in company with anyone else, or heard any words from him except a formal 'Good morning' when he passed by. It seemed even that members of the college tended quietly to move away out of his path . . .

It could be of course that people were a little in awe of him. Perhaps she was a little in awe of him herself. Yet he might have a part to play in the mystery surrounding Julius Farran's death. She remembered that he was a director, though non-executive, of the Farran Group, and that Andrew had remarked on his hours spent with Max and Bill McNair in Julius's room the day after Julius died. He seemed to have been in the group at Headlands also. She'd have liked to ask him some questions, but couldn't think of any pretext on which to do so.

She wasn't in awe of Carl Janner, however. They were old sparring partners. She had first known him in the early years of her incumbency at St Agatha's, when he was still an undergraduate and she was new to her post as college nurse. An unruly undergraduate he'd been, and something of a troublemaker even then; but four or five years later he'd come back as a junior fellow, his rough edges smoothed and his talent for troublemaking more sophisticated. After surgery she walked over to Back Court, where he had a somewhat poky set of rooms, such as St Agatha's provided for its unmarried junior fellows.

'Good morning, Dr Janner,' she said formally.

Carl looked up, grinning. 'Come off it, Imo,' he said. 'We've known each other since we were so high. I don't even let my students call me Doctor. But you don't often come to this neck of the woods. What can I do for you?'

'You can tell me about the Farran dossier,' said Imogen, coming straight to business.

Carl looked surprised. 'How do you know about the Farran dossier?'

'Robert Dacre told me.'

'I didn't know you knew him. How is the poor old sod?'

'Lonely and mournful. Physically he didn't look too bad to me. He could do with more exercise.'

'You've talked to him recently?'

'Yesterday as ever was. I hadn't met him before that.'

'So why were you meeting him now?'

Imogen had expected this question, and was prepared to give a straight answer. 'I've been worried about Julius's death. He talked about having enemies, and said I should remember that if I heard he'd fallen under a bus. And soon afterwards he was found dead after falling from a cliff, which seems suspiciously similar.'

Carl was immediately interested. 'Funny you should say that,' he said. 'I wondered myself what might lie behind it when I read the story in the papers. It sounds as if you think it might be murder.'

'I wouldn't put it as strongly as that. I'd like to know what happened, that's all.'

'What question are you asking yourself? Is it "Did he fall or was he pushed?" Because there's another possibility.'

'That he might have jumped,' said Imogen. 'Of course. But people I've talked to won't hear of it. He was simply not the suicidal type, they say.'

'Nobody can be sure of that,' said Carl. 'Lots of suicides come as a shock to everyone around. And yes, it was suicide that came to my mind. There were very good reasons why Julius Farran might have decided to top himself. And they're not mainly because of his enemies in the business world, though he certainly had plenty.'

'You mean?'

'The very thing you were asking about. The Farran dossier. Listen, Imo, what I said at that dinner wasn't the half of it. Julius Farran was holding off disaster by libel threats. I believe when he died he had about twenty writs out; gagging writs. But the pressure was growing all the time. Sooner or later, the explosion would have come.'

'And now that he's dead?'

'Well . . . Don't put it around to all and sundry, Imo, but although Julius is dead the story isn't. A friend of mine edits the Witness feature in a broadsheet Sunday paper, and we're working together on this. We're not in a hurry to break the story, because we want to have a book ready to follow it up. It should be a bestseller. Business scandals are a winner. There are thousands of people in the City who never read a novel but will pay up gladly for a good financial shocker. It's their equivalent of pornography.'

'Will you be discussing it with Mr Dacre, Carl?'

'Of course. He has a right to know what we're doing with his material. I expect I'll be seeing him in the next few days.'

'Do you think you could get him to tell his son what's going on?'

'His son? Derek? What makes you think of that? From what I've seen of Derek, he's pretty useless. Anyway, Robert's absurdly protective where Derek is concerned.'

'Do it for me, Carl. That young man needs rescuing from his obsession. If he could know that Julius was getting his deserts, even posthumously, it might just satisfy him. At least, there's a chance.'

'You know I'll do anything for you, Imo,' said Carl indulgently. 'Well, almost anything. Within reason, that is. If it's something I approve of. And if there isn't any other objection. OK, don't look at me like that, I'll see what I can do. For the moment, I've got something else on my mind. I'm meeting the student representatives, to plan the campaign against the cuts.'

'There was a meeting with the Master this morning, wasn't there?'

'Yes. A brief one. It didn't get anywhere. Sir William has no room for manoeuvre, he says. The abominable Wetherby is holding the purse-strings. Sir William suggests we arrange a discussion with Wetherby, but I can tell you right away that Wetherby isn't going to play ball. So we'll have to plan for direct action.'

'What form would that take?'

'That's what we have to decide. A demo, for sure; maybe a

strike against dining in hall; maybe in the long run withholding room rents.'

'And will it work?'

'Probably not. When the chips are down, the college holds the winning cards. If the students don't pay their dues, they'll be told they can't take their degrees until they do.'

'Will you warn them of that?'

'Yes, of course. But the mood they're in, it won't stop them. And I'm not going to discourage them. A bit of disruption will be a good thing. What this college and the university as a whole need is a lot more student militancy. Sometimes I despair at the absence of it. We're all so meek we encourage the powers-that-be to push us around.'

'You're still a revolutionary, Carl, aren't you?'

'Call me that if you like. I'm not ashamed of it. We've become a rare breed, I'm afraid.'

'What about your own career? Don't you stop to think about that?'

'I'm not too worried. I don't expect my contract to be renewed anyway; I've been too much of a thorn in people's sides. But there are half a dozen of the new universities who'd be glad to have me. I'm more worried about someone like Belinda Mayhew, who teaches a minority subject, such as classics. Classics doesn't benefit the economy, or so our masters suppose, and if it doesn't benefit the economy it's no good.'

'You don't share that view, then.'

'No, indeed. I may be a revolutionary, but I'm not an ignoramus. Classics is worth defending. Anyway, I'm a sociologist, and I'm not sure that sociologists have more economic value than classicists. Analysing society doesn't increase the gross national product any more than studying Aristotle. The rewards in either case don't appear on the financial bottom line.'

'You seem to me,' said Imogen, 'to be not so much a revolutionary as an all-round heretic.'

'OK,' said Carl, sounding pleased. 'Heretics of the world, unite. Join the club. Although, as Groucho nearly said, no club that I'd want to join would be likely to want me as a member.'

'You're a member of St Agatha's, though. Don't you feel any loyalty to the college?'

'I have lots of loyalty to the college. But reform of the university and college systems would benefit it in the end.'

'Hmm. And what about poor Sir William? He's terribly worried over the college finances. Do you really want to inflict more pain on him than he already has?'

'Sir William's a dear old boy. Of course I wish him well. But . . .'

'But if he stands in the way of the revolution it will just have to roll over him?'

'Come now, Imogen. You're stealing my lines and exaggerating them.'

'You're a dangerous man, Carl. I deplore you. I don't know why it is that I rather like you.'

'We'll leave it at that, Imo. Just for now, I have to go and stoke up the class war. Lots of love.'

Was he a dangerous man? Imogen wondered as she walked back to Fountain Court. Perhaps he was, but somehow she doubted it. Did really dangerous men have a sense of humour?

11

Andrew had gone by the time Imogen reached home. He hadn't left any message and hadn't made his bed. Typical, she thought ruefully. She was having tea with Fran when he came through on the telephone.

'I'm in the office,' he said. 'Clearing my desk. Max is in conference all day and won't see me. However' – there was satisfaction in his tone of voice – 'I've got around that one. Thanks to Fiona.'

'Fiona?'

'Yes. You know she's Max's PA now. His personal assistant. Very personal. She's living with him in the Hertfordshire cottage during the week. It's a neat little arrangement. Weekends she spends in her London flat and Max goes home to Rowena. And she says Max will be on his own in Hertfordshire tonight. He doesn't know it yet, but she's having an evening out with a girl-friend. If I go along in the late evening, I'll find him alone with a bottle of bourbon, she says. The perfect opportunity to beard him in his den.'

'Why should Fiona be doing this for you?'

'Oh, for old lang syne, I suppose. She may still have a soft spot for me. Or perhaps the odd pang of conscience for having thrown me overboard – not that Fiona's a great one for pangs of conscience. But I'm guessing she has other fish to fry. I don't really believe in the evening out with the girl-friend. Fiona's the kind of girl who doesn't go in for girl-friends. Max may have money and power, but he's pushing fifty, dammit, and she likes them younger than that. The girls in the office say she's been seeing a gorgeous hunk of twenty or thereabouts. In fact I'd be more surprised if she wasn't.'

'So Max is cheating on Rowena, and Fiona's cheating on Max?'

'Seems so. It'd only be poetic justice, wouldn't it?'

'But, Andrew, I'm a bit alarmed. Not about Fiona. From what you say, she can look after herself. But Max seemed to be on the point of violence at Welbourne yesterday. What if he turned even nastier?'

'Don't worry,' said Andrew. 'I'm not afraid of Max.' And he hung up before she could say any more.

Imogen had a hard day. She spent the afternoon in a committee meeting, discussing the affairs of a good but rather boring cause in company with people who seemed to have more time on their hands than she had. She was just sitting down to supper when she was recalled to college by a telephone call from the porters' lodge. There had been something of a fracas. Carl Janner and Clive Horrocks, accompanied by a small group of undergraduates, had attempted to see the bursar, and been turned away from his door. They had called a meeting in the junior common room for the early evening. As it happened, the lunch in hall had been a particularly dismal affair of nondescript soup, luncheon meat and limp salad, and a groundswell of grumbling rose quickly to anger. The result had been a surge of undergraduates across the Fountain Court to the bursar's rooms, where entry was again refused and a reluctant porter was barring the door.

'Nothing to do with me,' he said. 'I'm only doing as I'm told. And he says if there's trouble he'll call the police.'

This was an inflammatory message. Some thirty or forty students, with Carl and Clive leading from the rear, first banged on the door and then began to chant. The chant intensified, and developed into shouts of 'Wetherby out!' It happened that there was a meeting of the college rugby club going on in a nearby room, and some of the rugger players, either from political disapproval or from enthusiasm at the prospect of a rumpus, decided to break up the demonstration. A scuffle began in good spirits, but became unpleasant when two or three people came to blows, and still more so when Clive Horrocks, pushed by a hefty front-row forward, tripped over an ancient mudscraper and got a nasty cut on the shin.

By the time Imogen arrived, most of the combatants had drifted away to dinner in hall. She disinfected and bound Clive's cut, having ascertained that he'd had an anti-tetanus injection quite recently, and listened patiently to a tirade in which he threatened to sue the college. She knew he wouldn't. Then, on her way to the main gate and home, she was seized upon by Lady B. to render comfort and an extra dose of his daily medication to the Master.

Sir William was deeply upset. He had been hoping to cruise uneventfully through his last two or three years to retirement, but things were happening in the college that hadn't occurred before in his lifetime.

'To tell you the truth, Imogen,' he said, 'I am beginning to wonder about Wetherby. He came to us with high recommendations, but I don't think he was meant by nature for collegiate life. It seems that he slipped quietly away during the recent scuffle rather than facing the music. He isn't even in college at the moment. His car's gone from Back Court. It won't do, you know. And he's playing the financial cards very close to his chest; not telling us exactly what he's up to. However, I gather he has some master plan that will deliver us magically from our problems, and I do hope he'll be vindicated. Now, may I offer you a glass of sherry?'

Imogen declined with thanks and returned to Newnham to her neglected supper. She was joined afterwards by Josh and Fran, to whom she recounted the day's events. They sat late in the kitchen over a bottle of wine, Imogen and Fran worrying over what the college was coming to, while Josh, cheerfully convinced that like all financial crises this one would blow over in due course, reserved his worries for the college first boat. Colin Rampage had still not turned up for training. Tony Wilkins was currently taking his place, but he wasn't up to Colin's standard, and his promotion to stroke had left a weakness at six. Spies had reported that the Caius and Lady Margaret first eights were very fast and training hard, and St Agatha's had to bump them both in order to go Head of the River in the Mays. Hopes were beginning to fade.

'Now that,' said Josh, 'is really serious.'

At that moment, the doorbell rang, imperiously and non-stop. Imogen made her way wearily to the door, and Andrew staggered in.

'Oh, my God!' she said. His clothes were dishevelled, he had a developing black eye and a split lip, and there was blood on his shirt. 'It's Max, isn't it? Oh, Andrew, why didn't you have more sense? And why didn't I manage to stop you?'

Andrew, shaking and unsure of himself, could hardly speak. He sank into a chair.

'I thought the brute was going to murder me,' he said after a minute. 'I reckon I'm bruised just about all over. He said that if I went anywhere near him or Rowena again, he'd finish me off. He fucking well could, too. Though I did land one blow on him and give him a bloody nose.'

'You shouldn't have driven here in that condition,' Imogen told him. 'You're still in shock. You might have killed yourself, and some other driver as well. Now, get your clothes off and let me check you over, and then if there's nothing dire I think it's some dressings and a warm bath, and a double whisky if you're good, and to bed with you. I'll put your clothes in the washer. You can tell me all about it in the morning.'

'I think we're in the way, Josh,' said Fran, nudging her boyfriend from the room.

Andrew submitted patiently to Imogen's ministration, and by the time the whisky was reached had relaxed a little. But he wasn't going to stay quiet until next day.

'Max wasn't really going to kill me,' he admitted. 'But he gave me a hell of a fright. He'd been drinking and he was in a foul mood. He wouldn't listen to me. He just told me to get out, and when I stood up to him he lost his rag. I suppose I could bring an assault charge against him. Of course I'm not going to.'

'I think you're wise,' said Imogen. 'I think you should steer clear of Max from now on.'

'And leave him as monarch of all he surveys!' Andrew said. 'Running the Farran Group, making millions, grinding Rowena into the ground, having fun and games with Fiona and getting away with murder. Literally. Because I'm more sure than ever that he did for poor old Julius. That man would stop at nothing!' Andrew was silent for a minute, then said with a burst of sudden vigour, 'I'll get the bastard somehow if it's the last thing I do!'

'Oh, Andrew!' Imogen said. A wave of tenderness swept over her. Seeing him stripped, she'd remembered and noted afresh his slightness. Physically, he wouldn't have had a chance against Max. 'How can I make you look after yourself? And how will stirring up more trouble help Rowena? Think of her and be sensible. And for now, go to bed!'

It was five o'clock in the morning when the telephone rang. Imogen struggled out of sleep and into a dressing-gown, and went to answer it. A female voice asked anxiously, 'Is that Imogen Quy's house?'

'It is.'

'And is Andrew Duncombe there?'

'Who's calling?'

'It's Fiona. Fiona from Farran Group. I thought he might be with you. I need to speak to him, urgently.'

'He's in bed. You know what time it is?'

'Of course I do. You must get him up. I told you, it's urgent. I mean, really urgent. Life-and-death urgent.'

'Andrew's pretty groggy. He's been hurt. He may not be well enough to come to the phone. Can I tell him what it's about?'

'Tell him . . . Tell him I found Max when I came in.'

'You found Max? What do you mean?'

'Andrew will know what I mean. Get him to the phone, now! Please!'

Imogen went to the spare room and switched on the light. Andrew groaned at her touch and turned over, and she had to shake him awake.

'It's Fiona. She needs to speak to you, urgently.'

'Whatever time is it?'

'Five o'clock. Can you get up? She sounded desperate.'

Andrew climbed out of bed, looking bemused. He was naked, and his bruises were visible.

'Whatever . . . ?' he began.

'Here, put on my dressing-gown,' she said, 'and take it in the hall.' She went back to her room, and put her own telephone on the hook. It wasn't her way to listen in to other people's conversations.

But a minute later Andrew's voice came up to her, loud and agitated. 'Imo! Are you there? Pick up your phone! Quick!'

She did, and heard Fiona's voice. It sounded hysterical.

'Yes, I tell you. He was just lying there smothered in blood. And his head battered in – it's indescribable, it's horrible, it's worse than horrible, I heard myself screaming . . . Andrew, was it you? Did you do that?'

Andrew seemed unable to speak.

'Why did you? Why, why, why?'

Andrew pulled himself together. His voice was shaky. 'You mean he's dead?'

'Of course he's dead. Murdered! Didn't you know? You were there, weren't you? Was it you or was there somebody with you who did it? I can't believe it, I can't, but he is, he's bloody dead. Oh God, did I say "bloody"? It's not a joke, he's in the study, he's all bloody, there's blood everywhere.'

Andrew's voice was steadying. 'You're sure he's dead?' he said. 'You're really sure?'

'Sure? If you could see what I'm seeing! You'd never sleep again! Did you do it, Andrew, did you?'

Andrew said, 'I haven't killed Max. He was fine when I left him. We had a bit of a scrap, but I hardly touched him. He damaged me a lot more than I did him. I can't believe what you're telling me . . .'

'It's true, I tell you, it's true! I haven't gone crazy, even if I sound it.'

'OK, Fee, I do believe you. And believe me, I didn't kill Max. Somebody must have got in after I left. Have you called the police?'

'Not yet. I had to speak to you first. I've only been here for half an hour. I got home late. It was a night out, and you can probably hear how I am, I'd had a few drinks. I'm not really fit to see the police.'

Andrew had become calm. There was even a degree of snap in his voice. 'You must call them at once,' he said. 'Never mind what time it is. And I'm coming straight across to you. They'll need to talk to me, and the sooner the better. And Fee, for old times' sake, I'll rally round you if I can.'

'What will I tell the police?'

'Just tell them when you came in and what you found. What more can you do? I can't say I'm sorry about Max. I'm still trying to take it in. I'll be with you in about an hour.'

Andrew put down the telephone.

Imogen went down to him. He looked dreadful. His eye had closed up and was turning purple, his unshaven face had a ravaged look, his hair was rumpled. Imogen said, very quietly, 'I heard what she said. Andrew, my dear, I'll be on your side whatever happens. But you must tell me every last thing about what went on.'

Andrew said, 'I'm gobsmacked. When I left Max, he was triumphant, horribly triumphant, and a bit drunk. He'd made a mess of me and I'd hardly managed to lay a finger on him. I can still hardly believe he's dead, but he must be, and it wasn't me. Someone must have broken in and done for him. But, Imo, it must have occurred to you already, the police will have an obvious suspect. Me. There'll be lots of my DNA around. To say nothing of the marks on my body.'

Imogen said, 'All the same, you're quite right to go over there at once. As you said to Fiona, the police will want to question you in any case, and it will be best if you turn up of your own accord and give them straightforward answers. I'll come across with you and give you moral support. I'll drive, too, if necessary.'

Andrew said sharply, 'No. I don't want you to get involved. And it wouldn't serve any purpose.' He hesitated. 'It's a pretty unlikely story really, isn't it? There's a fight, blood all over, then one of the combatants goes off into the night and the other is murdered by somebody else. How can I not be suspected?' He hesitated, then, 'Imo, tell me truly, do you believe that it might have been me?'

Imogen said robustly, 'No, I do not. Not for one second.'

She spoke with certainty. She knew to the depths of her being that Andrew had not killed a man. She knew he couldn't.

'But you realise,' she said, 'that if we're right about Julius there have been two murders, both of the top people at Farran Group. And either it's another remarkable coincidence or there's a murderer still around.'

12

Imogen saw Andrew off into a grey dawn loud with bird-song, which seemed a mockery. Then she went back to bed, but not to sleep. Her mind was in turmoil. Though she had learned in her professional life that the most surprising people sometimes did unexpected and terrible things, she remained sure that Andrew didn't have it in him to be a killer. She played over in her head such scenarios as she could devise to explain what had happened during the night at Lilac Cottage, but couldn't make sense of them. It was clear, however, that Andrew faced interrogation and would have some explaining to do.

After a while it occurred to her to wonder about Rowena. If Rowena didn't yet know about her husband's death, she soon would. She had seemed to Imogen to be lonely and vulnerable, and whatever kind of husband Max had been this would be a huge shock to her. She might need moral support. Imogen decided it was not for her to break the news but she would get in touch as soon as she properly could. Then she fell asleep after all, and in spite of uneasy dreams and a couple of brief awakenings she overslept and was late for her surgery. There was no call from Andrew, and Josh and Fran had quietly gone out.

Surgery was uneventful, apart from a visit from Clive Horrocks to have his dressing renewed and to tell her he might not sue the college after all but he was going to launch a petition to have the offending mudscraper removed. He was aware that it was of venerable antiquity and was said to have been stumbled over by important personages of the past, but it was indefensible in these days when Fountain Court was totally lacking in mud. Imogen conceded that the scraper was now more a hazard than a necessity and sent him away muttering. Five minutes after the end of her surgery Sir William appeared, having come to request another extra dose of his medication.

'I shall be all right by this evening,' he said, 'but I must admit I'm still a little distressed. Wetherby seems to have been away all night and is still away. His secretary doesn't know where he is, and although of course he isn't obliged to stay in college all the time it's a busy period and he might at least have mentioned his absence to somebody. And there's a groundswell of opinion building up against him. I really don't like it.'

'Mr Wetherby is a director of the Farran Group, isn't he?' Imogen said.

'Yes. I'm not entirely happy about that either. He told us when he applied for the job here that he'd be retaining his directorship, but he gave us to understand that it was an undemanding kind of appointment, a sort of consultancy – an occasional board meeting, that sort of thing, not a serious call on his time. And we were so pleased to get an experienced accountant with a surprisingly modest view of what he should be paid that we snapped him up. But perhaps we were naïve. It seems he's more deeply involved than we thought.'

Imogen said, 'He may be even more involved now. I've just heard that Max Holwood, the chief executive of the Farran Group, has died.'

'Oh dear. And so soon after Sir Julius. I didn't even know he was ill. Wetherby must be upset. Perhaps he's been distracted lately. I shouldn't have made those uncharitable comments, should I?'

Imogen refrained from telling the Master how Max had died, or of Andrew's presence on the scene. Sir William would have to know before long, but for the moment he was more than enough upset already. She chatted to him gently for the next twenty minutes, and he left observing, not for the first or second time, that a talk with her always left him feeling better.

She carried her mobile phone with her all day, but there was no call from Andrew, and an attempt to telephone him produced only a routine voice mail message. The death of Max had been too late to make the day's newspapers. Next morning, still not having heard from Andrew and after a restless night, Imogen went out early for the morning papers, and discovered that there had been an earthquake disaster in the Middle East, with some hundreds of deaths and several British citizens among the missing. Gruesome pictures were splashed over the front pages, and Max's violent death, cut down in relative importance, was inside and down-page, its unpleasant details dwarfed by major catastrophe. The death, it was stated, was being treated as murder, and a man was helping the police with their inquiries.

Her heart bumped. That could only be Andrew. But she had a job to do, and went to her surgery as usual. She had barely arrived when there was a call from the porters' lodge to say that a policeman wanted to see her. Imogen braced herself with an effort, said crisply, 'Send him along,' and prepared to offer a cup of tea.

The policeman showed her his credentials. He was Sergeant Burwell from the Hertfordshire Constabulary: tall, with a small moustache and an authoritative though not aggressive air. He declined the tea, and asked Imogen if she was aware of the death of Mr Max Holwood. Imogen said she was. Was she aware of the circumstances? Imogen said cautiously that she understood he had died a violent death. How did she know? She had been told by Dr Duncombe, who had driven over from Mr Holwood's cottage.

The policeman nodded. 'We are talking to Dr Duncombe,' he said.

Imogen felt a nasty little spurt of anxiety at the turn of phrase: did 'talking to' mean interrogation, she wondered, and did it mean that Andrew was being treated as a suspect?

The sergeant noticed her unease, and said, 'We're only trying to find out what happened. I gather Dr Duncombe spent the night with you.'

'He spent the night in my house, yes.'

The sergeant gave her a straight look. The slight change of wording was clearly not lost on him. He didn't pursue the point and went on, 'He tells us he was in a distressed state when he reached you.'

'He was indeed.'

'In fact he had injuries?'

'Yes. Obviously you know about them. Do I have to spell them out?'

'No. Did he tell you he had been in a fight with Mr Holwood?'

'He did.'

'And did he tell you what it was about?'

This was a hard one to answer. Imogen said thoughtfully, 'Max sacked him a few days ago.' That was simple truth and might be seen as a sufficient cause of conflict. Asked for other reasons, she would have been in difficulty; she didn't want to discuss Max's infidelity, and still less did she want to talk about Andrew's suspicions of Max, which indeed events had probably proved groundless. She said quickly, 'But Andrew didn't attack Max. Max attacked him.'

'That is what he told you,' the policeman said. His tone was neutral, but the implication was obvious: that what Andrew said was only one side of the matter.

'I know Andrew well,' said Imogen. 'He's a peaceable man. I know he did hit Max, but that was in self-defence. I don't believe Andrew had ever swung a fist before in his life. Whereas Max could be violent.'

'Why do you say that? Do you know of occasions when Mr Holwood behaved violently?'

The only specific instance Imogen knew of was the incident in the churchyard. Reluctantly she described it. It occurred to her as she did so that she was drawing the sergeant's attention to the closeness of the two deaths. He might or might not find any significance in that; indeed, she wasn't really sure that there was any. He listened to her, then moved on.

'I believe you attended to Dr Duncombe's cuts and bruises. You're a nurse, aren't you?'

'Yes, I did, and yes, I am.'

'Dr Duncombe arrived back at the cottage in the morning having changed his clothes.'

'Yes. I borrowed some clothes for him from my lodger. His own were in a mess.'

'There was blood on them?'

'Yes.'

'What did you do with them?'

'I put them in the washer.'

'Oh.'

It struck Imogen forcibly that putting bloodstained clothing in the washing machine might seem suspicious. But it had been an obvious and ordinary thing to do at the time.

The sergeant went on without comment, 'What time did Dr Duncombe arrive at your house the previous night?'

'I didn't take special note, but I think it was around half past eleven.'

'Is there anyone else who might remember?'

'There are my lodgers, Fran and Josh. They were there at the time.'

The policeman made a note of the names. Then he asked, 'What time did he leave you this morning?'

'I do know that. It was ten or twelve minutes past five.'

'Could Fran or Josh confirm that?'

'No, they couldn't. They were fast asleep. I didn't see why I should wake them.'

'Would it have been possible for Dr Duncombe to leave the house during the night?'

'It was locked. He could have found the keys. But if you mean could he have slipped over into Hertfordshire and come back to Cambridge again between midnight and five o'clock without my knowing, no, he couldn't possibly, the very idea's absurd. He wasn't in a condition to do such a thing, anyway . . . Does that query mean you're suspecting him of murder?'

The sergeant waved the question away. 'Nobody's suspecting anybody of anything at the moment. I told you, we're just trying to find out what happened.'

'Do you know what time Max died, and how he died?'

'No. That's not what I'm concerned with. I'm here to ask you what *you* know.'

It sounded like a put-down.

The policeman relented. 'I wouldn't be supposed to tell you even if I knew,' he said, 'and I don't. The pathologist will report on that.' He closed his laptop. 'Now, could I change my mind about the cup of tea?'

Imogen gave him tea and biscuits. He took on a chatty tone.

She wasn't deceived; he was still fishing for information. She was wary; she had no intention of telling anything but the truth, but an incautious slip might damage Andrew. Having drunk his tea, the policeman got up to go.

'You're going to be around for a while?' he asked her. 'You're not on the point of going away somewhere?'

'No.'

'We might need to ask you some more questions. I can't be sure. Thank you anyway for your help.'

When the policeman had gone, Imogen called Andrew again, and at last got a reply.

'Sorry to have left you in the dark,' he said. His voice sounded weary. 'I've been put through the mangle. Two sessions, two inspectors and a sergeant, not much sleep. I'm going to bed now.'

'Where are you?'

'In my own flat. I've just got here. They haven't detained me, they've let me go home, but they've told me emphatically to stay around. They may be keeping an eye on me, I don't know. There are people hanging about outside; I don't know who they are and I'm not answering the door. But the cottage is where the action is; police have been crawling all over it. And I'm sorry for Fiona; she's been heavily questioned too, and the press are on to her, as you might expect. Nobody's been charged, so they have a free hand. The whole world will know that she's Max's current mistress – was, I should say – and you'll be seeing her face all over the papers tomorrow.'

'They can't suspect her, surely?'

'I shouldn't think so. She wasn't even the last person to see him alive – that was me – but of course there was plenty they wanted to know from her. And, Imo, I'm scared. One protection for me is timing; with any luck they'll know, if they don't already, that Max's death couldn't have happened before I left to drive to your house. You and your lodgers are my alibi, so to speak. But it's a nightmare. And although I detested Max I wouldn't wish him or anyone to be brutally murdered.'

'You realise, Andrew, that your suspicion of Max goes out of the window. It's hardly likely that Max got rid of Julius and then in turn somebody got rid of Max.'

'Unlikely but not impossible. It's a dog-eat-dog world they both lived in. However, I must admit that if somebody did get rid of Julius, then probably it was the same person who's done for Max.'

'In which case there's a double murderer at large. Does that thought frighten you?'

'Perhaps not as much as it should. I haven't room for any more fright at the moment. But, Imo, I think we should be out of contact in the next few days. It was my fault, not yours, that I got into this mess, and I'd like to keep you out of the picture if I can. And there'll be financial ramifications, terribly hush-hush, that I don't want to involve you in. You don't by any chance hold shares in Farran Group?'

'No. Or any others, for that matter.'

'And you don't read the financial pages?'

'No.'

'Farran shares are slipping.'

'They slipped when Julius died, didn't they, and then recovered?'

'Yes. But the City wasn't really worried. The general view was that Max was up to the job and might even be an improvement on Julius. The City thinks differently now, with both of the top men gone and no obvious successor. And, Imo, there were rumours beginning to float around before this latest disaster. Murders apart – if they are apart – there's something rotten in the state of Farran. Don't ring me, as they say; I'll ring you. Please. And now, forgive me, Imo, but you'll have to let me go. I need to get some sleep if I can. I'm alternately feeling a desperate need for it and feeling I'll never sleep again in my life.'

13

I mogen was busy during the next few days, and was glad there was so much to take her mind off her anxiety. With final examinations pending, there were many calls on her for pastoral services. As always, there were undergraduates panicking about the work they hadn't done, fearing disaster, needing reassurance and (in some cases) a nudge to pull themselves together and get on with it. There were emotional crises, referred to her by tutors and best friends and sometimes by the victims: relationships breaking down at the worst possible time under last-minute stress. Two or three of the younger dons shamefacedly revealed their anxieties over the future to Imogen, and by doing so relieved them. Somehow the whole college knew that Imogen was an ever-present help in times of trouble and didn't hesitate to resort to her. Additionally, there was a nasty flu-related bug going around, and a consequent demand for remedies, advice and sympathy.

She found time, however, to look apprehensively at the newspapers. The senior common room at St Agatha's sub-scribed to the entire range of them, not excluding the most lurid tabloids. The earthquake disaster still filled most of the front pages: pictures showed still more scenes of devastation, stories were of mounting casualties and of survivors dragged out of the rubble. Beside all this the death of Max Holwood was reduced to its proper proportion in the scheme of things. Coverage in most of the papers diminished. Investigations, it was said, were continuing vigorously; the police had several leads and were following them up. In short, there was nothing much to report.

There was one exception, the *Meteor*, which had got itself a minor scoop, most likely through a police leak. 'Mystery fight in murder cottage', it said; and the story was that there had been a violent struggle in the cottage on the night of Max's death. Elsewhere in the report it was stated that there had been clashes in the Farran boardroom and that star economist Andrew Duncombe had been dismissed. It wasn't suggested that Andrew was the murderer, but (Imogen reflected grimly) readers were all too likely to draw that conclusion. Alongside the article was a picture of Andrew with a glamorous-looking Fiona at a smart party the previous year, and the information that he had been her boyfriend before her association with Max. Things looked bad for both of them.

Though no one in the senior common room would have admitted actually reading the *Meteor*, the news spread quickly around the college. Andrew was still well remembered. Imogen was not mentioned in the report, though it was clear to her that that might come. Nobody spoke about the affair to her except Carl Janner, who observed with a wealth of innuendo that she too had once been friendly with Andrew.

The Master and senior fellows had something more directly disturbing to think about. Peter Wetherby had still not been seen or heard from.

'I don't like the look of it,' Sir William said, coming across the court to Imogen for a further advance on his medication. 'It's only four days, I know, and of course the man isn't chained to the college, but I wouldn't have expected him to disappear without a word to anyone. There may be a simple explanation – I hope so – but these are difficult days for us all and I'd have liked him to be around. We can't call the police as yet; we'd look so silly if he turned up a few hours later asking what all the fuss was about.'

Imogen said thoughtfully, 'We could ring the Farran Group.'

'I suppose we could,' the Master said, adding drily, 'That seems to be his other base of activity.'

But no one at Farran Group headquarters appeared to have seen Mr Wetherby lately.

Sir William had hardly left when Andrew rang.

'At last!' Imogen said, in a tone of mixed relief and reproach. 'I was beginning to wonder what was happening.'

'An awful lot,' Andrew said. 'I hardly know where to begin. You've seen today's *Meteor*?'

'I have.'

'Well, the *Meteor* story's out of date already. Imo, I'm in the clear. I'm still a witness in the Max affair, but I've been eliminated from the inquiry as a murder suspect.'

'Thank heaven for that. How come?'

'Well . . . officially I've no idea, but unofficially I know more than I really ought to know, thanks to Lord Robinswood.'

'Lord Robinswood! Where does he come in?'

'He's come riding over the hill to rescue the Farran Group. He's been chairman since Julius died, remember, though with Max in charge he wasn't much involved in running the group. There are puffs of smoke emerging from the financial pages of the press. The group's in trouble; we don't know how deep, but Robinswood has called me back to help find out. He says he found my letter of resignation still sitting on Max's desk, and he's torn it up. I'm back on the board; in fact it seems that technically I've never actually left it. And Robinswood has friends in every high place you can think of. How do you think he amassed a dozen directorships? Wherever he goes he can get behind the scenes, and he's found out behind the scenes why I'm off the hook. He may even have speeded it up.

'The fact is, Imo, the autopsy showed that Max hadn't been dead long enough for me to have killed him and got across to Cambridge when I did. Also, there were signs of another struggle, and of somebody else's DNA around. Max seems to have fought back enough to draw blood. According to Robinswood's source they haven't found a match for the other DNA yet. Or rather, they found matches in two brothers and a cousin in a back street in Darlington who'd never been within a hundred miles of Hertfordshire and could be abundantly vouched for. So that wasn't any help.'

'And the *Meteor*'s aspersions are dead?'

'Yes, the aspersions are dead but the story isn't. Having written me off as a suspect, the police are back at Square One. They're holding a press conference later today, but they won't have much to report. They haven't found the murder weapon, which apparently was a sharp-pointed knife, stiletto type, easy to dispose of. A window had been broken from outside, and there were fingerprints that they've not been able to identify; they weren't mine or Fiona's. The path below the window was paved and gave them no help. So the whole thing is wide open. Fiona's been able to give them one clue, however, for what it's worth. She thinks that as she was arriving back at the cottage in the grey dawn a car was driving away from it. It was only half light and she was over the limit – shouldn't have been driving – and not taking any particular notice.'

A wild surmise came into Imogen's mind. 'It wouldn't by any chance have been a blue Audi?' she asked.

'I don't know. Fee couldn't give a description, and by now she's been pressed so hard to remember everything that she might remember anything, true or untrue. I wouldn't trust her as a source of information. Why do you ask?'

'Our bursar is missing – the unloved Peter Wetherby. He drives a blue Audi. And somebody called him the smiler with the knife. What if that turned out to be all too accurate?'

'Sounds a bit far-fetched.'

'Yes, but . . .' said Imogen, becoming excited, 'Wetherby knew Max well and had access to his office. He could have known where a key to the cottage was, and borrowed or copied it. Or, even simpler, if he appeared at the door Max would have let him in.'

'Why would Wetherby want to kill Max?'

'I don't know. Wheels within wheels. Maybe Max knew something that Wetherby didn't want to come out. Or was going to do something that Wetherby didn't want him to do.' Imogen added thoughtfully, 'The Master doesn't want to report Wetherby's disappearance, but I think perhaps he should. Meanwhile, where's Fiona now?'

'She's in her own flat, with the boyfriend, dodging the press. There are photographs around which I gather are a bit spicy, and although the police have let her go the papers think there's still a story in her. But it's not the press she's scared stiff about. Somebody murdered Max and is still at large, and she doesn't know who it is or what his motive might be. She wonders if she might be next in line. Meanwhile the boyfriend's getting jittery and making noises about getting back to university in time for his exams. She thinks he's concerned for his own skin. Doesn't want to be involved in a murder inquiry. I think they may be coming apart. If they do and if she can sneak out without the reporters seeing her, she may come to my flat instead.'

'Oh, indeed. Andrew, you do rather tend to accumulate women in your life, don't you?'

'What do you mean?'

'Well, Fiona and Rowena, and dare I mention myself? I don't know of any others at the moment.'

'Oh, come off it, Imo! If she does come, Fiona will just be a temporary house guest. As between her and me, it's all quite innocent.'

'Does Fiona know the meaning of the word?'

'I think you're jealous.'

'Perhaps I am. But let's be serious. It's Rowena I'm worried about. Have you been in touch with her since all this happened?'

'Only once. I telephoned. She wasn't weeping, but I knew she had been. Somehow we didn't know what to say to each other. We'd lost our footing. I couldn't sympathise, and she knew I couldn't. And I didn't know what she might suspect. I just sort of stammered out that I didn't do it, and she said, "I know," and neither of us said anything more for about a minute, and then she said, "Good-bye."'

'You need to go and see her,' Imogen said.

'Lord Robinswood wants all my time at present, and then some. And it may not be good for Rowena for me to go and see her while the police are still hovering around and looking for suspects. Imo, why don't you go and see her?'

Imogen said, 'I've been thinking just that.'

After some hesitation, Imogen telephoned Rowena, wondering whether she would even be remembered, and if so whether Rowena would really want to see her. But Rowena's voice on the phone, though a little strained, was welcoming.

'Yes, of course I remember you. You were here with Andrew, the day Max stormed in. Stormed in with fatal paperwork, as it happened. I felt so sorry for you, having to put up with that unpleasantness. Although it was such a brief visit, I felt at once that you and I were on a wavelength. Do come.'

'You are sure?' Imogen asked. 'It must be a trying time, and I don't want to be intrusive.'

'You won't be intrusive. I'm distressed, of course, but there's nothing you can make worse, and nothing I'd like more than a friendly visit. And you know, it's a help to me that you're a new friend; the old ones, such as I have, seem to load me with such a lot of emotional baggage.' There was a moment's pause, then Rowena went on, 'You're not going to counsel me, are you? I've been offered that already by a policewoman, a local council official, and the bank. They can hardly believe I don't want it.'

Imogen disclaimed any intention of counselling. She decided that Rowena, though under strain, was not in a state of collapse, and that her words of welcome could be taken at face value. She would go to Welbourne All Saints next day if she could arrange it.

Bridget said, 'You're getting into debt, Imo, in the matter of days off, but OK, I'll take surgery for you.'

Sir William Buckmote said, 'Yes, I know, Imogen, I really must get myself off these tranquillisers, but just for today I still feel the need. Wetherby? I'm afraid he's still adrift. What did you say? Telephone the Hertfordshire police? Why Hertfordshire? Has he been breaking the speed limit, racing recklessly through Herts in that Audi of his and terrorising the public? No, of course not. But don't tell me any more just now, I've quite enough to contend with. I want to give him another day or two. I still think he'll be back as large as life with a simple explanation . . . All the same, he really should have told us.'

Imogen, driving Josh's battered Skoda, chugged along the motorway and through country lanes now luxuriating in early summer sunshine. The Skoda responded gamely if noisily, and got her safely to Stonegates. She had expected to hear the piano, as last time. It was silent, but Rowena appeared almost at once in the doorway and embraced her.

Her hair was on her shoulders; she wore a shirt and jeans. Her face, naturally pale, looked slightly drawn, but she was in full possession of herself and her voice was steady. Imogen had previously registered her as good-looking and now decided that she was beautiful; she had fine, dark eyes, handsome features and a look of intelligence.

'I feel as if I've known you for years,' Rowena said over coffee. 'As I said, I don't want counselling, but I do need to confide in somebody congenial.'

Imogen said, 'Tell me as much or as little as you want. It's a fine day; we could walk round the garden or the village and talk plants. Or might you possibly feel like playing the piano? That would be a treat for me.'

Rowena said, 'I want to tell you a great deal. There's so much that I can't tell any of the people I know already. Imogen, although murder is a horrible thing, and I'm still in shock from it, I can't, I absolutely cannot, be sorry that Max is dead. Does that horrify you?'

'It does startle me,' Imogen admitted. 'I suppose you're going to tell me why.'

'Yes. Max was a brute, that's why.'

Imogen had already formed that impression of Max. She waited for Rowena to go on.

'My father pretty well made me marry him,' Rowena said. 'I was so young – just nineteen – and I'd had the kind of sheltered upbringing that girls don't have any more. And Father – well, you didn't know him then, did you? – he was a force of nature, a powerful one. Hardly anyone could stand up to him; I certainly couldn't.'

'Why did he want you to marry Max?'

'It was dynastic, really. He hadn't a son; he wanted one desperately. He'd have thought it out of the question for a woman to run a company the size of Farran. For him the ideal woman would be decorative and bear male children. He thought I'd be fine for that. And if he couldn't have a son the next best thing would be a son-in-law who could himself beget sons and keep control in the family. But the son-in-law had to be a successor who would run the company the way he'd done it himself. He'd looked for years without finding one, so when Max came his way he was delighted. Max was very bright, very tough, very determined, a risk-taker, a man after Father's heart.'

'So it was a whirlwind courtship?'

'It was hardly a courtship at all; more of a fait accompli. Less than six months after I first met Max, I was married to him.'

'And did you love him at the time?'

'No. I didn't know what love was. Except that I love – loved – my father, and I knew he loved me in his way, though he didn't even try to understand me. It was as if he owned me and could do what he liked with me. He didn't bully me, exactly, he just assumed that he gave the orders and I carried them out. And I assumed it too; I'd never known anything else.'

'He didn't actually abuse you?'

'He didn't abuse me sexually. That came with Max, after we were married. Max was bestial and violent, and seemed as if he was driven by hatred. He inflicted sex like vengeance on an enemy; I'll spare you the gruesome details. And there were other women all the time; he didn't bother to conceal it. I'm sure he didn't treat them as he treated me. He couldn't have got away with it; but I was his wife, fair prey. I never told anyone how bad it was, least of all my father. I thought about divorcing Max, often, but it would have meant telling Father, who would have been appalled, and would have done something drastic, maybe even violent. I had the boys to think about, and my mother, who's so frail. Well, divorce is one thing that can't happen now.'

She was silent for a moment, then went on, 'Now of course everything's come apart. I've told you, I can't be sorry that Max is dead, but you can imagine, with that coming when it did, I feel as if the wheels have fallen off the world. I guess it's up to me to put them back on again. The boys are going to need me when they come home from school, and Mother doesn't seem to get any better, rather the reverse.'

Imogen said, 'There's steel in you, Rowena. You'll come through this all right, I know it. And I suppose you won't be in financial need?'

'No. My father made a settlement on me before the marriage, and arranged it so that Max couldn't get at it. Which was just as well. And there are my shares in Farran Group.'

Imogen decided not to pass on what Andrew had said about Farran Group the day before, but, remembering something he'd told her previously, Imogen said, 'I believe you're the controlling shareholder now.'

'Well, not really. My father didn't have a majority of the shares, though he had the biggest holding and called the shots. In an extremity the banks and investment companies who held most of the rest could have voted him out. Anyway, the reason Max arrived the day you and Andrew were here was that he'd brought some paperwork for me to sign, which gave him effective control over my shares. He was going to use them as collateral for a loan to carry out a big deal. I didn't object; didn't really think of objecting. It was the sort of thing he did, you know, borrowing big to make an even bigger profit; he and my father were wizards at it. I don't know what happened over that deal; whether it went ahead before Max died.'

Alarm bells rang loudly in Imogen's mind.

'Don't you think you'd better find out?' she asked.

'I expect I shall find out. I had a sympathetic phone call yesterday from Lord Robinswood. It's kind of him, when he's so busy. I've met him two or three times, and basically I think he's a nice man. But I won't be able to talk to him as I'm talking to you.'

'You've told me so much that I didn't have to know,' said Imogen, 'that you've encouraged me to be even more impertinent. I know that Andrew is fond of you. I wonder if you see a place for him in your life.'

Rowena had been calm and self-possessed all through the conversation, but now she looked embarrassed.

Imogen said quickly, 'You can tell me to mind my own business.'

But after a moment's hesitation Rowena said, 'I just don't know. I like Andrew rather a lot, and we have so much in common: music, for instance. He's very clever, and he has an interesting mind when he lets it run free. But we didn't seem to be getting anywhere. And Max would have murdered him if he'd thought we were lovers . . . Oh, God, murder . . . How could I use such a word? It was awful . . .'

It seemed for a moment that her calm would break down at last. But then Mrs Farran senior wandered into the room.

'Rowena, can you remember where I . . . ?' she began; and then, seeing Imogen, 'Oh, I see we have a guest. How nice.'

Rowena introduced Imogen. Mrs Farran said, 'Haven't we met before?'

Imogen said she hadn't previously had that pleasure.

Mrs Farran seemed worried. 'I'm sure we have,' she said. 'I'm quite sure we have. But I can't remember where or when it was. I'm afraid my memory isn't what it used to be. You must remind me, my dear. Where was it we met before?'

Imogen indicated, very gently, that Mrs Farran was mistaken. She herself was a little alarmed. Rowena's mother was probably about seventy – not a great age these days – but her movements were slow and uncertain and her speech hesitant.

'Darling, are you sure you should be on your feet?' Rowena said to her. 'You know Dr Random will be here any minute, and he's been telling you that you need bed-rest.'

'I'm perfectly all right,' the old lady said. 'At least, I think I am. I'm tired of being in bed. I'll just sit for a little in that armchair.'

Rowena gave Imogen a rueful look and said no more. Mrs Farran sat quietly for a minute; then, as if recollecting with difficulty social niceties of the past, inquired politely where Imogen lived, whether she had come by car, and what sort of a journey she had had. Imogen made suitable reponses and was told she had a nice smile. After a minute, Mrs Farran remarked conversationally, 'Did you know, my son-in-law, Max, has died? He was an important man, you know. He will be much missed.' Then, as if it were an afterthought, 'At least, I suppose there will be people who miss him. Oh dear, nothing is as it used to be. But you know, Isabel . . .'

'Imogen,' Rowena gently corrected her.

'You know, Isabel, Rowena looks after me so splendidly, she and Dr Random between them . . .'

It might almost have been the cue for a ring on the doorbell.

Dr Random had arrived. He was just as Imogen had seen him at Headlands: immaculately dressed, the beard neatly trimmed, the manner calm and confident, the picture of a rather distinguished physician to whom a patient's life and health could safely be entrusted. But he didn't seem pleased to see Imogen.

'Yes, I have met this lady,' he said coldly. 'On the previous occasion she did not see fit to tell me her name, but I have learned who she is. Miss Imogen Quy of St Agatha's. An excellent college, St Agatha's. I have acquaintances there.' He paused for a moment, then, addressing Imogen: 'I wonder if I might have a brief word with you when I have seen my patient.'

'Of course,' Imogen said. She forced a smile, though inwardly she felt uneasy. As at Headlands, she had the passing sensation of having seen him before somewhere, perhaps a long time ago. For all his smoothness, Imogen thought there was something in his look that suggested that the encounter had disturbed him. He turned away at once to Mrs Farran.

'Anne, my dear,' he said, 'you are really rather naughty. If you'd obeyed my instructions you would be in bed. Now, if Rowena and her guest will excuse us, I'd like us to go into your room, and let me have a look at you and see how you're getting on.'

He opened the door, and the old lady obediently trotted through it.

Imogen said to Rowena, 'I seem to be asking all sorts of questions today that I haven't any right to ask. But somehow there doesn't seem to be time to approach matters with due decorum. Frankly, do you trust Dr Random?'

'He's been my mother's doctor for many years. She trusts him. And he'd been my father's doctor for ever. He only has a very few patients these days, so I suppose she's privileged. She has a heart condition, and he does keep watch over her, quite conscientiously. He's not my doctor, though. I go to Dr Bennett here in Welbourne All Saints.'

'Do you *like* Random?'

'Frankly, no. He sets my teeth on edge, I don't know why. But he has a good reputation.'

'I'm wondering if there's something amiss with your mother besides the heart condition. Do you think you could get another doctor to see her? Ask for a second opinion?'

'She'd hate the very idea.'

Imogen felt she had intruded into Rowena's life as much as was tolerable. She let the matter drop.

Rowena said, 'Would you like to help me put out the lunch? It'll be simple. I have some smoked salmon and salad, and fresh bread from the baker today. And a bottle of white wine. Will that do?'

'It sounds like a feast.'

By the time they were ready to eat, Dr Random had reappeared. To Imogen's relief, he declined an invitation to join them.

'And how is my mother?' Rowena asked.

'Pretty much the same. She's gone to sleep, which won't do any harm. I'm keeping an eye on her. Ring me if anything worries you; otherwise I'll be round again in a week or two.'

Dr Random then asked Rowena courteously if he might speak to Imogen in an adjoining room. When they were alone together he was less polite. He spoke in measured, even weighty tones.

'I do not like the deception you practised on me,' he said. 'I like it even less after finding out more about you. I must ask you again, what were you up to?'

'I suppose it was a kind of game,' Imogen said miserably, inwardly cursing the fit of creativity that had caused Andrew to invent Aunt Laura and Uncle Herbert.

'It was not a game that amuses me. I am well aware that even now there are people who would like to impugn the memory of Sir Julius Farran, who would drag my old friend's reputation through the mud. I do not how they propose to do so, but for all I know you may be associated with them.'

Imogen thought of the dossier. But she and Andrew were not involved in it.

'We've nothing to do with anything like that,' she said firmly.

'Good. I hope not. However, for your own sakes, Miss Quy,
I warn you and Dr Duncombe not to become involved in any
way with enemies of Sir Julius. It might cost you, at the very
least, professional disadvantage. You will know what I mean.
That is, I hope, a word to the wise. And now I have a great
many things to do. Tell Rowena I will find my own way out.'

'What was all that about?' Rowena asked when he had gone.

There was no point in adding to Rowena's anxieties, Imogen thought. She said lightly, 'He was just giving me a message
to take back with me.' But she told herself that, while not
actually untruthful, she'd been more devious than she liked to
be.

After lunch, conversation became relaxed. They sat out in
the garden for a while, then Rowena played a Mozart piano
sonata to a standard that in Imogen's ears sounded professional, though Rowena denied it. By the time Imogen left to
drive back to Cambridge, she felt she had made a new and
surprisingly intimate friend; and also that she had new worries
to contend with. Was Rowena's mother getting the right
treatment? And what lay behind Dr Random's admonish-
ments?

Arrived home, Imogen went to her shelves and pulled out
the brochure she'd been given by the Headlands receptionist.
As might be expected, there was a photograph of Dr Random
in it. It was a good head-and-shoulders colour portrait and
imbued him with that air of distinction which no doubt helped
to bring him wealthy patients. She studied it closely and tried
in imagination to remove the neat beard and darken the
greying hair. A portrait emerged in her mind's eye; and with
it a memory began to emerge from the shadows. Somewhere,
some time – but she couldn't for the life of her remember
where or when – she'd seen that face before.

14

In the morning, Imogen found that the balance of her anxieties had shifted a little overnight. The potential significance of Rowena's disclosure that Max had gained control over her shares in Farran Group hadn't fully sunk in at the time. Who was in control of those shares now Max was dead, and what might have happened to them in the meantime? Andrew had spoken of little puffs of smoke rising from the financial pages. Obviously he was the person to ask. She wouldn't trouble him with probably empty threats from Dr Random, but control of the Farran Group was a matter of urgency. She decided to ignore Andrew's indication that he was too deeply buried under work to be disturbed. But a telephone call to his flat produced only his voice mail, and a call to Farran Group was fended off at reception level with the bleak reply that he was not available.

Imogen went into college half an hour too early for her surgery, and resorted to the senior common room, where the day's papers were laid out as usual. Her competences were many, but they didn't extend to a familiarity with the financial pages. She picked up the *Financial Times*, which seemed the most likely source of information, and was puzzling her brows over the columns of stock exchange prices when Carl Janner came into the room. He saw with interest what she was reading, and greeted her amiably.

'How are your shares doing today?' he inquired.

'I don't hold any shares. My worldly wealth is in my house and my pension expectations, such as they are.'

'So why are you wrestling with the *FT*?'

'I could tell you to mind your own business,' Imogen said without rancour. 'But there's no secret about it. I've been wondering what's happening to Farran Group.'

'Aha. I might have guessed. Your friend Andrew is back on the board. Why don't you ask him?'

'In a word,' said Imogen ruefully, 'he's too busy.'

'I'm not surprised. There's a lot to sort out there. There isn't anything leaping to the eye from the news pages today, which is a good sign. Let's have a look at the share price. Three hundred and sixteen and a half. It was about four hundred and fifty at the start of the year, with Julius still around, but it's taken a few knocks lately. Not surprisingly, with two top people dead and one of them murdered. But it's been rising a little this week, and I see it's up a bit more today. I'd guess that the City's reassured by having Robinswood in charge. He's the Number One blue-blooded all-purpose portable guru. And although Julius had captured and rather sidelined him, Andrew has a good name and it won't have done any harm having him back on board.'

'You take a lot of interest in the Farran Group, don't you?' Imogen said.

'I do indeed. Remember the dossier? Its time will come. May be at hand. Watch this space.'

Surgery over, Imogen rang Andrew's number again, but again got only the voice mail. She tried again at teatime, after supper and the next morning, with the same result. In early evening the following day, at last, her call brought him to the phone.

'Andrew, how are you? I'm worried about you.'

Andrew said, 'Imo, things are bad. I don't want to trouble you with them. Just wish me well.'

'Are you throwing me off the line?'

'I suppose I am. I told you, these are my problems, nothing to do with you. Leave them to me. Lots of love. I'll get in touch when I can see my way through.'

Imogen said, 'I'll be right over.'

Andrew made no reply and hung up. But she meant it.

On the platform at Cambridge station, she found Carl waiting for the train to come in.

'So,' he said. 'We meet again, rather soon.'

'Yes,' said Imogen, with misgivings.

'We talked about the Farran Group, didn't we?'

'Yes.'

'Imogen, dear, I'm glad you told me you hadn't any shares in it. If you had, I'm afraid you'd be running for the exit a bit too late. Tomorrow comes the crash.'

'How do you know?'

'Because the whistleblowers will be out. Nine thirty, at a press conference announced by Steve Larty.'

'Steve Larty! Isn't he a publicity man? Famous for making millions out of celebrity divorces and such goings-on.'

'The same.'

'I don't understand. Explain.'

'Two members of the Farran board – Bill McNair and Helen Alderton – are going to allege huge financial jiggery-pokery, before and after the death of Julius, with money disappearing into a black hole. It won't surprise me, of course, but it'll make the City wet its knickers.'

Imogen felt a spasm of anxiety. She said, achieving with some difficulty a level tone of voice, 'How will this make money for the likes of Steve Larty?'

'Oh, whistleblowing has its price. Financial scandals aren't quite the same market as sexual scandals in showbiz, but there's money in them all the same. And with a murder thrown in it's a peak time for selling stories.'

'And you have an interest in this, haven't you?'

'I have indeed,' said Carl smugly. 'I told you this morning to remember the dossier. Well, its time has arrived sooner than I thought. Financial scandals move fast. We've been working with the whistleblowers, of course. I'm going to meet my friend David and our agent tonight, and tomorrow we'll see publishers and newspapers. We'll be taking bids for book rights, serialisations, behind-the-scenes exclusives, the lot. And they'll be forthcoming.'

Carl was becoming expansive with self-satisfaction. 'Pity we couldn't get old Julius in his lifetime,' he said, 'but I think we'll make a bomb on this. And throw a brick or two into the capitalist system.'

'And you tell me this. Has it occurred to you that there are people who may get hurt? Such as Andrew. I may as well tell you that I'm on my way to see him now.'

'Good. You can bring him up to date with developments. I don't bear any malice towards Andrew; in fact I rather liked him in the old days. But when you join an outfit like Farran you deserve what comes to you. Nothing makes any difference now, anyway. Tomorrow, nine thirty prompt, the whistles will blow.'

Imogen said, 'You're a detestable creature, Carl. I don't believe you have any principles. In fact, I hate you.'

'Oh no, you don't. You may think you do for a moment, but you don't really. We're buddies, aren't we?'

'Possibly we were,' said Imogen.

Carl roared with laughter. 'The train's coming,' he said. 'Aren't you going to sit with me?'

'Not within a bargepole's length of you,' she said, and walked away.

The voice that admitted her on the entryphone to Andrew's flat was Fiona's. After what Andrew had said, she had more than half expected that, although it didn't please her. She had an uneasy feeling that Fiona was bad news. It was Andrew himself who opened the inner door. But she was startled by the way they both looked. Andrew's face was drawn and haggard and his greeting strained. Fiona had lost the poise and air of cool sophistication that had impressed Imogen on their one previous meeting, the day of the boardroom lunch. In place of the power dressing she wore rumpled jeans and a baggy sweater; she was without make-up and her hair straggled. She said, not smiling, 'Hello, Imogen.'

'You remember me then.'

'Of course I do. We met in the office. And Andrew has talked about you a lot.'

'Favourably, I hope.'

'Very much so.'

Andrew said, 'You shouldn't have come, Imo. I told you, you should keep away. You weren't there when Max died, but you were on the fringe and the police are still sniffing around. The less you have to do with me the better for you.'

'Friends don't keep away from friends who are having a hard time,' Imogen said. 'And it must have been dreadful for you both.'

Andrew said, 'I think it's been worse for Fee than for me. First Julius, then Max, then being grilled for hours by the police, then hounded by the press. And it's not only that . . .'

He paused. Fiona said, 'I can't sleep at night. I can't get the picture out of my mind of Max when I found him. And, frankly, I'm scared.'

'Somebody's got it in for the Farran Group,' said Andrew.

'As for that,' Imogen said, 'I heard some news this evening.'

'There are lots of rumours going around,' Andrew said. 'The group's in trouble, everybody knows that. Robinswood has sent in sniffer accountants, the sharpest in the City, he says, and we don't much like what's coming out.'

'So you don't know yet about the whistleblowers?'

'What whistleblowers?'

'McNair and Alderton.'

'Oh, my God. No, I didn't know about that. What are they doing exactly?'

Imogen told him.

Andrew said, 'McNair's a little rat. Alderton doesn't know anything except through him, but she's rancid with malice ever since Julius dropped her. McNair will make out that he didn't know what Julius and Max were up to, but of course he did, he was finance director. I was only on the margins as Julius's trophy economist. I'd better ring Robinswood now. Look, why doesn't Fee pour us some drinks while I do it? She knows where everything is. Mine's the usual.'

His usual was always a bourbon on the rocks, Imogen remembered; and she noted wryly that it still was and that Fiona knew it. For herself, she felt for once that she'd earned a stiff gin and tonic. Fiona drank white wine.

Andrew came back from the phone.

'Robinswood has just heard,' he said. 'He says he was going to call me. Steve Larty has invited him to the little show he's planned for half past nine tomorrow morning. As a courtesy, Larty says, but of course Robinswood knows courtesy doesn't come into it; he's only been asked so that the press can get at him and spice up the story. He wants me to go, too, and try to hide myself among the crowd. Our accountants and lawyers will be there. Then we go into a huddle with Robinswood and decide on our response. An exercise in damage limitation, I expect.'

'I meant to ask you,' Imogen said, 'since I believe Max got his hands on Rowena's shares, who actually controls the group?'

'As of this moment,' said Andrew, 'Martin Robinswood is in charge. By tomorrow night, who knows?' He smiled wearily. 'As for tonight, well, whatever happens we have to eat. I'll ring for a takeaway and we'll all have supper together.'

Over the lemon chicken and the beef with black bean sauce, he said, 'Imo, we've been in so much together. Now you're here, do you think you could stay overnight and come along to the presentation with me? It won't be a ticketed event, just a bit of a scrum. I can promise you it will be interesting.'

'I shan't be wanted at the high-level conference with Lord Robinswood and his band of experts,' Imogen said.

'No, but you can give me moral support at the event, and we'll have our own discussion afterwards. I've been wondering what will happen to our Julius quest now that our main suspect has himself been killed. We need to talk about that.'

'We do indeed. But I was planning to get the last train back to Cambridge,' Imogen said.

'There'll be more trains tomorrow. You can fix it for someone to take your surgery.'

'Perhaps Fiona should go to the presentation rather than me,' Imogen suggested.

'There is nothing I should like less!' said Fiona. 'Anyway, there may still be lurking reporters waiting to pounce.' She added, with surprising emphasis, 'Imogen, do stay!'

Imogen said, 'I've mortgaged my days off from here to eternity already.' As she got up ruefully to telephone Bridget – or should it be Alison this time? – she reflected that Andrew, for all the worries that surrounded him, was beginning to look more cheerful. He was enjoying, she thought with a touch of sourness, a comfortable domestic evening with two former lovers. And no doubt thinking of Rowena.

He said, 'Do you two girls mind sharing a room? You can have mine. I'll sleep in the boxroom.'

Neither of the women minded. Imogen found Fiona interesting, never having met anyone before with such fatal and apparently readily transferable charm. And Fiona's first remark to her as they retired was, 'This arrangement is so we can each know he isn't in bed with the other.' The thought had not occurred to Imogen, and she didn't deign to comment, but she felt free to ask a question that she might otherwise have thought intrusive.

'You have a boyfriend, haven't you? Where is he at present?'

'Probably at my flat, wondering where I am. But the real answer to the question, "Where is he?" is, "On the way out." I'm giving Colin his marching orders. He's unbearably jealous. He hated Max; in fact he'd threatened to kill Max himself, though I didn't take it seriously. He said he couldn't bear to think of Max touching me; wanted me to leave him. He seemed to think I could live alone in my own flat and he could live with me part-time until he finished at university. He couldn't see how unrealistic that was. Living alone just isn't me; it's not the sort of person I am.'

'Hasn't Max's death changed things?' Imogen asked.

'It hasn't changed Colin's nature. He's still jealous, or possessive if you like. He knows I've been friendly with Andrew again since Max died; well, sharing a sight as horrible as that and then being under suspicion has brought Andrew and me together. So now he's jealous of Andrew.'

Imogen, feeling that she was being impertinent but wanting to know, asked, 'And without cause?'

'Quite without. Andrew and I are on a new basis. Actually I'm rather enjoying being just a friend. And I don't think that affair would have lasted much longer anyway. Colin's drop-dead gorgeous, there's no denying it. I knew as soon as I set eyes on him that I just had to shag him. But what can you do with a man who doesn't talk about anything but boats? I like to keep away from the water. High sexual demand and no conversation doesn't add up to a viable lifestyle, does it?'

'I wouldn't know,' said Imogen. 'Did you say his name is Colin?'

'Yes, why?'

'Oh, I just wondered.'

Fiona had talked coolly, but later Imogen woke in the night and heard her sobbing. The sobs went on and on. Eventually she got up and moved across to the other bed. 'Tell me,' she said.

'I can't. There's so much, and it's so awful. I was asked to do something I shouldn't, and I did it. God, what a disaster. I've cost a life and I may have ruined thousands. I'm rich, and I don't want to be, but I can't give it away or it would make things worse. I don't know how I'll ever live with myself.' She sobbed again.

Perhaps Fiona wasn't as tough a cookie as she appeared, thought Imogen.

'Is it to do with Max?' she inquired.

'Yes. I wouldn't wish anyone to die as he did. But there's more, so much more. And really I can't tell. I only wish I could. I'm sorry to have woken you, Imogen. I'm feeling better now. Go back to bed.'

Imogen went back to bed, but felt wakeful and lay thinking. In the end Fiona went to sleep before she did. It was being borne in on her that the mystery she'd become involved in might be more complex than she'd imagined.

15

Steve Larty had called his press conference in one of a block of function rooms in a concrete and glass building near Finsbury Circus. It was none too big for the crowd that assembled. The national newspapers had been alerted and the morning's radio and TV bulletins had given prominence to the event. Andrew and Imogen slipped in inconspicuously and got seats towards the back of the hall.

Imogen had not seen Mr Larty before, even in photographs, and had vaguely imagined him as a vulgarly dressed, corpulent figure, more akin to the stereotype of a bookmaker than that of a stockbroker. She was quite wrong. He was lean, dark, fortyish, rather good-looking and wearing an excellent suit. Bill McNair and his wife sat at a table, one at each side of him, both looking pale and drawn. Lord Robinswood, tall, upright and silver-haired, was prominent in the front row, presumably in a place reserved for him.

Mr Larty stood to open the proceedings, waiting patiently until the photoflashes subsided. His accent was Rolls-Royce; his confidence was quiet but total.

'This meeting,' he said, 'has been called because Mr William McNair and his wife Helen, better known as Helen Alderton, both of them directors of an important financial institution, the Farran Group, have felt they can no longer remain silent about serious improprieties that have been going on. These improprieties, not to say embezzlements, have been taking place for some time, but have recently accelerated. There now appears to be a black hole of alarming size in the group's accounts. Mr McNair was until yesterday the finance director and Mrs McNair the personnel director. They have both resigned in order to be able to speak.

'Mr McNair had nominal responsibility for the group's finances, but as he will tell you the power was in the hands of the chairman and the chief executive. His role was to carry out their instructions. The chairman and chief executive were the late Sir Julius Farran and the late Mr Max Holwood. Both of these gentlemen, as you are all aware, have recently died, Sir Julius some months ago by a fall from a cliff, Mr Holwood, shockingly, by a brutal murder, the perpetrator of which has not yet been found. Mr and Mrs McNair will inform you of operations carried out by those two which they fear will have brought the group close to disaster.

'You may wonder why the McNairs have seen fit to put this information in the public domain when, as you will hear, there are clearly matters that call for police investigation. The short answer is that police investigation necessarily takes time but that financial markets move very quickly, indeed from minute to minute. The Farran Group has some thousands of shareholders, large and small. It is imperative that they be warned what is happening, lest the value of their shares should leak away without their noticing.'

There was a brief hubbub in the hall, during which Andrew murmured to Imogen, 'That's all crap. This won't prevent a crash, it will bring it on, fast.'

Somebody at the back shouted a question, which Imogen couldn't catch but to which Mr Larty replied, 'Of course the Fraud Squad will be involved. As soon as this meeting ends we shall put all the information we have in the hands of the police.'

As the chatter died down, Lord Robinswood stood up in the front row and called to Mr Larty, 'May I have a word, please?'

Larty said suavely, 'Of course, Lord Robinswood,' and, to the meeting, 'Lord Robinswood, as no doubt you know, was elected chairman of the Farran Group when Sir Julius died. Would you like to come to the microphone, Lord Robinswood?'

'I think I can make myself heard from here,' Lord Robinswood said. 'I have three things to say. First, I fail to understand why Mr and Mrs McNair could not have come first to me with their anxieties. That would have been the obvious thing to do.'

Bill McNair said, 'But we did. You brushed them aside.'

There was another outbreak of talk. Andrew muttered, 'Perhaps they did, perhaps they didn't. How can we know?'

Lord Robinswood said coldly, 'I have no recollection of any such approach. The second thing I have to say is this: that the Farran Group's lawyers are here in the hall and will be listening closely to every word. If anything slanderous is said, we shall not hesitate to take any action that may be required, if necessary to the point of seeking an immediate injunction.'

'Quite, Lord Robinswood, quite,' said Larty, unruffled. 'But of course any allegations of malpractice will concern Sir Julius and Mr Holwood, and your lawyers will be well aware that one cannot libel the dead.'

'The third thing,' Lord Robinswood said, 'is that immediately before the start of this meeting I requested the London Stock Exchange to suspend trading in Farran shares. They will by now have done so.'

There was more hubbub in the hall. From the back came a thin scatter of boos. Andrew said to Imogen, 'The boos will be from shareholders, but there aren't likely to be many of them here. It's mostly journalists. For them it's a story more than a financial catastrophe.'

Steve Larty called for order. Then Bill McNair got up to speak. He was nervous and hesitant – unimpressive, it seemed to Imogen – but warmed up a little as he went on. He began with an account of the origins of the group, which he'd joined in its early days. He described its early operations and its expansion by buying other companies, sometimes turning them round and other times selling them, invariably at a profit.

'Julius wasn't a gambler,' he said. 'He took risks and he wasn't too scrupulous, but he always knew what he was doing. He was a brilliant manager of risk. As he got older and the group grew, the deals he did were bigger and bigger.

'He kept on cutting corners – I think he couldn't help it, it was in his nature – but by the time he was seriously rich he'd begun to be more interested in reputation and social status. He didn't care about money for its own sake, because he'd got plenty, though he still liked to bring off a big coup. But he knew his record was murky and the classier people in the City didn't look on him as "one of us". He worked hard for his knighthood: cosying up to politicians, donations in all the right places, sponsoring sports and concerts. Oh yes, Julius knew how to play the great game. He got his K, he got everything.'

'He got Helen, too, didn't he?' called a voice from the back. There were one or two titters.

Larty made a gesture to McNair that was clearly a signal to go straight on, and he continued. Though his words and tones had been neutral, Imogen had detected a note of bitterness in his last few remarks. Perhaps, as Andrew had suggested earlier, he'd worked for Julius all those years in a state of quiet resentment.

Then, said McNair, along came Max. Julius, who had long been concerned over who was to succeed him, welcomed him with open arms. Max's marriage to Rowena followed shortly afterwards – it was almost a kidnapping, McNair added, in what was clearly an aside – and he was established as chief executive. From then on, power shifted gradually from Julius to Max, although Julius still held the trump card of his controlling shareholding. It was getting obvious that Julius was past his best; he was aware of it himself, was drinking heavily and becoming more and more paranoid about real or imaginary enemies.

But whereas Julius had prospered by taking considered risks, Max was a gambler, and although he had all of Julius's boldness he had none of Julius's judgment. Power going to his head, he had made wild moves, finally plunging the free assets of the group into buying Bionomials, a Californian bio-technology company poised on the frontier between the science of life and the art of medicine. The price was high. Bionomials was reported to have developed a gene therapy technique which would cure or control neurodegenerative diseases, relieving a great deal of suffering.

Unfortunately the technique had failed at a late stage to get approval from the Food and Drugs Administration, with disastrous consequences. To make matters worse, it turned out that the patents and licences under which Bionomials was operating didn't belong to it but to its founder, a Dr Biebner, personally. The value of Bionomials had crashed, and the banks that financed the Farran Group's purchase had demanded their money back. Max had borrowed heavily, and would be unable to repay.

McNair finished by giving an account of innumerable complex financial jugglings, involving strings of improbable-sounding companies and a worldwide variety of tax havens. Imogen found these hard to follow, although a few words such as bond and mortgage and debenture stood out and sounded ominous. It seemed clear, however, that large amounts of company money had disappeared unaccountably into the void, both before and after Julius's death. The position of Farran Group appeared to be irretrievable.

Mrs McNair, otherwise Helen Alderton, added to the indictment some details of inflated staffing costs, unfulfilled obligations and the raiding of the pension fund for money to throw into the void. She was interrogated from the floor about her relationship with Julius, which seemed to be of more interest to some of those present than the intricate financial details. She agreed that she had been Julius's mistress for some years, but said the affair had ended amicably.

'That's a lie,' said Andrew to Imogen under cover of surrounding chatter. 'She hated his guts.'

Steve Larty brought the proceedings to a close. Mr and Mrs McNair, he said, had come into the open at considerable cost to themselves. They had lost their well-paid jobs and expected to run the gauntlet of publicity. But the actions they had exposed were reprehensible in the extreme, and they had acted from a sense of public duty. He and they applauded Lord Robinswood's call for dealings in Farran Group shares to be suspended. They would give all possible help to those who would be involved in sorting these unfortunate matters out, and hoped that in spite of everything there might yet be a happy end to the story.

'Some hope, I'm afraid,' said Andrew as he and Imogen made their way out among a throng of people all talking at once on their mobile phones. 'It's a can of worms that's been opened.'

On the pavement Lord Robinswood signalled to Andrew. After a brief greeting to Imogen he told Andrew, 'I'm going round to the Stock Exchange now. We'll have a meeting with the lawyers and accountants in the boardroom at twelve. I'll see you there.'

'That gives me time to walk you to King's Cross,' said

Andrew to Imogen. 'Thank you for coming with me. Let's talk about all this later on.'

'It sounds horrible,' Imogen said.

Andrew said, 'There may be worse to come. The McNairs are keeping a lot of juicy stuff back for sale to whoever buys the story. I don't know how long the boardroom meeting will go on; it could be hours. Martin Robinswood and I have been digging around for days, and so have the accountants. Forensic accountancy they call it. But there's still a lot we don't know. I wasn't in the inner circle while it was all going on, and neither was Martin. Only Max, McNair and the missing Wetherby really knew what was going on.'

Then his mobile rang.

'Yes, Fee, yes,' he said. 'Look, I'm sorry. It sounds like a crisis. But I'm caught up in a bigger one. I'm sorry, it really is much bigger. Why don't I get Imogen to come round to you? She's better at these things than I am.'

'What things am I better at than you?' inquired Imogen.

'Oh, you know. Emotional problems. Wrecked lives. That sort of stuff.' He said into the phone, 'She'll be there,' and switched off the phone.

'Hold on a minute,' Imogen said. 'Aren't you assuming too much? Where do you want me to be, and why?'

'At the flat. It's Fiona. She's having a showdown with Colin.'

'Colin's other name wouldn't be Rampage, by any chance?'

'I think that's his name, yes.'

'I'll certainly be there,' said Imogen. 'Sounds like a crisis.'

She could hear the shouting from outside before she got to the door. Words like 'bitch' and 'whore' sounded out from a stream of incoherent invective. Fiona opened the door to her and almost fell about her neck.

'For God's sake,' she said, 'get this idiot off my back!'

Colin Rampage stopped in mid-shout.

'Miss Quy!' he said, startled. 'Fancy you being here!'

'Hello, Colin!' said Imogen. 'It seems I've arrived at an awkward moment.'

She knew him, of course. She'd seen him several times at St Agatha's, crossing Fountain Court as if he owned it, or on one occasion coming to her to have a sprained wrist bound. He was as handsome as ever, and she couldn't help responding instinctively to the abundant maleness of him. It wasn't surprising that Fiona had found him irresistible. Aged twenty or perhaps twenty-one, big, muscular, he was the epitome of golden youth. A shirt wide open at the neck displayed a splendid torso with a light, intriguing fuzz of curly fair hair. At the moment he was standing in startled and abashed silence.

'We weren't expecting anyone,' he said in an apologetic tone when he'd recovered some equanimity.

'So it seems,' she said. 'Should I go away, or could I possibly help?'

'Oh, don't go!' said Fiona. 'Don't! Don't leave me with this crazy – this crazy adolescent! Just help me to get rid of him!'

'Why, you . . .' Colin began again. 'You . . .' He paused to find an epithet.

Imogen said, 'Calm down, Colin. Fiona, why don't you go and make us some coffee? Don't be in too much of a hurry.'

Fiona seemed all too ready to escape.

Imogen motioned Colin to a chair. He subsided, with an air of acceptance.

'You were shouting abuse at her,' she said severely. 'You don't really hate her, do you?'

'Yes, I do,' he said. 'No, I don't. Sometimes I do, sometimes I don't.'

'Do you want to stay in a relationship with her?'

'I don't know. It's the same. Sometimes yes, sometimes no.'

'Can you specify, when yes, when no?'

Colin thought for a moment. Then, 'Yes, I can,' he said. 'If I sit and think about it, I think there's no future in it. She's years older than I am, and she has form, if you know what I mean. I didn't know at first, I thought she loved me. That was naïve. I'm just another guy to her. Heaven knows how many she's had before me. She won't come clean; maybe she can't remember. She didn't even tell me about Max to start with.'

'But at other times?'

'At other times it's nothing to do with thinking. I just want her like hell, bugger the past and bugger the future. Sometimes I hate her and want her like hell at the same time, and that's a hard one to deal with.'

'Shall I give you an outside opinion?' Imogen asked.

'Look, this is my business,' he said crossly. 'I haven't asked to be told what to do!' Then, a moment later, 'Sorry, Miss Quy. Yes, please, go on. I'm in a spin about it all, don't know where the hell I am.'

Imogen said, 'I'm not going to moralise about Fiona. She is what she is. She's sexy and hugely attractive, and she knows her market price. I don't suppose she's the least bit intellectual, but she's bright and shrewd and determined. After all, she attached herself to two rich men in succession; that wasn't accident. She doesn't herself see a future in you. Colin, be honest with yourself. You're out of your depth with Fiona.'

'Out of my depth is the word. I seem to be fathoms under. But, Miss Quy . . .'

'Imogen.'

'But, Imogen, I don't know how to say this . . . Fiona's terrific, she's a revelation, I didn't know it could be like it is with her. I mean, there are plenty of girls in St Ag's, and I've been around a bit, but compared with Fee they haven't a clue.'

Imogen said, 'I've given you a diagnosis. Now do you want my advice?'

'I suppose so, yes. But I don't promise to take it.'

'I'll give it anyway. Colin, I think you should accept that this has run its course. Be thankful for what Fiona's given you and bid her a fond farewell. She'll be relieved, and once you're out of her orbit so will you. To take your mind off her, you could try mending fences with the college.'

'They certainly need mending,' said Colin ruefully. 'I know I made a hash of my Tripos papers. I'm not looking forward to seeing my results. Dr Barton used to think I'd get a first, but last time I saw him he shook his head and said I should be thankful if it was a two-two. I think he was relieved I even turned up for the exams.'

'All for love and the world well lost?' said Imogen.

'You think it can't be worth it, don't you?'

'You're the only one who can decide whether it was worth it, Colin, and you might change your mind. But there are other costs besides dropping a grade in your degree. What about rowing?'

'Oh, don't remind me. I'm out of the first eight, and there isn't time to get back in. They've all been training like mad. You need to be in condition. And I'm not going to get that Blue I was expecting.'

'But you have another year, don't you, Colin? Time to make up ground in all directions.'

Imogen realised as she spoke that there was a question mark over the next academic year. If St Agatha's turned out to be in real trouble, could his third undergraduate year be affected? Well, there was no point in worrying him about it at this stage.

Colin said seriously, 'I'll think about what you're saying, I really will.'

Fiona appeared in the doorway, balancing a tray with a coffee pot and three cups. Colin looked up.

'But isn't she a stunner!' he muttered.

Imogen rang Andrew's number when she got home, but there was no reply. Late in the evening he rang her.

'We're still digging,' he said, 'and we shall be for quite a while. The can of worms is well and truly opened. The accountants are professionally gloomy, though they may be relishing the thought of lots of highly paid work ahead. There's no market in Farran shares, officially, but unofficially there are dealings at a quarter of yesterday's price. So the whistle-blowers are bringing about the result they were supposed to be trying to avert.'

'I got a bit lost when Bill McNair went into the details,' Imogen admitted.

'The details are massively complicated. But here are one or two nasty ones for you to digest. Rowena is a big loser. Max mortgaged her shares in the group and it doesn't look as if there'll ever be money to pay off the loan. His estate will be insolvent.'

'My God, Andrew. Hasn't she suffered enough? Her father dead, her husband horribly murdered, and now this!'

'I'm afraid for her. I don't know what her other resources may be. And for another, St Agatha's College. It lent eighteen million pounds to Farran Group on the security of a high-interest bond. Which will now be worthless . . . Have you ever heard of a Cambridge college going bust?'

16

The Master always went to bed early. Imogen decided not to risk waking him with the bad news. He might as well, she thought, have one more peaceful night's sleep before it broke. Later she was sorry and felt the decision had been a mistake. If she'd told him, he would have had a dreadful night but at least he'd have been prepared for what happened the following morning. As it was, he was caught off guard. At first he could hardly believe it. In fact he couldn't at first understand it. While still in his pyjamas he'd had a call from the *Meteor*, which had had to tell him of the disaster and how it affected the college. By the time he finished an interrupted breakfast there had been four more calls from press and radio.

Not realising the scale of the affair, he told the first two inquirers that financial issues were a matter for the bursar, that the bursar was away and that the college didn't know when he would be back. From the response to this information he quickly realised that it served only to heighten curiosity, and thereafter he declined to comment.

Meanwhile, the news was reaching the college from various quarters. Overnight, dons who had heard or watched the late news programmes had been telephoning each other anxiously. Imogen was in the senior common room early and found it already crowded. Members were clustering around spread-out newspapers and anxiously discussing their contents. All the papers headlined the story on their front pages, excepting the *Galaxy*, which featured the cavortings of a young actress with three pop stars and an Alsatian dog. The news released in mid-evening by Lord Robinswood had not been fully assimilated, and the emphasis was less on the victims than on the size of the black hole in the Farran accounts (variously estimated at from two hundred million to two and a half billion pounds) and on the villainies of the late bosses of the company. Two or three papers had leading articles criticising Lord Robinswood as chairman for not knowing of their depredations or, worse, knowing of them and failing to stop them.

Imogen was not surprised, soon after breakfast, to see the Master approaching her surgery. She expected a request for his tranquillisers, and was pleased when he didn't ask for them. But she was alarmed to note how worn and weary he looked. He was stumbling along like a man twenty years older.

'I think you ought to see your doctor,' she told him. 'Just for a check-up. You really don't look well at all.'

'I'm due for an MOT, you mean? I'm afraid I'd fail it ignominiously. In fact I'm thinking today that I ought not to be on the road at all. Have you heard the news, Imogen?'

'Yes.' There was no point in trying to soften it. 'Isn't it terrible?'

'I haven't quite taken it in as yet. But I'm afraid it seems catastrophic. It's that man Wetherby. There's still no sign of him, by the way. I don't suppose he dares show his face. I'm rueing the day we took him on. It seems he turned the college's assets into cash and invested the lot in a corporate bond issued by the Farran Group. Eighteen million pounds! It was going to pay eight per cent interest and double our day-to-day income, but what good is a promise of eight per cent interest if you lose your capital? We're not a rich college, you know. It's practically every penny we have.'

'Is this bond going to be worthless?'

'We don't know. We're told it may take months to sort out the mess at Farran. We certainly won't get anything back at present.'

The Master sighed deeply. 'You know, there have been twenty-three masters of this college before me, dating back to 1552. Most of them were good and able men, two or three were lazy or incompetent, and at least one was a thumping crook. But none of them managed to lose the entire wealth of the college.'

'There are the buildings and grounds,' Imogen pointed out.

'Yes, of course. Extensive and beautiful, as the guidebooks say, but in financial terms they're a liability rather than an asset. We have to maintain them. And what are we going to maintain them with? You know, Imogen, I really think that having let this happen I shall have to resign the mastership.'

'You must be charitable to yourself. It isn't your fault.'

'It is. I should never have let Wetherby get a free hand as he did. Anyway, if a ship goes down the captain is supposed to go down with it, and in a sense I'm the captain of this ship.'

'The ship hasn't gone down yet, and you must stay at the helm until it does. Let's hope it doesn't. We need you, William.'

It was the first time Imogen had addressed the Master by his first name. She was surprised to hear herself doing so, and to perceive that she'd taken his hand.

'I'm not a money man,' he said. 'We need someone with a grip on the college finances to survey the damage, fast, from our own point of view, and work out what we're to do about it.'

'Could you persuade the former bursar to come out of retirement for a while? Dr Honeywell?'

'Honeywell's part of the problem, not the answer. He ran the college into trouble through incompetence, and it looks as though Wetherby may have run it on into ruin. I wish we hadn't lost Andrew Duncombe. He has the sort of mind we need. I suppose there's no way we could get him back?'

'Andrew's deeply involved at the other end of the affair, trying to sort it out at Farran. I expect he's working all hours.'

'Oh dear, oh dear. However, I've asked the domestic bursar to take over at our end for the time being, young Malcolm Gracey. He's pretty bright, isn't he?'

'He is,' said Imogen.

'And a friend of yours?'

'He's a good friend,' Imogen said. 'He's asked me to partner him to the May Ball.'

'Excellent, excellent,' said Sir William; and then, his brow clouding, 'But I'm not sure the May Ball will take place. It depends on how bad things are. Perhaps Malcolm will be able to tell us. We'll be calling in our accountants to help him, of course. We must all hope for the best. And now, I mustn't stay here talking. There's a lot to do.'

The next three or four days were the most miserable at St Agatha's since Imogen's arrival seven years before. A rough assessment of the college's position emerged. The loan to the Farran Group had been almost the whole of its free assets. A few remaining investments could be realised and resources called upon, and commitments could be met at a reduced level for a few months. But spending would have to be cut on a scale far beyond the economies already imposed by Peter Wetherby. Scholarships and research grants would have to be withdrawn, salaries reduced, faculty without secure tenure and college servants dismissed, cuts made in all directions. And, said the Master, addressing an emergency meeting of the Governing Body, none of these savings would be enough. St Agatha's would have to apply to the colleges' joint fund, which normally assisted the poorer colleges, for help on an unprecedented scale.

'And if they stumped up on a big scale, of course they'd want to supervise us,' the Master said. 'Which wouldn't be nice at all.'

'We could go cap in hand to Trinity,' said Dr Barton. 'Trinity's rich enough.'

But this remark met a deafening silence. Going cap in hand to Trinity, members felt, would be the ultimate indignity.

Sir William offered his resignation. It was unanimously rejected.

St Agatha's had some unwelcome press publicity. That its losses could be ill afforded became common knowledge. Two or three papers, including the *Meteor*, picked up the story of the vanishing bursar, but couldn't get far with it, because Peter Wetherby seemed to have left no traces. Meanwhile the Farran Group filled many columns of newsprint, as ripples spread outward from the disaster. Imogen was not busy, since full term had ended and most undergraduates had gone down. She spent more time than usual reading the papers, and was distressed by what she read. The college was only one of many losers, though among the biggest. Several subsidiaries and smaller companies that had been dependent on the group looked like collapsing; jobs were being lost and pension funds in trouble. The newspapers were reporting stories of individuals of modest means who had lost everything and didn't know how they were going to rear their children or survive in old age. At St Agatha's, younger fellows of the college came to Imogen to confide their worries and ask anxiously whether she knew when the economy axe would fall; she didn't.

One morning Malcolm Gracey came to see Imogen in his new capacity as acting bursar. He had a sheaf of letters in his hand.

'I have a dreadful day ahead of me,' he said. 'I have to give bad news to about a dozen people. I could just put the letters in their pigeonholes, but I feel that isn't good enough. It's only decent that I should go to them in person. And I'm afraid you are first in line.'

Imogen quailed inwardly. 'Am I getting the sack?' she asked.

'No, no, of course not. Not you. But I'm afraid the college won't be able to pay you your usual retainer for the vacation.'

This was a blow, but not a fatal one. 'I can survive,' she said. 'I won't even need to get a job on the checkout at Tesco. My parents left me a small income and I have my lodgers. And of course if I'm really needed I can be called in, whether I'm paid or not. I expect there are some who are hit harder than I am.'

'Yes, there are. Some junior fellows have to go. Some aren't fired but don't get their appointments renewed.'

'Belinda Mayhew? Carl Janner?'

'Yes, and others. Mostly they'll have been expecting it; they were warned when the first round of cuts was being made. Senior fellows are being asked to take a voluntary reduction, and they'll all agree. But the worst sufferers will be staff: two porters, a gardener, half a dozen people in the kitchens. Those who stay will have to do more work. It's a bad business. And the awful thing is that although we have to do it, it won't make much of a dent in the deficit.'

'Are the accounts in a mess?'

'Oddly, perhaps, not at all. In fact Wetherby had begun by clearing the confusions left behind by Dr Honeywell. We had no trouble getting into his computer, and everything's in meticulous order. Unfortunately his dominant activity was realising the college investments and accumulating the monstrous sum that he lent to the Farran Group, with the result we all know about.'

'It's the May races next week. Will they be affected?'

'No. The Boat Club is a separate entity from the college.

Luckily its funds are intact. But – I hate to tell you this, Imo; it's a big disappointment – the May Ball is off.'

Imogen gulped. In spite of the Master's hint, it was a shock. St Agatha's only had a May Ball every third year. She'd looked forward to it. Maybe there would never be another.

'Yes, it's a disappointment,' she said. 'But I suppose we have to see it in proportion. There are worse things happening than that.'

'Let's do something else together as soon as possible, shall we?'

'That would be good. Malcolm, it would be a bad joke to tell you to have a nice day today. But accept some useless sympathy.'

'Thank you. I'll get on with delivering the bad tidings. 'Bye for now, Imo.'

One caller was plainly unaware of the present difficulties. Colin Rampage put his head round the door of Imogen's surgery, and seeing no one else there invited himself in. He seemed rather pleased with himself.

'I just came to thank you, Miss Quy,' he said. 'You caught me at the critical moment and put me right. I'm glad I had the sense to see it.'

'You mean you've broken with Fiona?'

'Yes, I have. After you left I thought it over. And as soon as I went away from her the spell broke. I actually felt free. I remembered all the things that I hadn't been keeping up with. And, you know, Miss Quy, actually sex isn't everything.'

'No, I suppose not,' Imogen observed, a shade drily.

'I've talked to my tutor. He was terrific. Gave me the prodigal son treatment. Says I'll have slipped a grade this time but I'm coming back next year and he thinks I'll be in line for a first in Part Two. How's that?'

'Impressive,' said Imogen.

'And what's more, Jimmy Downes wasn't too bad. He's the captain of boats, you know. I expected a real bollocking from him. Well, I got one, but I'd been expecting a worse one, if you know what I mean. He won't reinstate me in the college boat; says it wouldn't be fair to throw Tony Wilkins out of the first eight, with the May Bumps just coming up.'

'No, I suppose not.'

'I'm back in training, though. I was out in a skiff at half six this morning, in the gym at seven, got up a good sweat, showered at eight, felt better for it . . .' He hesitated, then frowned. 'I was right, wasn't I?' he said. 'I mean, like I said the other day, Fiona's a stunner, but she's a stunning bitch.'

'Don't call her that,' said Imogen. 'She's the sort of person she is and you're the sort of person you are, that's all. I think you were only meeting on one level. And as you so wisely observed, sex isn't everything.'

'No,' agreed Colin. Then he grinned. 'But it was good while it lasted. Anyway, I came to thank you, Miss Quy. May I call you Imogen?'

'I've told you, you may. Now get along with you.'

At lunch-time, Fran and Josh were both out. Imogen ate a slice of bread and butter and an apple, not really feeling hungry, and then, restless, wandered around the house. In the sitting-room her eye fell on the brochure for Headlands, still lying open with its face to the floor. She turned it over, and looked again at the portrait that had stirred her memory. Once again she tried in the mind's eye to strip away the beard and darken the hair. Suddenly a recollection came to her, and she thought she had it. She went to the computer in Josh's room, which she had his standing permission to use, and searched the web for a name. It delivered, and gave her the name and date she was looking for, but not much information.

Imogen got into her car and drove to the University Library. It wasn't far, and she would normally have cycled, but she was excited and wanted to know more. She went to the microfiche room and scrolled through issues of newspapers around the date she'd noted. A certain Dr Philip Snetterton had been accused of the murder of eleven elderly patients, who had died unexpectedly while in his care. His trial had lasted several days and made headlines, not least when in the end he was acquitted for lack of evidence. The newspaper stories were accompanied by pictures of a man whose face looked remarkably like that of a younger Dr Random.

Her thoughts turned inevitably to Andrew. Andrew had not been in touch with her since the day of the whistleblowers. This was not surprising; he must be busier than ever with Farran Group affairs. There was no reply from his flat, so she rang the group head office. At least there was someone to answer the phone; and the voice was familiar. It was Fiona's.

'Hello, Fiona,' she said. 'It's Imogen.'

'Oh, hello,' Fiona said. 'I've been intending to call you, Imogen. I want to thank you for disposing of that tiresome boy.'

'I didn't dispose of him exactly,' said Imogen.

'Well, he's gone, and am I glad!'

'He seems quite happy, too. It's good to have pleased both parties.'

'Also, I meant to say, forget the things I told you at Andrew's the other night. They weren't true. I was over-wrought.'

Imogen reflected that memory could not be switched off like electric light, and that a statement once made could never be fully annulled. But there was no point in pressing the issue.

'How are things in Farran Group?' she asked.

'Desperate but not serious, to coin a phrase. I'd rather be here in the office than hiding from the press. As a matter of fact, I think the press has lost interest in me. And here I am. I'm Lord Robinswood's PA now. I'm rather liking it, actually. And him. He's a hundred-per-cent gentleman all the way through. Although he's terribly busy, poor dear.'

'And what about Andrew?'

'Oh, he's even busier. He's working all hours, day and night. I never thought he could be such a workaholic.'

'Is it possible to speak to him?'

'Well, I don't know. He's given strict instructions that no calls should be put through. But seeing it's you . . . Hold on a minute, Imogen, I'll try him for you.'

It was two or three minutes before Andrew was on the line. He seemed even more weary than when they'd last spoken.

'I'm still slogging away in the Augean stables,' he said. 'So is his lordship. Little did he think when he added Farran to his collection of directorships that it was going to land him in all this. I must say he's buckling down to it. And he and Fiona are hitting it off like nobody's business. But to add to the stack of troubles, the police investigating Max's death are also crawling all over the place, turning up Farran records. They're looking for business enemies, people who might have had a motive to do Max in. There are quite a few of them. But it seems they're still not getting anywhere with the inquiry.'

'Andrew, can you give me five minutes?'

'Just about.'

'I've been thinking about this whole business, from Julius's death onwards. Because I'm sure that it's all one big complex, if only we could sort it out. It can't be coincidence that first the chairman, then his second-in-command, are removed from the scene in quick succession and soon afterwards we find that the group they built up is in ruins. And that St Agatha's, where we both heard Julius denounced, is one of the principal sufferers. There's something sinister behind all this. I'm sure that somewhere there's a key that will unlock the whole thing, and I'm beginning to feel I'm on the way to finding it.'

Andrew said, 'Imogen, dear, I'm dealing with a major financial disaster. There was one murder for sure: Max's. It was horrible, and I hope they catch the person who did it, though I'm not confident that they will. But as for Julius, I've rather lost interest. What I'm working my socks off for at present is trying to sort out the Farran Group mess and see if there's anything we can do to reduce it.'

Imogen felt put down. She said, chagrined, 'I just feel everything may be linked together. I've been thinking for some time that the key I'm talking about might be at Headlands, where they had that strange conference the night Julius died. And today I've found something mindblowing.'

'Have you?' He didn't ask what it was.

'Do you remember the case of Dr Philip Snetterton?'

'No.'

'Try harder. Thirteen years ago. A sensational affair.'

'I'm sorry. I need to concentrate on the here and now, not thirteen years ago.'

'Andrew, will you just listen? Dr Snetterton was charged with causing the deaths of eleven elderly ladies, six of whom had made wills in his favour. He signed their death certificates, recording death from natural causes. Until the last one, there were no inquiries made. He said he'd been treating them all, usually for high blood pressure; they were at high risk, and their deaths weren't surprising. He was acquitted on grounds of insufficient evidence. And of course eleven acquittals don't add up to a conviction. But half a dozen cases of old ladies who'd died and left their money to their doctor is rather a lot.

So although he went free everyone thought he must be guilty really. What if now he's grown a beard and is up to his old tricks under the name of Random?'

'What reason have you to think Random is Snetterton?'

'I've seen pictures of Snetterton. They were in all the papers. They look just as you'd imagine Random would have looked a few years ago. If you took the picture in the Headlands brochure and subtracted the beard, you'd have the same man.'

Andrew sounded impatient. 'Honestly, Imo, this time you really have let your imagination get the better of you. False identifications are temptingly easy to make, and after thirteen years how can you possibly be sure?'

'I can't be sure. But when he saw me at Rowena's he came down on me like a ton of bricks and told me never to darken his door again. Why should he do that unless he had something to hide?'

'Well, we played silly-buggers with him, didn't we? It was my fault, I admit. It's not surprising that he doesn't like us. But it's a long, long jump from that to being a mass murderer, even if this Snetterton actually was one. And it's all very well to say everyone thought he was, but after all an acquittal is an acquittal.'

Imogen said, 'Hang on a minute, Andrew. Let me go on. If he really was a killer, he might well have killed Julius, mightn't he?'

'And Max as well?'

'That's a bit problematic. Such a different method.'

'I'll say it is. My own theory is quite simple. I think Max killed Julius and some person or persons unknown killed Max. And that was gruesome but it was also good riddance.'

'Andrew, don't you think that if Random is Snetterton he has to be confronted? It's an ethical question. There may be people in danger now. Including Rowena's mother, who is a patient of his. If he really was up to the same business as before it would be a matter for the police, of course, but I'd rather be sure before bringing them into it.'

'You can say that again. They'd laugh you out of court.'

'Well, I want to go up there and face him with it. And there are leads to follow up. You remember old Ben in the pub at Eastham; I thought he was on the point of telling us something interesting but you choked him off. I'd like to talk to him again. How about another trip to the seaside, Andrew?'

'Honestly, Imo, I couldn't possibly take a day off. I don't know when I'll get one. At the moment it feels like never. And, frankly, I think you're proposing a wild-goose chase.'

'All right, Andrew. In that case, I think I'll go there on my own.'

'Yes, why not, if you must? But don't blame me if you're sent off with a flea in your ear.'

Imogen thought, He just wants to get me off the line. She said, 'I'll do that tomorrow. For now, I'm going to call Rowena.'

Andrew's sigh was audible. 'When am I ever going to see her?'

Imogen said, 'That I can't tell you. But I'll give her your love.'

'Oh, yes, Imo, please do. All my love, tell her.'

So much, she thought, for tact.

On the phone, a couple of minutes later, Imogen gave Rowena the exact message.

Rowena said, '*All* his love? Every last drop? He can't be serious.'

'I think he is.'

'He must have some for other people. He loves you, for instance.'

'In his way,' said Imogen. 'His rather limited way.' She went on to ask, with some anxiety, 'How is your mother?'

'Oh, pretty much the same. Frustrated that she can't do anything much. And I'm afraid her memory doesn't get any better.'

Imogen had a wild urge to ask whether the first Mrs Farran had made a will, but realised that it would be impossibly impudent. Yet a frail and vague old lady might fall an easy victim to persuasion.

'Is she still a patient of Dr Random?' she asked.

'Yes, she is. I sounded her about making a change, but as I thought she won't hear of it. And I'm not going to press her, Imogen. I've grasped that you're not happy about Dr R., but she trusts him and I don't know anything against him. We've known him a long time. You'll forgive me if I let it drop.'

She sounded decisive, even perhaps a little cool. Imogen wished them both well and hung up.

17

I mogen drove up to Headlands in some trepidation. Confronting Dr Random was not a pleasant prospect. She had wondered on the way whether she shouldn't simply report her suspicions to the police. But she also thought it likely that they would respond with disbelief. She needed firmer grounds on which to act.

At the reception desk she gave her name and asked to see Dr Random. This time he bustled out of his private room almost immediately. He signalled to the receptionist to leave her desk.

'Miss Quy! What are you doing here?' he demanded. 'I should have thought it would be clear from our last encounter that you are not welcome.'

Imogen looked him in the eye and said, 'Good morning, Dr Snetterton.'

She had worked out that if she was wrong and there was no connection, he would be bewildered, but that if he was Snetterton the greeting would shake him. It did. The instant reaction of shock was unmistakable. But in a matter of seconds he had recovered, and the shock had turned to anger.

'Miss Quy,' he said, 'I was once Philip Snetterton. I was acquitted on extremely serious charges. It's obvious that you know about them. In spite of the acquittal, there was strong public feeling against me. For a while I had police protection; I was given a new identity and moved to a new location. In time the furore died down; I had not been struck from the medical register and could make a fresh start. Over the years I first built up a small private practice and later developed the speciality that resulted in Headlands. Obviously you are aware of this, and no doubt it is why you gained access to Headlands on a pretence.'

Imogen in turn was startled but had time to recover her equanimity. 'No,' she said, 'we didn't know anything about it then.'

'Curious. Extremely curious. However, you will now under-stand my strong reaction to your inquisitiveness. Well, Miss Quy, let me assure you that the medical authorities and the Eastham police are aware of all the facts. Undoubtedly they will keep an eye on me for the rest of my professional life. It's a cross I have to bear. However, I have to say that these same authorities have been helpful in keeping the story from being spread around. It is not known in these parts or to potential patients at Headlands. Though I have committed no offence, I would be ruined if the truth were known. I am serving a life sentence from which there is no appeal.'

Imogen was silent as she tried to take this in.

Dr Random continued, 'You may be sure that I'm extremely careful in my care of patients and above all in the certification of deaths. I must never arouse suspicion.' He smiled thinly. 'So you will understand that your knowledge of the past is alarming to me. May I ask how you came by it?'

Imogen told him.

'Have you shared the information with anyone else?'

'With Andrew Duncombe. He wasn't very interested.'

'Is he likely to spread it further?'

'Very unlikely, I should think. I'll tell him not to.'

'And may I have your assurance that you yourself will not pass it on?'

'I have no intention of passing it on.'

Dr Random's manner thawed from the strictly formal to the almost confidential. He smiled again, this time in a way that she could well believe attractive to his patients, then said in a quiet, casual tone, 'You know, Miss Quy, the possession of confidential and potentially damaging information is a responsibility.'

'I understand that.'

The doctor added, in an offhand way, 'It can even be dangerous.'

'What on earth do you mean by that?'

'A general observation, not one with any specific reference. Good-bye, Miss Quy. Thank you for being so understanding. Do take care, won't you?'

He smiled again as he showed her out.

Imogen walked slowly to her car and stood beside it, thinking hard. From what Dr Random had told her it seemed unlikely that his patients were at any risk; and it wasn't an offence to be attentive to old ladies. He might even *like* old ladies; and solicitous care of them, while it might well be lucrative, couldn't be considered culpable. But she knew she still didn't like or trust Dr Random; and what had he meant to convey by that last remark?

It was rather early for lunch, and she had a lot to think about. She decided to walk into town along the cliff, leaving the car where it was, in the ample space in front of Headlands. It wasn't as fine a day as when she'd been here with Andrew, but not a bad one for walking: breezy, with scudding clouds and intermittent blue sky. On the cliff-side path, she felt a little nervous, as from time to time the wind caught her, though it was blowing on shore and wasn't going to carry her over the edge. From a distance she glimpsed a single human figure. On nearer approach she saw that he was at the fatal spot where

Julius had fallen, and was standing at the seaward side of the protective fence. He was staring down as if communing with the sea below, and didn't appear to see her.

She recognised him at once. It was Derek Dacre, whom she had last seen at Julius's graveside.

'Do be careful!' she said. 'It gives me a fright, seeing you there!'

He turned, vaulting the fence, and faced her.

'Haven't I seen you before?' he asked.

'Yes, you have,' she said, and reminded him. As she spoke, the thought came unbidden into her mind: could he be revisiting the scene of a crime?

He said, 'Well, you know about Bastard Farran. I've been coming here sometimes, just to rejoice at what happened to him. Still, this may be the last time.'

'You mean you'll forgive and forget?'

'I'll never forget what happened here. I'm printing it on my mind now, every detail of it, to make sure I don't. But I have to turn my back on it. You know, move on. Carl said so. You know Carl Janner?'

'I know him well.'

'He's a great guy, isn't he? He's awesome. I never knew anyone like him. He has fire in his belly. And now he's working on a book that will demolish Bastard Farran's name for ever. Wow! I only wish I could bring Farran back to life long enough to see it.'

'So you'll be satisfied at last, Derek?'

'Not *satisfied*. I'll never be satisfied. I don't *want* to be satisfied. But I'll know it's the best thing that can happen, the way things are. I'll settle for that. Get my life back. And it's all thanks to Carl!'

'And your father as well, perhaps?'

'Poor old Dad! Well, he's coming round.'

'It's for the best,' said Imogen. 'Congratulations to both of you.'

She felt inclined to congratulate Carl, and herself as well, as she went on her way. But as she continued along the path, she turned matters over once more in her mind. The chain of disasters that had culminated in the apparent ruin of St Agatha's, and hundreds of employees and shareholders in the Farran Group, had stemmed from this cliff top. Julius's death, which had brought Max to power, was officially accidental and might actually be so, but the mysterious gathering in Headlands described by Lisa and never mentioned at the inquest seemed suspiciously like some kind of conspiracy. Andrew had been convinced, and she only slightly less so, that Max had murdered Julius, but Max's own death made that seem unlikely, since it would require the existence of two murderers. Perhaps it should not be ruled out, however, especially since the deaths had been so totally different in kind.

Julius and Max both had enemies, that was for sure. Max's succession to power had brought on the crash, but it seemed to have been in the making already, although Julius's brilliant juggling might have kept the balls in the air indefinitely. She didn't know who the outside enemies might be. Somehow she couldn't believe in Robert Dacre as the perpetrator of a violent, or any, murder.

Carl Janner as a suspect was a new thought. He had a motive; while Julius was alive his cunning exploitation of the libel laws would have deterred publishers from risking publication of the famous dossier. Now, with both Julius and Max out of the way, he could go ahead and probably make a great deal of money. But there was no reason to think Carl had been anywhere near Headlands at the time of Julius's death, and she couldn't believe that a bloody murder such as that of Max was Carl's style.

It looked as if the culprit, or culprits, must be looked for among the Farran directors. She couldn't see Lord Robinswood as a suspect. There was no advantage to him in these deaths; he'd been infinitely more comfortable drawing his fees for rather slight duties than he now was coping with the cartload of troubles that had descended on him. If there was a conspiracy at Headlands he wasn't in it; nor, so far as she knew, were the whistleblowing McNairs or the marketing director, Hancock, who'd hastily resigned on the day of their revelations. Dr Random and Lucia Farran were clearly in the front line where Julius was concerned, for his death would clear the way for their marriage and no doubt endow Lucia with a great deal of money. And perhaps Julius, having known Tim Random for many years and probably knowing of his earlier identity, had a hold on him that Random would be glad to break. That left as a suspect the elusive Peter Wetherby. If only he could be found, much would become clear.

Was Fiona a possibility? There seemed no motive for her. She had been comfortably ensconced as mistress of Julius, and on his death had moved on to Max. And, remembering Fiona's agonised voice on the telephone the morning Max's murder was discovered, Imogen knew in her bones that Fiona couldn't have done such a deed. Yet there was still the dark secret that had so distressed Fiona in the night-time at Andrew's flat. She must speak to Fiona again.

Musing thus, Imogen arrived in Eastham. She made her way to the Fishermen's Arms, looking for Ben, with whom she and Andrew had talked on the earlier visit. Reviewing the conversation, she remembered a remark of Ben's that she'd have liked to follow up, if Andrew hadn't been so keen that they should get on their way.

The sun was stronger now, and the wind had dropped.

People were sitting outside on benches at homely wooden tables in the front garden. Ben was on his own, gazing glumly into his near-empty pint glass.

Imogen said, 'May I join you?'

Ben didn't recognise her at first. 'I can't stop you,' he said without enthusiasm.

'You don't remember me, do you? I was talking to you here, back in the spring. I'm Imogen.'

'Oh aye. I remember now. The one with the fancy name. Where's your feller?'

'Andrew isn't with me today.'

'That's him. Andrew. He bought me a drink.'

Imogen took the hint and renewed his pint. She said, 'You're on your own again. You were telling me about your pal Charlie, who'd got some money and left town. Has he never turned up?'

'No. Not seen hide or hair of him since. I still miss him.'

'I'm interested in Charlie.'

'You're about the only person in the world who is. Nobody wanted to know Charlie, except me. Well, he was scruffy, and he was sleeping rough, and he didn't shave all that much. And, tell you the truth, he ponged a bit, although you got used to it, at least I did. And he'd drink too much if he had the money for it. Then he'd sleep it off in that place I told you about halfway up the hill, a sort of grassy hollow where we'd go for a bit of peace. You could call him an outcast. But he was all right really, he was a good friend, wouldn't harm a fly. He was in the trade as we call it here' – Ben winked – 'that is, getting drink to them as was taking the cure at Headlands and was desperate for liquor. Charlie would get it for them and pass it in through the window. Of course, he'd charge them three times the price. Private enterprise, you might say.'

'But he gave up the trade and left town. Was it because he'd made his pile?'

'No, no, he drank the profits, such as they were. But he made a friend, and I wish he hadn't, seeing it turned him away from me. There was a feller, a patient as they called them, whose room was on the ground floor, and he got interested in Charlie. They'd talk at night sometimes, through the window, when Charlie was delivering. He told Charlie he had talents that was wasted and he could make something of himself, but he'd have to start by smartening himself up. He gave him the money to buy himself a suit. I'd have said that was a daft thing to do, Charlie would only spend it on booze for himself and be flat out for a fortnight. But there you are, folks can surprise you. Charlie bought the suit. I saw him in it a day or two later and his own mother wouldn't have known him. He'd cleaned himself up and had a shave and a haircut. And a day or two after *that*, without a word, he was gone. Nothing left of him but his old clothes, and they wasn't up to much, I can tell you. I reckon the chap must have given him money as well, maybe a lot of money, or what would have seemed a lot to Charlie, and he just lit out of town. Thought he'd go off and make his fortune, maybe. I don't know the whys and wherefores of it all. Don't suppose I'll ever know now.'

Ben sighed deeply and finished his pint. Imogen went and bought him another.

'Did you ever hear any more about his benefactor?'

'No. Never knew who he was. Never tried to find out. But I was upset to lose Charlie, still am. I tell myself, some day he may come back as sudden as he went. Who knows?'

Imogen asked, 'Can you remember just when this happened?'

'Before I met you the first time, must have been, seeing I

told you he'd gone. But I reckon not that long before. Can't say exactly.'

'Ben, what became of Charlie's old clothes?'

'They wouldn't have been no use to nobody. Wasn't worth a penny, I'd have thought. I've still got them somewhere. Thought I'd keep them for him, in case he came back. He'd have pawned the suit and spent the money and he might be glad of them. But it hasn't happened. Why do you ask?'

'Just curiosity. Ben, tell me about your own life.'

Ben, warming to the unaccustomed audience, gave Imogen a long rambling account of an early life in poverty, of low-grade jobs and spells of unemployment, of a middling-happy marriage, a wife who'd died younger than she should, and two children, one in America, whom he never saw. 'But it's a lonely life when you get to my age,' he concluded. 'Charlie meant more to me than you'd think.'

Imogen listened with interest. Getting up to go, she thanked him. Seeing her pull out her wallet and gauging that she might intend to give him a present, Ben waved it away.

'I'm better off on the pension than I ever was before,' he said. 'I don't want money from nobody. But you can buy me one more pint. I'll drink it for Charlie.'

Imogen walked back along the cliff path to Headlands, where she'd left her car. Normally she'd have walked with eyes wide open to her surroundings, rejoicing in seascape and cloud-scape, noting the clumps of thrift and heather along her way. But now her mind was fizzing with excitement; she felt she was near to completing the Farran jigsaw. Two or three more pieces and she'd be there.

It had been a day of surprises, and there was another to come. Going for her car, she encountered Lisa, the girl with whom she and Andrew had walked from Headlands into town.

Lisa was pushing her bike from the house towards the road.
She recognised Imogen at once, leaned the bike against the
wall, and went over to her, smiling.

'Hello, Lisa,' Imogen said. 'How's things?'

'Looking up. I got a new job. With Daphne at the flower
shop.'

'So you're saying good-bye to Headlands.'

'Good-bye and good riddance. I'm working out my notice.
Finishing at the end of the week. I can't tell you how glad I am.
There's something about that place that pisses me off.'

'I must admit,' Imogen said, 'I wouldn't want to work there
myself.'

Lisa said, 'I was thinking of you the other day. I remember
telling you about the little party in the small parlour the night
Sir Jules Whatsisname died, and you looked very interested.
Well, one of them came here a week or two back. He was here
two or three nights, just visiting. He put his car in the base-
ment, which you can do by going in the back way, but it's a bit
tricky to get in and nobody does it much. He looked a bit
agitated and never left the house.'

'Which of them was it, Lisa?'

'It was the one with the moustache. I knew him at once.'

'But he's gone now.'

'Yes. Left in the night. One night he was here and next
morning he'd gone.'

'And his car? Was it a blue Audi, by any chance?'

'That's it. The car went too.'

'Well, thank you, Lisa.'

'You thought there was something tricky going on there,
didn't you?' said Lisa shrewdly. 'Maybe something suspicious?'

Imogen realised that Lisa herself, while not wanting to get
involved, was interested in that little group that had met in the

small parlour. But she didn't feel it was up to her to tell Lisa that this was a first sighting of the elusive Peter Wetherby.

'Sir Julius's was an unexpected death,' she said, 'but it was quite a while ago now.' And without elaborating on this uninformative statement she wished Lisa well in her new job and waved her on her way.

18

Imogen had given up any expectation that Andrew would telephone her. It had been a one-way process recently. So she was surprised when, a few minutes after her return from Eastham, he rang.

'You haven't heard from Wetherby?' he asked.

'No, but I've heard *of* him. He was briefly sighted at Headlands a few days ago. Nothing since that I'm aware of.'

'Well, I have news for you. It's for Malcolm Gracey, really. In fact I called him a minute or two ago but got no reply.'

'He's around somewhere. I saw him just now as I came into college. Can I give him a message?'

'You remember the eighteen million pound bond issued to St Agatha's?'

'How could I forget it? The cause of our threatened ruin!'

'Well, we've found that a commission of four per cent was paid to Peter Wetherby by Farran Group for securing the investment.'

'Whew!'

'And you realise, Imo, four per cent doesn't sound a lot, but this is four per cent of eighteen million. A cool seven hundred and twenty thousand pounds. That's money.'

'I can't even imagine it. Where do you think it's gone?'

'It's probably gone the way such money often goes. To a magical little island in the Caribbean that makes it disappear and reappear as required.'

'Can we get it back?'

'We'll try. We've got the police looking for Wetherby now. If we can get hold of him we'll shake his pockets, so to speak. But his pockets may be empty.'

'Andrew, I've been to Headlands today and I have things to tell you. I've spoken to Dr Random, and he admits he's Snetterton. But he says the powers-that-be know all about him. Effectively he was given a fresh start when the case against him collapsed all those years ago and he's been a model practitioner ever since.'

'So he's in the clear?'

'He's in the clear on one dimension. It seems that even if he was guilty once, he's put the past behind him. Old ladies are safe from him. On another dimension he's not in the clear at all. I'm more sure than ever that there was a conspiracy and it centred on Headlands.'

'Oh. That's interesting.' But it seemed that the matter of the St Agatha's bond was of more immediate concern to him. 'Excuse me for now, Imo,' he said. 'I'd like to try Gracey's number again. I need to put him in the picture.'

'Yes, of course,' Imogen said. 'But before you hang up, listen. I think I'm on the verge of finding out what really happened to Julius. And if we can find that out, with any luck it will lead us to Max.'

'I don't think the police are getting anywhere over Max.'

'Maybe they aren't. I was talking about *us* getting somewhere.'

'About *you* getting somewhere is what it'll have to be.'

'Oh, Andrew, Andrew. I love you very much – well, I love you a little bit – but there are times when I despair. After all we've been through together, are you opting out?'

'I think I am, really. I'm rather like President Ford, who it was said couldn't walk and chew gum at the same time. I've such loads of financial gum to chew on that I can't really think of anything else.'

'Oh well, so be it. While you can still think up silly metaphors there's hope for you yet. I won't trouble you with the reasons why I think I'm hot on the trail. However, in that connection I need to speak to Fiona. Is she available?'

'Fiona's not in the office today. Robinswood's given her a day off. She'll be out shopping, probably. When in doubt she goes out and buys expensive clothes. It seems to cheer her up.'

'She's in need of cheering up?'

'She's up and down. Sometimes she's on a high, sometimes depressed, sometimes tearful, which she never used to be. She has something weighing heavily on her mind that she won't talk about.'

'I might even be able to guess what it is,' Imogen said.

'Well, good luck. I'll ask her to call you. And now I must get on masticating my cartload of gum.'

Fiona rang the next morning, a fine Saturday. She sounded in high spirits.

'Imogen!' she said. 'What can I do for you?'

'I'd love to have a talk with you. Face to face if we can.'

'Fine. Where and when?'

'I could come across and see you. Take you to lunch.'

'What a bore for you. Look, Imogen, it's aeons since I was in Cambridge. I've happy memories of it by the dozen. Half my early boyfriends were at Cambridge. Why don't I come over and take you to lunch? Let me do that, please. We'll go somewhere really nice, expense no object.'

'I don't think you should. I'm the one who's asking a favour.'

'Nonsense. I insist. A Cambridge day! Lovely! Just book somewhere good and tell me how to find you!'

Fiona arrived in a bright yellow open sports car. Her fine blonde hair was blown enchantingly around her head, and she was wearing a bright, light, longish summer dress and high-heeled sandals. Her bare arms and ankles were perfect. Floating through the streets of Newnham Croft and across Lammas Land towards the restaurant, she drew admiring eyes from all directions. Imogen felt bathed in reflected glory.

Over lunch, Fiona chatted happily. She inquired after Colin Rampage, and was told that when last seen he'd appeared to be thriving and still the idol of female undergraduates.

'A nice boy, really. All he needs is to grow up. You know, Imogen, one comes to realise that youth isn't everything, or even nearly everything. There's a lot to be said for maturity and experience. In men, anyway . . . You know what? I think I'm rather falling for Martin Robinswood; he's so distinguished, and very good-looking, and he's a widower. And sixty-five is no age at all these days. I'm beginning to think I may be the marrying kind at heart. I can quite imagine being actually married to Martin.'

'You'd be Lady Robinswood.'

'Yes, wouldn't that be fun? I'd quite enjoy being milady. And Martin is really top flight; he mixes with royals and such. Yes, I know what you're thinking. An advance on Julius and Max. Well, you know, Julius is – was – quite a dear, really, when he wasn't in tycoon mode. As for Max, he was a mistake, I admit. He was pretty awful; I won't go into details but I wouldn't have stayed with him much longer. His death was horrible, though.'

Fiona's face suddenly clouded over.

'Oh God!' she said. 'Oh God! Imogen, whenever I think of

it, it knocks me over. And do you know, I have nightmares! I mean, literally, nightmares, dreams from the pit.'

Imogen said, 'It's not surprising. I expect they'll go away with time.'

'I hope so. It's awful. And the worst thing is, I feel so guilty, so loaded with guilt I can't bear it.'

The elation had totally left her. Her tone now was the one Imogen had heard in the night-time talk at Andrew's flat.

Imogen said, 'You can't really be guilty. You're not telling me you caused Max's death, are you?'

'Well, I didn't kill him or encourage anyone to kill him. But if it hadn't been for me it wouldn't have happened. And I don't just mean leaving him on his own that night, I mean more than that. I just shouldn't have been with him at all if I hadn't behaved the awful way I did.

'It was the money, Imogen. Money stinks, you know. I ought not to have it and yet I'm spending it; I have to, somehow, seeing it's there. And it gives me a buzz, for a while. This dress I'm wearing, for instance. It made me feel so good this morning, at the top of the world. And now, wham, it was only a fix, I'm back at the bottom. I couldn't really marry Martin, even if he asked me to, it'd be such hell for him when I'm down.'

She wept a little, then dabbed carefully at her eyes.

'And I'm truly sorry to do this to you, Imogen. When you said you wanted to talk to me, you can't have expected this.'

'I may be doing something awful to *you*,' Imogen said. 'But I have to. You mentioned the money. It was that initially, wasn't it? The root of all evil?' She took a deep breath and went on. 'It was your price, wasn't it?'

'Yes, it was, and I took it. I took the money and ran. I welshed. Well, it wasn't entirely the money; I just couldn't go through with it. Anyway, I ratted. And the disasters stemmed from that.'

'Not only from that,' Imogen said.

'The worst ones did. Murder was worst. And a lot of good it all did me. I could give the money back, but it wouldn't mean anything to him if I did. I may as well have the quick fixes.'

Imogen said, 'You know now that I know. And I'm going to follow it up; I have to. I've worked out *who* he is, but I don't know *where* he is. Will you give me the address? And are you prepared for the consequences, whatever they are?'

'Yes,' said Fiona. 'I've kept it to myself long enough. Let the sky fall.'

Imogen took her pocket diary from her handbag and tore out a blank page. 'Write it on that,' she said.

Fiona wrote, in a clear, round, schoolgirlish hand:

Dr J-F Lalande
51 Quai d'Anjou
Ile St Louis
Paris 4
France.

While she was in the Ladies', making further repairs to her face, Imogen paid the bill and ordered a taxi. Back in Newnham, they found Fran and Josh in the house. Fiona recovered, talked animatedly, and asked to be taken punting. Josh agreed eagerly, took the punt-pole and rejoiced in the sight of Fiona reclining elegantly on the cushions. Fran was mildly jealous. Afterwards, Imogen made tea for everyone, and Fiona insisted on driving herself home.

'I'm glad you know,' she said to Imogen as she left. 'It's a relief to get it off my chest. It's a kind of . . . what's that Greek word for it?'

'Catharsis,' said Imogen.

She was steeling herself already for what had to follow.

19

It was a grey day in Paris. Imogen checked in at the modest hotel in the Latin Quarter where she'd stayed on an earlier visit. She lunched at a small restaurant in one of the streets around the Place St-Michel and walked through to the quays. Opposite her, dividing the River Seine, was the Ile de la Cité, with the looming presence of Notre-Dame. Map in hand, she turned right along the quay, which became the Quai de la Tournelle, and crossed the footbridge to the Ile St Louis.

At another time she could have spent a happy afternoon here. The island had missed out on Parisian modernity. It had no flashy hotels or fashionable stores, no Métro, not much traffic. Its soul seemed still to be at rest somewhere between the seventeenth and eighteenth centuries. On the long narrow street of St Louis en l'Ile that formed its spine, dignified façades hobnobbed with craft shops and those selling every-day needs. She loitered a little along this street, apprehensive about driving to a close the mission that had brought her here; she peered briefly into the tiny garden at the island's prow, and at last turned north and westward to the Quai d'Anjou, facing the northern arm of the Seine and the right bank. A low wall separated the narrow street from the brown, strongly flowing river; at the landward side was a row of tall houses of majestic presence.

Majestic was almost the word, for most of these houses bore plaques recording discreetly their one-time glory as residences of dignitaries of pre-revolutionary France: a Ministre du Roi, a Président de la Diète d'Empire, Seigneurs of doubtless splendid domaines, a Capitaine au Régiment de la Reine, a 'peintre et Valet de Chambre de la Reine Mère'. They had come down in the world a little but not much: dignified dowagers of architecture, still well preserved and stately, though almost all were now divided into obviously expensive apartments.

Each house was entered through a broad and high archway, in which were set double doors with elaborate antique knockers. Most doors were closed, but one stood open, revealing a pretty paved courtyard with a fountain, currently inactive, and an array of flowering shrubs. Imogen arrived at number 51, which was near the end of the street, and stopped in front of the black-painted, forbiddingly solid doorway. There was nothing to indicate who might live there. She put a hand to the heavy knocker, lifted it, and hesitated, gathering up the determination to bang it against its metal plate; and as she stood there she was saved the need because the door opened and a youngish man in a hat emerged. He raised the hat to Imogen, stood aside for her to go in, muttered an absent-minded 'Madame!' in passing, and went about his business.

In the courtyard, beside a little doorway that had probably once been the entrance to a concierge's lodge, was a plate with half a dozen names, a bell-push against each of them. The one next to the bottom read: Dr J-F LALANDE.

A broad stone staircase curved round two sides of the courtyard; Imogen took it in preference to the lift and now stood in front of a handsome panelled door, with beside it a bell-pull. She tugged at this, and from deep in the apartment could hear a bell jangle. It seemed a long wait before there was any response. She had a sense of unreality, and with it apprehension. She didn't know whom she should expect to see; if someone came it would very likely be a maid or a receptionist, or she might find herself in the presence of a bemused medical personage and at the end of a wild-goose chase.

But when the door opened she was looking straight into the face of the man she had come to see. And although it was what she'd hoped for and expected, it still gave her the shock of the impossible.

'Miss Imogen Quy!' said Sir Julius Farran. 'Well, well. This is a surprise. Come inside, Miss Quy!'

20

With the lumbering gait she remembered, Sir Julius led Imogen through an impressive entrance hall into a large, elegant room, with carved marble fireplace, above it an ornate gilded mirror, elaborate decorated cornices and a chandelier with the grace of a living thing. The dark, heavy furnishings were of a later and clumsier period.

Sir Julius was wearing a loose grey sweater, slacks and sandals. As he turned to face her, Imogen noted that his complexion was still high, he looked unhealthily overweight, and his eyes were slightly bloodshot. There was no sign or scent of alcohol about him. But, at a swift appraisal, he looked to have gone downhill physically since she'd last seen him.

However, if he had been discomfited by Imogen's appearance on his doorstep, he had soon recovered. His tone of voice was calm, almost suave.

'What brings you to this pleasant backwater?' he inquired.

'I came to see you, Sir Julius.'

'Of course you did. Are you on your own?'

'Yes.'

'There isn't someone lurking around the corner? Or a couple of visitors from Scotland Yard?'

'No.'

'And you haven't got some nasty little machine secreted about your person?'

'No again.'

'I'm glad to hear it. Now, obviously you're in possession of information the general public doesn't have.'

'Yes. That you are alive.'

'Indisputably. How did you come by this knowledge, Miss Quy?'

Imogen didn't want to involve anyone else. She said, 'For the moment I think that's my business.'

'Very well. Putting that on one side, what do you propose to do with what you know? Obviously you have a purpose in coming to see me today. Are you here as my nemesis, or as an angel of wrath? Or is it a question of money? The price of silence, perhaps?'

'It's not that,' Imogen said. 'I haven't decided yet what I'm going to do. It depends on what you can tell me about two deaths and a financial crisis. The deaths are of a person called Charlie on the coast near Eastham and of Max Holwood in his country cottage. The financial crisis is of course the collapse of the Farran Group. I think you know more about that than anyone else and might be able to do something about it.'

Sir Julius said, 'Miss Imogen Quy, you are venturing into dangerous waters. Has it occurred to you that you could be putting your own life at risk? I'm merely playing with possibilities, you understand. We are here a few feet from the River Seine. In its time, that river has received the bodies of a great many people whose deaths remained unsolved mysteries. It's a convenient disposal system. Think about that.'

Imogen said, keeping her voice steady, 'You're trying to frighten me. It's an empty threat. You couldn't get away with it. I left this address with the hotel I'm staying at, and I left letters behind me in Cambridge telling the whole tale.'

Sir Julius said, 'You're a brave, not to say a foolhardy

woman. Those measures would not protect you. I have half a dozen passports in various names. European borders are very porous. I'd be over the hills and far away faster than a person could say "Interpol." However, Miss Quy, we don't need to be confrontational. I have thought for some time that the nemesis I mentioned would come to me one of these days. And if it has to come, I would rather meet it in your friendly form than in any likely official one. Why don't we talk things over together? I can offer you tea, Miss Quy, or, as you allowed me to call you on an earlier occasion, Imogen. Would you like that?'

Imogen, somewhat surprised, said she would. Sir Julius shambled across the room and rang a bell. A stout elderly woman appeared, and stood impassively as Sir Julius, speaking loudly, gave her instructions.

'Amélie is my housekeeper,' he told Imogen. 'She's rather deaf. She's the soul of discretion; in fact she has to be, because she can't hear a word of what's going on.'

Amélie brought in a tray with tea and a plate of petits-fours. Imogen accepted the tea but declined the petits-fours.

Sir Julius said, 'Well, here we are, totally in private, alone you might say in our little world. We can continue discussing the matters you raised. Hypothetically, you understand. Nothing is admitted and everything could be denied if necessary.'

Suddenly Imogen was cross. 'I didn't come here to play silly games,' she said. 'I don't want anything hypothetical, I'm trying to find out what really happened. Let's begin at the beginning, shall we? You, the rich and distinguished Sir Julius Farran, supposedly fell off a cliff at Hell's Elbow on the coast near Eastham while intoxicated. Your wife and your doctor attested that the body found there was yours. But here you are, as large as life. The false identification couldn't conceivably be a mistake. Somebody else fell over that cliff, and not by accident. I believe it was an elderly man called Charlie. Let's stop beating about the bush, Sir Julius. Who pushed him?'

'Imogen, my dear, please don't try to bully me. It won't work. It wouldn't be as easy as you think to denounce me. You know very well that if you went to the police their first response would be to laugh at you. However, I'm quite willing to talk to you, on the basis that what I say to you is confidential, at least for the time being.'

'I'm not promising anything,' said Imogen.

'Very well. Correspondingly, I'm not admitting anything and could deny everything. Now, what was your question?'

'Who pushed Charlie over that cliff? Was it you or Tim Random or Max?'

'It could have been an accident, you know.'

'And he could have fallen into your clothes? And been mistaken for you by your wife? Really, Sir Julius, come off it! If you're going to be frank with me, please start now.'

'All right. I did the deed myself. Next question.'

'Why did you do it?'

'I expect you have a good idea already. It's really quite simple; perhaps a little too simple. Cherchez la femme, they say; and it's astonishing what havoc can be wrought by a fatal female. A man who thinks himself shrewd and experienced can be thrown dizzyingly off balance by an infatuation.'

'You're talking of yourself and Fiona.'

'Yes, of course. I'd convinced myself, and she'd convinced me, that in spite of the age gap she was genuinely fond of me. I was nearly seventy and ready to hand over control of the group. I'd always thought that if and when I retired I'd go to Paris and pick up a project I'd put on hold all those years ago. And now I had the dream, the infatuated dream, that I could take Fiona with me and we would live happily there together.

'You don't need to tell me it was absurd. I knew it was, really, but all my life I've been used to getting what I wanted and I thought I could get it again. And Fiona said she was willing. I wasn't of course so innocent as to suppose that money never entered her thoughts, or that my being rich and elderly wasn't a consideration. But I didn't mind that; it's only sensible. People who claim not to care about money don't impress me; they are either naïve or hypocritical, usually the latter. I didn't think Fiona was either of those things.'

'I think actually she was quite fond of you in her way,' Imogen said.

'I'd like to believe it. Anyway, I'd long thought that a neat and economical way of retiring would be just to disappear and be presumed dead. There was a naughty clergyman, some forty years or so ago, who did just that. He was on holiday with his wife at the seaside. He went, supposedly, for a morning swim in the sea; his clothes were found in a neat heap on the beach, he was presumed dead, and his wife, with whom he was on good terms, received a large sum from his life insurance. Unluckily for both of them, a former parishioner ran into him at some resort on the Continent with a pretty young mistress on his arm.

'That was what I was planning to do – more carefully, of course – when I checked in at Headlands. I'd confided the plan to Fiona and motivated her with a handsome sum of money. A quarter of a million pounds, paid down cash in advance, a prosperous lifestyle in Paris to follow, and, to be brutally realistic, the likelihood of my death in the not too distant future. She knew I'd had a quadruple bypass operation and had a somewhat gloomy prognosis. I was offering her a good package, and she accepted it. I think she thought it was rather a lark.

'And then along came Charlie. If I'd believed in God I'd

have said Charlie was a godsend. The night after I arrived in Headlands there was a tap at the window, and outside was this disreputable-looking figure offering to procure liquor for me, at an outrageous price. I only bought from him to please him; I drink more than I should, but I'm not addicted, and my being at Headlands was really in preparation for disappearance. One thing that instantly struck me about Charlie was that he was just about my height and build, though nobody would actually have mistaken him for me.

'I made friends with Charlie, talking to him through the window. I told him what a clever fellow he was, how he had all it took to be a business success if only he'd wash and shave and get a decent suit. He took it all in; he was so impressed he'd have swallowed anything I told him. I gave him money to buy a suit and to clean himself up, and I said I'd meet him outside Headlands, so we could have a walk and a talk, and discuss a business plan for him. I would stake him with a few thousand pounds: a vast amount by his standards. I told him I wasn't supposed to go out and it wasn't possible in the daytime, but I could get hold of a key, get out and meet him at a time we fixed the following night.

'I thought it quite likely that he wouldn't turn up, but he arrived more or less clean and sober and proudly wearing the suit. It was a bright night; we went as far as Hell's Elbow and stood there a minute. I pointed out to sea and asked if he could see a ship out there. And as he looked out I just gave him a hard shove from behind and over he went. It was easy.'

Imogen said, 'But Tim Random and Lucia identified the body. They couldn't have thought it was you. There was a conspiracy, wasn't there?'

'You can call it that if you like. I was the prime mover. They knew what I was going to do, and what they had to do to round off the operation.'

'I'm wondering why they should do it. Wasn't it risky for them?'

'A little. But there was no reason for the police or the coroner to be suspicious. It was a clear identification by the two people who should know best. And Tim and Lucia had reasons for being willing to help. Tim was an old friend, and was vulnerable; I knew more about his past than had ever come out, and more about his present activities than was comfortable for him. Lucia would get very large insurance money, and the pair of them could marry, which they wanted to do. Max knew about it as well, and was delighted. He was desperate to take over Farran as chief executive; I really believe he'd have killed for it if necessary.'

'Just as you killed Charlie?' Imogen said; but Sir Julius ignored the interruption.

'In the end,' he concluded, 'I made mistakes of judgment, and I shall have to pay for them. The biggest mistake was in trusting people. I trusted Fiona and she bilked me; took the money and didn't come. I thought Max capable of running Farran, and he ran it straight into disaster by a mad gamble. I can't forgive myself for being so stupid.'

Imogen said, 'You really see this as just a matter of mistakes of judgment? As a brilliant plan that would have worked perfectly if people hadn't let you down? Doesn't it trouble you that this was a human life you were throwing over the cliff?'

Farran said, 'A singularly useless human life. A drunken sot of an old tramp, no good to anybody. He told me when we were talking together that nobody cared whether he lived or died.'

'That wasn't quite true,' Imogen said. 'He had a friend called Ben. Ben still misses him. And Charlie had hope. He thought you were going to set him up in business.'

Farran shrugged his shoulders. 'He couldn't have run a business. He couldn't have run anything.'

'But you led him on to think he could.'

'Please, Imogen, let's not waste time. I am not interested in Charlie, living or dead. He was just a bit of human debris.'

Imogen said, outraged, 'I don't know how you can speak like that and still be a human being yourself.'

'You mean I'm some sort of monster. I don't think so. I'm merely rational. Most people don't dare to be rational.'

'What about Max? Did you look on him as a bit of human debris, too?'

'That's an absurd comparison, and you know it. Charlie was of no importance. Max was powerful and dangerous. He was doing a great deal of damage. It had to be stopped.'

'And you decided to stop it by killing him.'

'You are a very clever lady, Miss Imogen Quy. I was impressed by you when we first met, and I still am. It would be a great loss if you were to be removed from the scene. But how are you so sure that it was I who killed Max?'

'It was the logic of the situation. Max, as you've just said, was running the business you created into ruin. You were in a unique position to commit a murder, since you were dead. And you are absolutely ruthless. Who else could so have combined the motive, the opportunity and the psychological capacity to commit a brutal murder?'

'Your logic is impeccable, so much so that there's no avoiding the conclusion: I must have done it. As indeed I did.'

'I can't see the whole picture, however. Didn't you hand control to Max when you disappeared from the scene? You brought your troubles on yourself.'

'I've already admitted that. As I told you, I was besotted at the time and wanting to head off for a private paradise. I'd persuaded myself that Max would go on running the group as

I had done. After all, I had hand-picked him to be my successor. And he was in many ways like me, though more of a gambler. How much more of a gambler I hadn't realised. I couldn't bear to see what he was doing.'

'When did you decide to kill him? And were there other reasons?'

'It was a decision that had built up over several weeks, and that came to a head that night.'

'It can't have been on the spur of the moment, since you went to Lilac Cottage armed with a lethal weapon.'

'I was indeed armed with a lethal weapon. A beautiful, wicked little stiletto that I killed a man with once before, in a fracas in the back streets of Naples in my youth. I went to the cottage that night prepared to use it, though still hoping I could persuade Max to reverse his policies. I phoned Fiona, who of course knew I was still in the land of the living, and who was eager and willing to be helpful so long as she didn't have to meet me face to face or give me any money back. When I told her I wanted to talk to Max in private, she told me she would be out until very late on that particular night. She seems to have forgotten that I wasn't the only person who knew of her intentions, and young Andrew Duncombe was also heading out for Lilac Cottage.

'I flew from Paris to Luton; I'd rented a car under one of my spare names and I drove across, arriving at the cottage late that night. There was already a car parked in the drive, and as I approached the door I could hear a furious row in progress. I didn't want anything to do with that. I got back in my own car, drove a little distance down the lane, and waited until the other car drove away. Then I let myself in – I've always had a key to the cottage – and went in search of Max. I found him in his study looking dishevelled and a bit shaken, halfway drunk and dabbing away at a cut lip. He wasn't pleased to see me, and he didn't want to talk business.

'I asked him if it was true that he'd put in a big bid for Bionomials. He said it was. I told him he was crazy; Bionomials was too big and too expensive for Farran to swallow. Also that Dr Biebner, who founded it, is an old friend of mine from long ago, and I'd heard from him that its new drug was having problems with the FDA. Max told me he knew more about Bionomials, and more about pretty well everything under the sun, than I did. We had a long, complicated, bad-tempered argument, during which Max drank more bourbon and lost whatever self-control he'd started with. In the end he told me to sod off and go back to being dead.

'Even at that point I might have decided to go away and let him stew in his own juice; but as I was getting ready to go I asked him about the row that had been going on just before my arrival. He told me that it was with Andrew Duncombe and that it was about Rowena. I pricked up my ears, of course, on hearing my daughter's name, and asked what he'd been doing to her. And he told me. He didn't spare any of the gruesome details, and emphasised the pleasure he'd had in inflicting what was virtually torture. It was unspeakably vile. So then I saw red. I had my stiletto ready and I'd learned in a hard school how to use it. I stabbed him once in the heart, in the right place, and twice in the stomach to make sure. It was the heart that did the job; he died while I watched.'

'And you drove away rejoicing?'

'Not rejoicing; how could I, after what had happened to Rowena? But glad I'd done what I did, as I still am. I locked the door and broke a window from the outside, drove back to Luton, left the car at the airport and flew home. I knew of course that once I had got away from the scene there was no way that suspicion could fall on me. Dead men don't commit crimes.'

'Didn't it occur to you that Andrew would be suspected?'

'It did, when I was on the way to the airport. But it didn't worry me. There was no way they were going to pin it on him. He couldn't have broken that window, covered with blood as he'd have been, without leaving his mark on it. And there were going to be DNA traces and fingerprints all over the place that weren't his. Myself, I've never been fingerprinted. The indications would point to an intruder. I expect they're still looking for one.'

Imogen said, 'You'd just murdered a man in the most horrible way. You seem to take it very lightly.'

'I don't feel any compunction over Max. He got his deserts. You know, nobody on this earth will grieve over Max. Rowena won't. His death is an order of release for her.'

'Does Rowena know that you're still alive?'

'No. I couldn't burden her with the knowledge. She still thinks I died at Hell's Elbow.'

Imogen was incredulous. 'How could you do such a thing to her? I saw Rowena in tears at your funeral.'

'Of course a woman is upset when her father dies. But it has to happen sooner or later, doesn't it? We adjust to these things. I thought probably when it was all safely buried in the past she might be let into the secret, though I wouldn't let her know it had cost lives. Rowena is so sensitive and high-minded, she'd not be able to bear it.'

'You astonish me, Sir Julius. It all sounds so unnatural.'

'The alternative would be worse. And I made sure she'd be well provided for.'

'I think you and I are on different planets. As for the burden of knowledge, you've laid that burden on Fiona. She's deeply unhappy over it. And it's not just that. Fiona may not have cared much for Max, but to find him murdered was shattering. She's still horribly disturbed and having nightmares.'

'Fiona has been well paid. I'm not trying to get my money back. I don't take responsibility for her feelings.'

'Do you care about all the people who are suffering from the collapse of Farran Group? Employees of Farran Group and its subsidiaries? Its agents and suppliers and firms that depend on it for their own business? And shareholders? Thousands of small investors?'

'The famous widows and orphans who always star on these occasions! Somehow or other, in spite of the sob stories, they never actually starve. I'm sorry for the poor dears, but only up to a point. People who can't afford to lose their money shouldn't go in for risk investments.'

'And what about St Agatha's? It's one of the big losers.'

'Oh, yes, I read something to that effect. St Agatha's. My alma mater, though its treatment of me was not very benign. How much is St Agatha's in for?'

'Eighteen million pounds. Almost its total wealth. Peter Wetherby invested it in a corporate bond issued by Farran Group; that is, Max.'

'And now it's worthless, I expect. That man's a fool. Let me offer you a valuable lesson, Imogen, which can be expressed in just seven words. Namely: greed and ignorance are a fatal combination. Remember that. However, eighteen million isn't very much.'

'It sounds like more than pocket-money to me,' Imogen said.

'About the amount of capital you might find in a small to middling business. I suppose St Agatha's is a small to middling business. I've bought and sold outfits worth more than that before breakfast.'

Imogen took a deep breath, suddenly filled with inspired indignation. 'A small to middling business!' she said. 'I'll tell you what St Agatha's is. It's a home of learning built up by a great many people over a great many years. It's an architectural and historical and cultural glory, it's a triumph of mind over time, it's an irreplaceable treasure, that's what it is. It can't be allowed to fail!'

'Your loyalty does you credit,' Sir Julius said. He spoke drily, but he was clearly impressed. 'You know,' he said, 'I could find that amount of money out of my own resources. No problem. I've never been a good college man, but maybe this is my chance. There's nobody and nothing I need to provide for, and I've told you I haven't much of an expectation of life. Why not?'

Imogen said, 'That would be wonderful, but it doesn't seem right to rescue St Ag's and leave all those employees and investors in the lurch.'

'What is Farran Group's deficiency?'

'According to Andrew, when I last spoke to him, the ballpark figure was about four hundred and eighty million, and still counting.'

'That really is money. I'm afraid I don't have four hundred and eighty million in my back pocket.'

'You're the founding father, the heart and soul of the Farran Group if it has one. And you're said to be a world class financial wizard. Can you wave your wand, undo all that damage, put things back as they were?'

Sir Julius said, 'Now you're being absurd. In the real world, complex and difficult problems can't be resolved by wand-waving, much as the politicians would have us believe that they can. Could I rescue Farran Group? The short answer is that I don't know. Without having the full picture, I couldn't even try. I certainly couldn't do it on my own. It might be an interesting challenge. But remember, being dead tends to disqualify one from further action.'

Imogen was silent.

Sir Julius went on after a pause, 'I think all this brings us back to the first question I asked you. What do you propose to do with the information you have?'

Imogen said, 'I have more information now, haven't I? You've told me you committed two murders. There's no getting away from it, my duty is to hand it over to the authorities.'

'To the police? As I said before, they'd probably laugh at you.'

'I don't know about that, but I suppose I'd tell Andrew, and through him Lord Robinswood. And Lord Robinswood would be taken seriously. He has access to all the powers-that-be, certainly up to commissioners of police, probably up to the Home Secretary.'

Sir Julius said, 'If you denounced me, I can assure you I would not be captured and punished. I should be forced to leave my pleasant home here and look for some safer, no doubt more remote sanctuary, far from the brilliant French doctor who looks after me here. It might well be the death of me. My doctor tells me I have no right to be alive in my present condition anyway. And it would certainly remove any prospect of salvation for St Agatha's, let alone the employees and the famous widows and orphans.'

Imogen said, 'You're asking me to keep quiet, aren't you? I can't. Not about two murders.'

'You're a perilously moral person. It could be terminal. Are you really not afraid of ending your life in the River Seine?'

'No.'

'You're quite right not to take fright. I'm not going to dispose of you. I wonder why. I must examine my own motives. Perhaps the reason is that I like you. Are you sure you wouldn't care to join me here in Paris?'

'Sir Julius, please don't joke about this. It's serious.'

'You don't know that I'm joking. But I take it the answer would be a decided negative. Now listen carefully, because I'm going to be very serious indeed. Events are closing in on me, I haven't much time, and I don't intend to be tried for murder. I have something to suggest to you. First, you mentioned Martin Robinswood and Andrew Duncombe. Yes, of course you must tell them what you know. I take it they will believe you?'

'It will shake them to their foundations. But yes, I think they will.'

'You can take them my card, with a signature they'll recognise and a telephone number they can call. And put a proposition to them: that they give me a month and their co-operation, and see if in that time I can start a turnaround for Farran Group. If I haven't visibly achieved anything by then they can denounce me.'

'And if you have achieved?'

'Then don't you think I could be left in peace?'

'Not really. It wouldn't cancel out two murders.'

'Oh, very well. Then let me take my offer to the limit. I don't value the balance of my life at all highly; I've been in contact with a clinic in the Netherlands that would help me out of it if need be. Suppose I say that, win or lose, I will settle my – what's the phrase? – debt to society in a month from now? Unless of course I've died of natural causes before then . . . You're looking unhappy, Imogen. Are you still in moral difficulty?'

'I don't know. I'm confused.'

'You must share your moral dilemma with Martin and Andrew. They have more responsibility than you have. I have to say that for most people getting results is apt to weigh more than ethical considerations. Robinswood's a man of the world, and one of its great fixers. I'm sure he can sort out a moral dilemma.'

Imogen's mind suddenly shot off at a tangent.

'You mentioned a project you intended to take up. What was that?'

'It was a study of fifteenth-century Florence. Does that surprise you? I'm not an illiterate, you know. Even for me, money isn't everything. But I'm afraid it'll never be finished. My health won't stand it.'

'That was the age and place of Machiavelli, wasn't it?'

'And of others, such as a constellation of great artists. Odd that you should mention Machiavelli. Perhaps it indicates your opinion of me. Actually Niccolo Machiavelli *is* rather a hero of mine. I'm studying his writings and the responses to them. There's a wealth of material.'

'Machiavelli thought promises could be broken if not convenient, didn't he?'

'He was, shall we say, flexible.'

'Why should you expect me, or Lord Robinswood, to trust a promise from you?'

'Imogen, my dear, I am not a fifteenth-century Florentine, I am a present-day Yorkshireman. Yorkshiremen are famous for driving a hard bargain. But, having driven their bargain, they can be relied on to keep it. You can trust me. And now I am going to take you out to dinner, at the excellent restaurant on the other bank.'

Imogen, slightly dizzy, said, 'I don't think I should. I'd like to get back to my hotel.'

'You feel you can't touch pitch and not be defiled? Come now, don't be holier-than-thou. A good dinner doesn't commit you to anything. Then you can sleep on the matter, and if you're so inclined you can shop me to the authorities tomorrow morning.'

'On that understanding,' said Imogen, 'yes, thank you. I shall keep an eye on you to see that you don't eat or drink too much.'

'That might be one way to the exit,' said Sir Julius Farran.

21

B ack in Cambridge, Imogen went to bed but not to sleep.
With her mind in a whirl she tossed and turned, read a
couple of chapters of her current bedside book, tossed and
turned again, went downstairs and made herself a cup of tea,
returned to bed and still remained wakeful for what seemed
like hours. Then in the end she fell deeply asleep and slept
until long after her usual time of rising.

The telephone woke her. She didn't at first recognise the
voice.

It was crisp, masculine and urgent.

'Miss Quy?' it said.

'Speaking.'

'Miss Quy! This is Martin Robinswood. What have you
been up to?'

Imogen didn't waste time in asking him what he was talking
about. She said, in the calmest voice she could manage, 'I've
been speaking to Sir Julius Farran on the Ile St Louis.'

'You spoke to a person who said he was Sir Julius Farran.'

'It was Sir Julius Farran. I know him perfectly well.'

'But you realise this is preposterous. Sir Julius has been dead
for six months.'

'It was Sir Julius, and he's certainly alive; at least he was the
other night, when I watched him eat a good dinner. But he's
not in good health. He has a very serious heart problem.'

Lord Robinswood said, 'You're asking me to believe the

impossible. I'm beginning to do so. I had a call from Paris half an hour ago, and it sounded like Julius's voice. I thought it must be an impostor, or a joker. I was about to put the phone down, but the voice positively commanded me not to. And there's just a trace of Yorkshire in Julius's accent that comes out from time to time. You have to know him as well as I do to detect it. That went a long way towards convincing me. But you realise, if he did turn up alive it would set half the financial world into a flat spin? If it really was him, he must have faked his death.'

'He did. I spent an afternoon and evening with him. He gave me a full account. He also gave me his card with his signature on it, to show you in case you didn't believe me. He was as surely Sir Julius Farran as I'm Imogen Quy.'

'He referred me to you,' Lord Robinswood said, 'for further details. He sounded tired and short of breath, and wouldn't stay on the line. And of course I remember you, from that boardroom lunch. Andrew here says you're a reliable witness. But if this is true . . . I don't know whether it's good news or bad news but I do know it's shattering.' He paused for breath, then repeated with emphasis, 'Shattering!'

Imogen said, 'It's shattered me, too. I don't know what I ought to do. Sir Julius said I should share the responsibility with you.'

'I don't think the responsibility is yours to share. I'm the chairman of Farran Group. The buck stops with me. But, Miss Quy, at the moment you know more than I do. Sir Julius said you would tell me the full story. Will you?'

Imogen said, 'I'll do my best.' She had run through it several times in her own mind, and now repeated it, trying not to omit anything.

When she came to the murders, Lord Robinswood broke out in an agonised tone, 'Oh, no, not that!' At the end he said,

'So Julius claims he can pull Farran Group round in a month?'

'Not quite that. But he thought he could turn it round and set it on the upward path.'

'That's still a tall order. It's all I can do to keep it from liquidation. But if anyone could manage it, it would be Julius. Tell Andrew what you've just told me. I need to discuss it all with him.'

Coming on the line, Andrew said, 'I overheard some of that. So Julius faked it and is still alive?'

'He is.'

'And he killed Max?'

'He did.'

'Well, that's one good deed the old villain did, anyway,' Andrew said. 'Does Rowena know?'

'I can't be sure, but I don't think so. Her father hasn't told her, certainly.'

'She's had a terrible time, you know, Imo. She's so sensitive, not a toughie like you. She was desperately upset at the funeral. I don't know which is worse for her, to know or not to know that it was all a fake . . .'

'She may not have a choice,' Imogen said. 'It may all come out anyway.'

'She needs someone to look after her. Could be a job for me, do you think, when all this is over?'

'She and the boys,' Imogen reminded him.

'Oh, yes, the boys. I met them once. Nice kids. Could do with a father; I mean a real father, not like Max. I like boys. Used to love kicking a ball around . . . I wouldn't mind at all being a dad.'

Imogen thought, when he hung up, Does he understand himself any better than he understands me? As an insensitive toughie I'm a total failure. Just now I feel pummelled to a jelly.

★   ★   ★

Lord Robinswood telephoned again half an hour later. His tone was brisk and decisive. 'Miss Quy,' he said, 'you are not, absolutely not, to disclose to anyone what you have discovered about Sir Julius until I tell you you may.'

Imogen bridled. 'Lord Robinswood,' she inquired, 'what right do you have to give me instructions?'

Lord Robinswood said, 'I apologise,' though he didn't sound apologetic. 'Shall we say I most urgently request you not to do so until you hear further from me. This is a matter of such sensitivity, with such huge possible consequences, that we really cannot let the news emerge without the fullest consultation. I must ask you to believe that my request is for the benefit of all concerned. The responsibility, as I said before, is entirely mine. I shall be in touch with you again as soon as possible. Will you accept this assurance?'

'I suppose so,' Imogen said doubtfully.

'Thank you. May I take it you haven't in fact told anyone?'

'Not a soul.'

'Are you aware of anyone who knows?'

'Well, Lady Farran – Lucia – and Dr Random must know about the faking. And Fiona. I'm not aware of anyone else.'

'Fiona won't talk. Lucia and Tim have good reasons not to.'

'I'm unhappy about it,' Imogen said. 'I've always been told that truth will out. I seem to remember a bit of Latin from my schooldays. "*Magna est veritas* . . ."'

'"*Et praevalebit,*"' Lord Robinswood concluded. '"The truth is great and will prevail." I'm afraid there are a good many people around who would greatly prefer that it didn't.'

Empty mugs and crumbs of toast told Imogen that Fran and Josh had breakfasted and gone. It was long after her own breakfast time and she wasn't hungry. Alarm and despondency were settling in on her, and it was a grey, dismal day. She cycled into college, where the atmosphere had no cheer to offer. Dr Barton, the Senior Tutor, whom she encountered crossing the court and invited into her room for coffee, told her that letters were being received by every post from prospective undergraduates who'd been accepted by St Agatha's and had now changed their minds and decided to accept their next-best offers instead.

'They show creditable ingenuity in devising insincere explanations,' he said. 'What they mean is that they're afraid we'll go bust.'

'We shan't really, shall we?'

'No, not quite. But Malcolm says we're peering over the fence and not liking what we see on the other side.'

Imogen hadn't spoken to Malcolm Gracey for several days, and decided to drop in on him in the bursar's office. She found him with weary face and his head down over paperwork. He wasn't optimistic about the chances of recovering the commission paid by Farran Group to Wetherby, and pointed out that in any case seven hundred and twenty thousand pounds didn't go far when set against the likely loss of eighteen million. He had just circulated an apologetic memorandum among the junior dons and research students suggesting reluctantly that if they had attractive job opportunities elsewhere it would be advisable to take them.

'I hate having to do it,' he said, 'and you can imagine the reaction. People I've spoken to have been very forbearing. They know it isn't my fault. I daren't tell you what they're saying about bloody Wetherby. However, you're safe, Imo. You'll be on the payroll again from the start of full term.'

'I'm wondering about my lodger,' Imogen said. 'Frances Bullion.'

Malcolm pulled a face. 'I know Fran, of course,' he said. 'Nice girl. But I'm afraid . . .' He didn't finish the sentence.

★   ★   ★

Imogen stopped off on the way home to lunch and bought strawberries and cream, to which Fran was particularly partial. She reflected ruefully that May Week – that carefree time celebrated, absurdly, in June, when examinations were over and the student world made holiday – was imminent. She would have been going to the May Ball with Malcolm if it hadn't been cancelled. He'd tactfully refrained from mentioning it today, and she supposed he would be spending that night hunched over the college books, or their electronic equivalent.

She found Fran and Josh at home for lunch and sharing a lugubrious bought lasagne. Fran had her copy of Malcom's memorandum on the table in front of her, and pushed it across to Imogen without a word. She looked as if she was managing with some difficulty not to cry. Imogen knew that Fran had the following year's research planned out and was looking forward eagerly to pursuing it. She might now have to get a job. Josh, who'd been attempting clumsily to comfort her, came up with an idea.

'Hey, strawberries and cream!' he said. 'And the sun's coming out. Look, it's the first day of the Bumps. Why don't we take these and a nice cold bottle, and go down and watch the fun?'

The weather was indeed brightening. Imogen seized on the suggestion with rather more enthusiasm than she actually felt. Fran smiled wanly and agreed.

Down on the river, the May races were in full swing. College crews lined up in some half-dozen divisions of seventeen or eighteen boats each and raced, division by division in single file, each crew trying to catch and bump the boat ahead and thereby move a place higher up the river. The boat that headed the top division after the four days of racing would be Head of the River.

The lowest divisions rowed first, and Josh led Imogen and

Fran to Grassy Corner, where the less able and less serious crews were apt to get into tangles, run into the bank, make questionable bumps, shout confused orders at each other and generally keep the bystanders entertained. Later in the afternoon they migrated with other spectators to the finish upstream, where the fastest crews would show their paces. St Agatha's first boat was lying fifth in the top division, the highest it had ever been, and had cherished since last year the ambition of making a bump each day and finishing Head.

Excitement grew as the leading boats appeared. The top three had rowed over with order unchanged; the hope was that St Agatha's would have bumped the fourth. Disappointingly, it hadn't; on the contrary the St Agatha's boat had itself been bumped. Josh, whipping out his mobile, communicated with some unknown power further down the river and swore loudly.

'It's Tony Wilkins! I knew he wasn't up to it as stroke. He's all nerves. And would you believe it, he caught a crab at Ditton Corner and was bumped quicker than you can say "Bloody idiot!" In fact there're two bloody idiots: it's Colin Rampage's fault for cutting all that training and getting himself thrown out of the boat. That puts paid to our chances of going Head.'

Imogen said mildly, 'What a shame.' Fran said nothing. Both of them had matters on their minds from which they'd been briefly diverted. But Josh was loudly disgusted. 'As if it wasn't bad enough the college being ruined,' he complained, 'we have to have bloody Wilkins catching a crab!'

At breakfast time next morning, the phone rang and the caller was Rowena. She was clearly distressed.

'It's my mother, Imogen,' she said. 'She's done something silly. Could you possibly talk to her? She was impressed by you, although she still refers to you as Isabel. She thinks of me as a child. She'll listen to you, but I don't think I can get her to the phone. It confuses her. Look, Imogen, I know this is something of an imposition, but if you happen to be free . . .'

'I'll come right over,' Imogen said.

The first Mrs Farran had been primed for her arrival and seemed stimulated by it. Conversation until lunch was pleasant if inconsequential. After lunch, Rowena said to her mother, 'Why don't you tell Imogen about the Birthday Girls?'

'Oh yes, I should have mentioned them. It was so nice, the Birthday Girls meeting again. You see, Imogen – it is Imogen, isn't it, or is it Isabel? – years and years ago, when we all had children of the same age growing up together and we all lived in Welbourne St Mary, we formed a kind of little group of friends who met in each other's houses and so on, the way one does. There was Eileen and Monica and Alison and me. And we decided we'd have a special lunch together four times a year, on the birthday of each of us in turn, at Hixton House, which is a rather special restaurant a few miles away. So we did for a few years, and we called it the Birthday Girls' Lunch, but when three of us moved away it all lapsed. And then this year Eileen had the wonderful idea of getting us all together once more. The Birthday Girls' Lunch revived! We had it last week!'

The old lady was glowing as she recalled the occasion.

'Of course, we realised it was probably the last. Eileen is going strong, but the rest of us are in poor health for various reasons, and it was quite an effort, though it was worth it!'

She launched into an account of the lunch, course by course, followed by a narration of the activities of her three friends over the years and an analysis of their respective medical conditions. Imogen judged that all this was doing her a power of good.

Eventually Rowena said, 'You haven't mentioned Dr Random.'

'Oh, yes, of course, I should have told Imogen – or is it Isabel? – before, but I'm afraid Dr Random wasn't at the front of my mind. Isn't that awful of me? Yes, you see we were all patients of Dr Random when he was in practice in Welbourne, and we found that three of us – Monica and Alison and I – are still his patients after all these years. We're among the privileged few he's kept on since he gave up practice to take over that place at Eastham where they do such wonders for people who – how shall I put it? – imbibe too freely. And, you know, he does it as a public service, really, and is going to set up a research foundation . . .'

Rowena said, prompting her, 'Wasn't there something about your wills?'

'Oh, yes, that's so interesting. We found we were all helping with the good work, because we've all independently remade our wills so as to leave all we could afford to Dr Random, to support the wonderful work he's doing. After all, none of us are poor, and our children are all grown up and prosperous. Dr Random can really use that money when the time comes.'

She broke off as if a thought had just struck her, and said, 'Of course, I wouldn't have done such a thing if it had meant depriving Rowena, but Rowena, bless her, told me some time ago that she was well provided for and wanted me to do just what I wanted with my own money. And helping Dr Random is just what I want to do. Now, I've been chattering away for long enough. I think it's time I had my rest.'

When she'd left the room, Rowena said, 'I don't like the sound of that, do you?'

'Emphatically, no. I'm horrified. *Are* you still provided for, by the way?'

'Oh, yes. My father carefully ringfenced the money he gave me on marriage. There was no way Max could get his hands on that. But I remember that you had doubts about Tim

Random and would have liked Mother to change her doctor. And now I'm wondering if you know something I don't.'

Imogen said, 'You've never heard anything about Dr Random's past?'

'I've always known there was something a bit dubious, but it was long ago and my father said he'd lived it down. And Mother's so devoted to him, I hadn't the heart to wrench her away. But when a doctor persuades old ladies to change their wills in his favour . . . well, frankly, I'm scared.'

'You're right to be,' Imogen said. 'He's a persuasive man. He persuaded me he'd become as pure as the driven snow. But now I'm going to tell you what I know about his former history. I'm afraid it may shake you still further.'

When she'd finished, Rowena said, 'What do we do now?'

'This is too much for me to handle,' Imogen said. 'It's one for the police. Luckily I have a friend there. He'll be more than interested.'

Rowena said, 'I can't tell you what a comfort you are. I'm isolated here, you know, apart from Mother, and she's a responsibility rather than a support.'

'Are you keeping in touch with Andrew?'

'Not really. He's always busy. He's got so much on his plate. When I speak to him on the phone he's so harassed. I just wish I could see him here in the flesh. See him and touch him.'

'You told me you could be serious about Andrew.'

'Yes. I know now, I could.'

'He seems to be working every minute of the day,' Imogen said. 'But it must be possible for him to have a break some time. Leave it to me. Leave everything to me.'

Back at home, she tried to telephone Andrew but found he was once again unavailable. She had better luck with Mike Parsons, who listened patiently, unshockably, to what she could tell him about Dr Random.

'You do get into things, Imo,' he observed. 'But with a track record like yours . . . Yes, of course I take it seriously. It's not in my parish. You remember I have a mate at Eastham? I'll get him to look into it for a start. He'll find out what they know about this Dr Random. It sounds as if they should be on to something if they're not already. Three old ladies changing their wills in favour of a doctor with a past . . . The name Random rings a bell somewhere . . .'

'He identified the body of Sir Julius Farran.'

'That's right, I remember now. You thought there was something fishy about it and I thought you were wrong for once. Hey, I suppose it isn't on the cards that your Dr Random killed Sir Julius?'

'I'm quite sure he didn't,' Imogen said.

22

Imogen telephoned Andrew at eight the next morning and this time got through to him. As soon as he heard her voice he interrupted.

'Imo! Have you seen today's papers?'

'Not yet.'

'Sensation. Bionomials shares have rebounded. Dr Biebner has come out of his retreat in Maine – or was it Alaska? – and is handing his patents back to the company. He says it was an oversight that they stayed with him personally. Nobody believes it, of course. Nobody knows what to believe, except Martin Robinswood and me. We know that it's Julius's doing. He and Biebner have a long and complicated relationship. Julius has scratched his back or squeezed his arm or something, and this is the result. As Farran Group is for better or worse the parent company, we get a rebound too.'

'Does that mean the crisis is over?'

'Not that, I'm afraid. There's still a question mark over the new drug. But it's a start. We're off the floor. St Agatha's bond may be worth something yet. We shall see how it goes.'

'Is there a decision yet about whether Sir Julius is to be exposed or kept under wraps?'

'I have a message for you from his lordship. He says it would be madness to blow the gaff now when things seem to be taking an upward turn and Julius may still have shots in the locker. He asks you to trust him and hold on for the present.

He insists that it's his responsibility and you have nothing to worry about.'

'I worry about the morality of it.'

'A conscience like yours must be quite a handicap. Honestly, Imo, we have to let it run for a while. Confidence is everything in the markets. And didn't Julius ask for a month?'

'Yes, he did.'

'Leave it, then. Look, do you understand, this is good news. G-O-O-D news. Martin will be in touch with you himself, I can promise you.'

Imogen changed the subject. 'Rowena's in distress, Andrew. She doesn't know that Julius is alive. She's still at a loss without him and upset over Max's horrible death. And now she has a worry over her mother, who's made a will in favour of Dr Random.'

Andrew's sympathy was instant. 'I need to go to her,' he said. 'And Martin knows it's high time I had a day off. I'll manage it within a day or two. I'm aching to see her, Imo, honestly, I'm just aching.'

'Go to her and ache no more,' said Imogen; but she felt a slight ache in herself.

It was still not nine o'clock. Imogen went to the senior common room, where the newspapers had arrived and there was a buzz of conversation, hopeful-sounding at last. As a news story, Bionomials' recovery of its patents hadn't been dramatic enough to make the front page of any paper except the *Financial Times*, though it was prominent in the business pages. Imogen looked around in vain for Malcolm Gracey, wondering if he had seen it. He was not there, and she walked across the court to the bursar's room, expecting to find him at work.

She tapped and pushed the door open, and then recoiled in

astonishment. Malcolm was at his desk, and standing beside him was the tall, lean figure of the bursar himself.

Peter Wetherby was not the upright, self-possessed and aloof-looking person she remembered. His face was white and drawn, his manner nervous, his expression slightly hangdog. He looked at Imogen but said nothing.

Malcolm rose from his desk and said, in a formal tone, 'Miss Quy! I'm glad you have arrived just now. We are having a conversation which I think requires a witness. As you see, Mr Wetherby has returned. He has brought something with him.'

Wetherby said, in his dry, usually precise voice which now sounded uncertain, 'I have brought two things with me. One is my letter of resignation as bursar of St Agatha's. The other is a banker's draft.'

Malcolm pushed a piece of paper across the desk to Imogen. She picked it up and looked at it. It was a draft drawn on one of the big banks in favour of St Agatha's College, and was for the sum of seven hundred and twenty thousand pounds.

'One doesn't like to entrust an item of this size to the mails,' Wetherby said, 'or I would have spared myself this interview. It is the commission I received from the Farran Group for negotiating the issue of a bond for eighteen million. Four per cent is not a high rate of commission, but it adds up.'

'It certainly does!' Imogen said. She had never seen anything like such a sum of money in her life.

'I don't know how you had the nerve,' Malcolm said to Wetherby. 'Or the greed.'

'Making that amount of money by means of a single act is a big temptation,' said Wetherby. 'I won't spell out to you in detail the reasons I had for succumbing: a rapacious ex-wife, a schizophrenic son, a large mortgage and many debts. I don't ask for sympathy. I am merely, as you see, returning the money.'

'We would have pursued you for it,' Malcolm said.

'I think you'd have had some difficulty. But I regret what I did. It will cost me heavily. I was already in trouble with my professional body – that's why I had to leave my former job and was willing to come to St Agatha's for half the salary – and I've no doubt that I shall be struck off its register. However, you needn't allow me the luxury of self-pity. I've found myself a clerical job in the West Midlands, and can survive.'

Imogen sensed that the man was in fact sorry for himself, and to her surprise felt some degree of sympathy.

Malcolm was made of sterner stuff. 'You can't walk away just like that,' he said.

'It's not actually a crime to take a commission on a deal.'

'Come off it. You were in breach of your duty to the college.'

'The letter now in your hand is addressed to the Master. It's a resignation and a full apology. It's up to him, or perhaps to the Governing Body, what he does about it.'

'I believe the Master is in college and at the lodge. Shall we go and take your letter to him in person?'

'I don't wish to see the Master. It wouldn't be an agreeable occasion for either of us. You can hand him the letter. I shall just fold my tents and go.'

'Well, I don't suppose I can arrest you,' said Malcolm, sounding as if he would have liked to do so. 'But I want your address, please.'

'It's on the letter,' said Peter Wetherby. 'Excuse me, Miss Quy, would you please stand aside? I'm on my way out.'

'So the fellow has a conscience after all!' said the Master.

'I doubt it,' said Malcolm. 'If the crash hadn't happened, he'd have got away with that monstrous commission. It was in Farran Group's books, not the college's. After the crash it had to come out, and did. He must have realised he couldn't hide himself away for long. He was acting in his own best interest by handing back the money.'

'You're a cynic, Malcolm,' the Master said. 'I prefer to take a charitable view. The poor fellow must have had a sad and anxious time. How could he not have been deeply troubled in his mind?'

'So what will you do, Master?'

'It rests with the Governing Body, not with me. I spoke the other day to Professor Sutherland, and he thought as a lawyer that Wetherby when found would certainly be open to civil and probably to criminal proceedings. But that was before he repaid his ill-gotten gain. I can't feel it would be good for the college to initiate any action against him. That's the line I shall take.'

Malcolm looked across at Imogen and made a despairing gesture. The Master intercepted the look.

'You think I'm an old softie,' he said. 'Well, maybe. I've lived a long time. Taking a hard line becomes less appealing. We shall see what happens. Now, are you two free this evening by any chance? Caroline and I will be having a quiet supper together in the lodge, which does happen occasionally. Would you like to join us? She'd be delighted. And we will try not to talk about the crisis.'

Malcolm and Imogen accepted gladly. 'But as for not talking about the crisis,' Imogen said, 'do you think that's possible?'

'Well, no, not really,' said Sir William ruefully.

On her way back across Fountain Court, Imogen encountered Carl Janner.

'You've heard the news, Carl?'

'Of course. And I'm tracking it on the web. The climb-back is continuing this morning.'

'And how does it affect your publishing project?'

'Favourably,' Carl said.

'Don't just give me that smug smile, Carl. Tell me why.'

'It's keeping Farran in the news. With luck there'll be more cliffhanging days ahead. And for us all news is good news. If Robinswood saves the day, that's headlines. And if it all goes pear-shaped again, that's headlines too. A win-win situation. Our publishers have upped the print order already.'

'I expect you're going to make a lot of money. Does it worry you, the contradiction of being a rich socialist? Shouldn't you give up either the riches or the socialism?'

'An old question, and I'll give you an old answer. It's perfectly possible to be both. You can use the riches to advance the socialism.'

'And cut off the branch you're sitting on? Or is it that your socialism is for other people while you yourself live a comfortable bourgeois life? I'd say that puts you in a morally exposed position.'

'It's all been said before, my dear. And will all be said again.'

'And you'll go on your way rejoicing.'

'I'm rejoicing at the moment. By the way, I was speaking to Bob Dacre the other day. He remembers your visit to Tuesday Market, and sends his regards.'

'How is he getting on?'

'Oh, rather well. He's seen a proof of our book and likes it; says so far as he's concerned old scores are now settled. He's congratulating himself that when he sold the business he took cash instead of the alternative, which was shares in Farran Group. And it seems young Derek has found a girlfriend and Bob's convinced he's going to marry her, though personally I hope she'll have more sense. Bob's dreaming of buying him a house conveniently nearby, setting him up in business in the town, and having grandchildren. He may be deceiving himself, but for the moment he's a happy man.'

'Good luck to him,' said Imogen.

Going home for lunch, she found Fran composed though still looking doleful, and had the pleasure of telling her that things seemed to be looking up. Josh, always optimistic and inclined to think that the worst would never actually happen, was quickly convinced that all would soon be well. His mind was a mile or two away: on the riverbank.

'We didn't see you last night, Imo,' he said. 'It's great news. Colin Rampage is stroking the college first boat. The captain of boats swallowed hard and asked him to take over. And yesterday we reversed Wednesday's bump. Caught them easily on the Long Reach. So we're back where we started. But with only two days left we can't go Head. At least, not this year. But next year, well, Colin will still be available. We'll make it then!'

Supper with Sir William and Lady B. was a pleasure, and none the worse for the congenial company of Malcolm. On Saturday morning, Andrew telephoned.

'Farran stayed on the upward path all day yesterday,' he said, 'and today's not a trading day. There's still a long way to go. Let's hope it continues on Monday.'

'I shall be in the Lakes by then,' Imogen said. 'I'm going on a walking holiday with Lucy and Emma. Had you forgotten?'

'No.'

'I bet you had. Anyway, we leave tomorrow morning. Two weeks of bliss, away from it all.'

'Well, my news is that I've actually got a day off,' Andrew said, 'today as ever was. You can guess what I'm doing with it.'

'Making a beeline for Welbourne All Saints and Rowena.'

'Got it in one. How do you think I'll make out with her?'

'I don't know exactly what you mean by making out. It's a suggestive phrase. But I'm sure Rowena is fond of you.'

'Imo, my intentions are, to coin a phrase, honourable.'

'What was it the man said in the Fielding novel? "His designs were honourable, namely to rob a lady of her fortune by means of marriage." I hope that's not what you have in mind.'

'Don't dare say such things. I want to marry her, repeat, I want to marry her, and not for her money.'

'She might come without any. It's possible she'll throw it into the Farran pot as a matter of conscience. She's spoken of that.'

'Perhaps that's a bit less likely now than it was a few days ago. But, Imo, I'd want to marry her if she hadn't a penny.'

'You're in the starry-eyed phase.'

'I know what you're thinking. My first marriage failed horribly. But I've learned a lot since then, thanks partly to you. With Rowena I could make it work. Wish me luck.'

'Dear Andrew, of course I wish you luck. And I wish her luck as well.' She hoped the last remark wouldn't be taken as carrying an innuendo that Rowena would need it.

And it wouldn't have done at all for him to marry me, she thought.

Andrew said, 'Thank you, Imo. May I ring you tonight and tell you how I've got on?'

'Yes, please. I'll be packing my rucksack for the Lakes. Don't leave it too late; we're starting early.'

He rang as promised. The message was brief. 'Everything's fine. I'm staying overnight.'

23

Imogen spent two happy weeks of assorted sunshine, wind and rain with Emma and Lucy in the Lake District. They walked round Derwentwater and Buttermere and Loweswater; climbed up Catbells and over Haystacks, visited the haunts of Wordsworth and Ruskin, drove to deep Wastwater and busy Bowness. They swam in Crummock Water, saw a play at the Theatre by the Lake in Keswick, bought gingerbread in Grasmere village and silly things in tourist shops. They stayed mainly in bed and breakfasts, never read a newspaper, and saw little of the news but television headlines.

Imogen's recent worries, distant geographically, seemed also to dwindle in her mind and to become slight and far away. She returned to Cambridge sun-tanned and feeling fit and reinvigorated, and was met by Fran with the words 'Look at this!' It was a circular from Malcolm Gracey to recipients of his warnings, advising them not to act too hastily because it seemed that all might not be lost after all. When Fran had danced out of the house, dragging Josh by the hand to celebrate at the pub, Imogen rang Malcolm.

'I feel a bit of a Charlie, blowing hot and cold,' he said, 'but I couldn't let people go on suffering when things are looking quite good after all.'

Imogen asked whether Belinda Mayhew and two or three other friends had received the hopeful news, and was assured that they had.

There was a stack of letters, which she decided could be left to mature for a day or two, and there were four messages on voice mail, which she played. The first was from Andrew, early in her time of absence, and consisted solely of the words 'Joy, oh joy!' She smiled and moved on. The second call, made a week later, was from Rowena, whose voice sounded distressed. Imogen rang her at once.

Rowena said, 'Imogen, you're back from holiday. I can't tell you how glad I am to speak to you. Imogen, I know my father is a alive. And I know you know.'

'How did you find out?'

'I saw him! Otherwise I wouldn't have believed it. It was such a shock, I can still hardly believe it. I saw him, Imogen, only a few days ago. I was here at Welbourne, at the piano, and he came into the room, quite silently. I turned, and there he was. I felt as if I'd seen a ghost. He stood there beside me and he said one word, "Beautiful." He meant the Schubert of course, not me.'

Imogen asked the first question that occurred to her: 'How was he?'

'He looked very poorly. He told me about the quadruple bypass and about his doctor's warning. He gave me the impression that he hadn't long to live. But I was so bowled over by seeing him alive that I couldn't really take it in.'

Imogen said, greatly daring, 'Are you glad you've seen him?'

'The honest answer is, I don't know. I'd wept for him once, and learned to live with his death. It's possible I'd have been happier left in the dark. It doesn't seem there's any future in it. He said I would never see him again. He wouldn't stay, and he forbade me to follow him.

'He had a message, though, and it was a bit odd. He said he thought I'd never known he loved me. And of course I knew he loved me, I'd always known. How could he have been so unperceptive? But he was a strange man, of course. I knew he wasn't a good man, I knew how hard and ruthless he could be. I was ashamed of him often, but he was my father. Still is, I suppose. I wish I knew what will become of him.'

Imogen said, 'You must have talked to Andrew about it.'

'Of course. And I found that Andrew knew already. It seems Martin Robinswood had more or less ordered him not to tell. I think Andrew should have refused the order. We almost had our first tiff about it. I love Andrew, he's bright and witty and affectionate, and he's musical, but he's not a strong character. And he hadn't understood how it would feel to me. I suppose men do tend to be a little short on emotional intelligence.'

'I've noticed the phenomenon,' Imogen said.

'But I shall marry Andrew if he asks me, and if he doesn't I shall ask him.'

'Then he's a lucky man. You're going to be the strong one, Rowena. Keep a firm grip on him and he'll be a good husband.'

'Imogen, I know you were close to him at one time. I haven't the right to ask, but did you ever think of . . .'

'Marrying Andrew? Well, I admit the thought crossed my mind from time to time, but it went away again. It wouldn't have done for either of us.'

Rowena said, 'Andrew and I are both going to see Martin Robinswood tomorrow. He's fixed up a crucial meeting. Andrew's sure Martin will be asking you to be there. I do hope you can make it. And, Imogen, let's get together again as soon as we can.'

'Trust me,' Imogen said.

The third voice mail message, from Lord Robinswood, was a request to ring him as soon as possible on his private number. His voice, when he answered her, was more cordial than before. 'I shall call you Imogen if I may,' he said. 'My name is Martin.' He inquired about her holiday, then asked whether she had been keeping up with the news. Imogen said she hadn't.

'You'll be glad to know,' he told her, 'that the recovery of Farran Group has continued. The likelihood is that in the end all debts will be repaid, including the St Agatha's bond. I've been getting a great deal of undeserved credit. Actually the principal factor is that since Dr Biebner handed those patents back to Bionomials the prospects of getting approval for the crucial drug have mysteriously improved. Whether it's chance or influence or some intricate machination I don't really know. I'm inclined to suspect that it's the last of these and that Julius is behind it somewhere.'

'So you think Julius has delivered the goods?'

'I do. But in the last few days we've lost touch with him. Either Andrew or I had been ringing him in Paris every day, but suddenly, without warning, he went off the line. His telephone wasn't answered.'

'He might be ill,' Imogen said.

'That occurred to us. We have contacts in Paris, of course, and we sent an agent to the Ile St Louis address. He found that M. le Docteur had vanished overnight, leaving no trace except an envelope addressed to his housekeeper and containing a sizeable gift of money. The housekeeper is deaf and bewildered and can't provide any information.'

Imogen said, 'You know what he promised.'

'That he'd settle his debt to society. If you thought that meant he'd take his own life, I always had my doubts whether he'd carry it out. He's let you down. Are you surprised?'

'Yes, I am, actually. I thought he did mean that. However, he'd also told me how easily, as he put it, he could be over the hills and far away.'

'Well, there we are. We're left with a problem; at least,

Andrew and I are. Do we go on keeping the truth about Julius from coming out, and if so, for how long? I think really we're in your hands, Imogen, since although you might have a hard time at first in getting yourself believed, you'd be able to do so eventually, and we'd be in trouble. Even with Julius himself still missing, there would be convincing proof available that his death was faked – an exhumation, for instance. And anyway the question would soon be put to me and I wouldn't be able to deny it. So I think the next step has to be a conference of those who know what the truth is, to decide what we do next. And those who know now include Rowena.'

'I know. I've just been speaking to her.'

'I've asked her and Andrew, and Lucia and Tim, to come to my flat at twelve noon tomorrow. Fiona will be there, of course; she also knows. It's very short notice for you, Imogen, but the matter's urgent and I hope very much you can make it. Can you?'

'I can and will,' she said.

The fourth message was from Mike Parsons and was another request to call back. She did so at once.

'Imo,' Mike said, 'you've been taken in by a con man. Your precious Dr Random hasn't been washed white as snow at all. His true colour is dirty grey. It wasn't true that he was allowed to stay on the medical register. He was acquitted of murder but struck off for all kinds of bad behaviour in the events surrounding the affair. He hasn't any right to call himself a doctor, and neither Eastham police nor the medical authorities knew about his past.'

'Oh my God, how could I have been so dumb?' Imogen said.

'You just took his word for it all, didn't you?' said Mike.

'He was so convincing, I swallowed it hook, line and sinker. I didn't think to check. Of course I should have done.'

'Most of us believe what we're told most of the time, or the world wouldn't go round. Still, next time you read about people being fooled by a plausible liar, you'll know how easy it is. Don't fret, love. You've done a public service by putting us wise to him.'

'What about those old ladies I told you about, the Birthday Girls?'

'They'll be all right. There's no charge laid against Snetterton alias Random at the moment, and it may take a while before there's a case for prosecution, but we have our ways of looking after people at risk. I'll keep you in touch.'

Imogen hung up, chagrined by her own credulity; and as she struggled to come to terms with all the information she'd just been given the recent pleasures of the Lake District were pushed ruthlessly out of her mind. She was in turmoil over the weight of the decisions to be made.

24

I n his apartment overlooking Green Park, Lord Robinswood greeted his guests courteously. Imogen arrived a little
early. Fiona was already there, looking very much at home and
dressed with the most stylish of casual chic. Five minutes later
Andrew and Rowena arrived, and, almost before the door had
closed behind them, Lucia and Tim Random. The atmosphere was uneasy. Though most of those present knew each
other well they had little to say to one another and no one
seemed pleased to be at the meeting. Lord Robinswood,
however, did not appear to notice any frigidity, spoke affably
to all and poured champagne.

'You may all congratulate me,' he said. 'Fiona and I are
engaged to be married.'

Fiona took his hand, looking happy and pleased with
herself. Imogen caught her eye and was sure they were both
remembering their recent conversation in Cambridge. You
have to hand it to the girl, she thought; she certainly gets to
where she wants to go.

Lord Robinswood invited everyone to sit, and himself
settled into an armchair obviously placed to show that its
occupant was in charge of the proceedings. He seemed quite at
ease, with the manner of a diplomat who has come through
many crises and is undaunted by the thought of one more.

'You all know why I have asked you to be here,' he said. 'I
am now, for my sins, the chairman of the Farran Group, and

we in this room are the ones – the only ones, apart from Peter Wetherby – who know that Sir Julius is still alive. We have to decide what to do about it. I have here a letter from Wetherby saying he doesn't wish to take part in our discussion and will accept whatever we decide. He seems to have gone to earth, somewhere in the West Midlands. I doubt we shall ever hear from him again.'

Tim Random said, 'I am here under protest. I don't see how there can be any question. There is only one course of action we can take: namely, none. So far as the world is concerned, Julius is dead. An inquest was held and arrived at a verdict. Nobody has queried it; nobody has any reason to query it. Julius is not going to denounce himself. For heaven's sake, let's be thankful that so much of the damage done by Max has been retrieved, and let sleeping dogs lie!'

Lord Robinswood said, 'I can't close down the discussion just like that. We're talking about a matter that's already caused huge concern and publicity, and could cause world-wide scandal. There are all sorts of issues involved, both moral and practical, and we have to address them.'

Tim Random said, 'Don't be a hypocrite, Martin. Never mind moral issues; when the chips are down we just have to look out for ourselves.'

Andrew said, 'I can understand Tim's attitude. He and Lucia have a lot to lose. If the truth came out they'd be in deep trouble for giving false evidence and conspiring to pervert the course of justice. Incidentally, their marriage would be invalidated and they'd be in the dock for bigamy. It's not surprising that they want it all kept dark. But by aiding and abetting Julius they set moving the whole train of horrors, and it's fair to say that any consequences were brought on themselves. There may be a case for concealment, but I don't think we should opt for it on their account.'

Tim Random bristled. 'I know you, Duncombe!' he said. 'You were sniffing around Headlands in company with Miss Quy. I hope this meeting is not going to take any nonsense from that woman. I have to say that she is not only inquisitive and interfering, she is malign. I have just had intrusive and possibly damaging inquiries made by the local police into another matter, and I believe they were inspired by her.'

Lord Robinswood, unruffled, said, 'Please, Tim, allow me to stick to the present issue. As I was saying, there are moral and practical questions involved, and some issues that are both. Perhaps the first thing we have to consider is whether we *can* keep everything dark. There's a saying that the truth will out, and one can never be sure that it won't emerge from some unexpected quarter. As you pointed out, there has never been any suspicion over Julius's death. Apart from Wetherby, who has abundant reasons for lying low, we don't know of anyone outside this room who knows that the dead man wasn't Julius. But the evidence will be there in his grave for centuries to come. And something might come out as a result of investigations into the murder of Max, although as I understand it the police are not getting anywhere and it's quietly sinking out of sight.

'Overall, it's a question of risk assessment, and risk assessment in these circumstances is guesswork. For what it's worth, my guess is that there is a ninety per cent chance that if we keep quiet Julius will, so to speak, stay dead.'

Nobody contested this proposition. Lord Robinswood went on, 'What we have to decide is whether to speak now or for ever hold our peace. It's an either/or question, and I for one am not prepared to leave it open. The next practical issue is, what are the respective costs and benefits of bringing the facts into the open?

'As chairman of Farran, I suppose my duty is to put the

interests of Farran's employees and shareholders first. At present, things are going rather well, and I am being regarded as a miracle worker. The City is looking kindly on me. It rates confidence highly and hates uncertainty. A resurrection of the late and much reviled Julius Farran at the heart of an enormous scandal would, to put it mildly, not be welcome to the City and in the short and medium term would do a lot of damage.

'There would certainly be a heavy personal cost to Tim and Lucia. There could also be serious trouble for Andrew and myself as directors of Farran; it could be said that we have a broader duty of disclosure regardless of the consequences.

'The next question: who would benefit from disclosure? It wouldn't bring Max Holwood or the unfortunate Charlie at Eastham back to life. It wouldn't, in my view, benefit the staffs and shareholders just mentioned. So what benefit would there be? This is where we move from practical to moral considerations. Is there an absolute and all-overriding obligation to Truth with a capital letter: that it must prevail because it is an unquestionable good in its own right? Miss Quy, you have listened patiently to my exposition, but I think you have strong views on this.'

Imogen said, 'I'm not a moral philosopher and I haven't thought about it in abstract terms. What troubles me is that Julius Farran by his own admission has murdered two people. It would stick in my throat to say, "Well, we'll let this pass because it causes problems if we report it." Without putting capital letters to the word Truth, I do think we have a duty. You could call it a public duty.'

Lord Robinswood said, 'That is in fact the absolutist case.'

'Well, not absolutely,' Imogen said. 'If it was a minor matter I mightn't be too fussy. But murder is murder.'

Fiona asked, 'Am I being consulted?'

Lord Robinswood said, 'Of course.'

'Well, I think if Julius has got away, good luck to him. I know he was an utter bastard in all sorts of ways, but he did have another side to him. I got a letter from him yesterday. He says, "Keep the money, it's yours. You were fun while you lasted." That's generous, considering how I treated him.'

Imogen asked, '*Are* you going to keep the money?'

'No, I'll throw it into the Farran kitty, except for what I've spent. I can afford to. I'm going to marry a rich man, aren't I, Martin?'

Lord Robinswood smiled rather thinly.

Andrew said, 'The person we absolutely have to consult is Rowena.'

Rowena had been looking increasingly distressed. She said, 'Of course in principle I agree with Imogen. But it's a desperately hard principle to apply. I know my father did terrible things and I can't defend them. But when all's said and done, he is my father, and he's old and ill. How could I say, "Yes, let them hunt him down," even for such a principle? Especially when it doesn't seem to hurt anyone else to let things stay as they are?'

Imogen said, 'They probably wouldn't catch him. He told me he had multiple passports and European frontiers are porous. I'm sure he knows the necessary strategies for getting away.'

'Yes, but still . . . to have my father a hunted criminal, a known murderer, and in even deeper disgrace . . . Well, I've no right to oppose it but I can't pretend it wouldn't hurt horribly. And then, there's the effect on the boys.'

Tim Random observed sourly, 'It's all very well for Rowena to talk. Whatever happens, she's in the clear. And Julius made sure he provided abundantly for her outside the firm.'

Rowena said, 'He gave me the house as a wedding present,

and I'm keeping that. I shall steer the rest back into Farran Group as soon as the lawyers can sort out how to do it. I can get a job teaching piano. It will be the first time I've earned my living, and I'm looking forward to it.'

Lord Robinswood said, 'Well, Imogen, it devolves on you in the end. It seems that from a practical standpoint no one anywhere would benefit from a disclosure. No one can prevent you from doing as you yourself think right, but perhaps you should ask yourself whether you ought to hold on to your own moral rectitude if it is at the expense of others. A difficult question, but one that you must face.'

Imogen said, 'You're a very clever man, Lord Robinswood. You've managed to shift the moral burden from the rest of you on to me. For the moment I'm at a loss. As you say, it's an either/or situation and I'm in it; either I act or I don't. There isn't a compromise. How long have I got to decide?'

'Not very long, I'm afraid. If there's a dramatic announcement to be made, then it's up to me and I mustn't delay it.'

The silence in the room was audible. Into the midst of it broke the opening notes of *Eine Kleine Nachtmusik*. They came from Imogen's handbag.

'Damn!' she said. 'I'm sorry. I forgot to switch the mobile off.'

'Take your call in the hallway,' suggested Lord Robinswood.

Glad to have even a short break, Imogen slipped out of the room. The caller was Mike. Imogen sat down in a deep armchair conveniently placed in the carpeted corridor beside a table with a flower arrangement on it.

'Good moment?' Mike asked.

'Well, not exactly,' Imogen said.

'I'll be quick. I just want to let you know,' Mike said, 'my pal at Eastham says they're following up massively on Random.

He may or may not have done anything wrong in the last few years, apart from pretending to be a doctor when he isn't one, but if he intended any jiggery-pokery with old ladies and their wills he'll have been thoroughly warned off it now. You and your friend can sleep sound of nights.'

'That's a relief,' Imogen said. 'Thank you, Mike.'

'And, Imo, just as a matter of interest, there's been another death by falling at Hell's Elbow. Not an important person this time; only an old tramp who'd been missing for months. His friend, Ben Somebody-or-other, identified him. There'll be more outcry about the spot being dangerous, but there you are.'

'Thank you again, Mike,' Imogen said, and switched off the mobile. She was thinking hard as she slipped it back in her handbag.

An old tramp who's been missing for months? That sounds like Charlie. A friend called Ben who's identified him? It must be the Ben I met, and it must be the Charlie he told me about. There couldn't be two Bens and two Charlies. But Charlie's dead. It doesn't make sense.

Then it dawned on her. When she'd upbraided Julius Farran over the death of Charlie, she'd mentioned Ben to him. Julius had been in England and visited Rowena. Perhaps he'd had one more thing to do. One last thing.

Julius had rewarded his housekeeper generously. He would have rewarded Ben generously. For the use of Charlie's clothes. For the identification.

With the shock of surprise came a wave of relief. The moral burden rolled away from her. There was no longer a question of bringing Julius to book for his misdeeds. Julius had avenged himself. It was all over.

Imogen went back into the room. 'Sorry to keep you waiting,' she said. 'I've been making up my mind, and I've done so.

I agree with the meeting that there's nothing to be gained by making it all public. Sir Julius Farran won't be seen again. In his own words, he's over the hills and far away. The moral problem's been overtaken by events. It's for the best if we just let the years grow over it. Whether that's the right decision I'll never know, but I've made it.'

'And we shall all applaud you,' said Lord Robinswood.

25

T he gathering broke up with relief rather than cordiality. Lord Robinswood and his fiancée did not press anyone to stay. Out on the pavement, Tim Random grabbed the first taxi, and he and Lucia disappeared without a word of farewell. Imogen reflected grimly that Random was still heading for trouble, and it served him right.

Rowena, her arm tucked into Andrew's, said, 'Why don't we three walk in the park?'

There had been an early faint haze, but the day was now clear and fine. It was going to be lovely, though the leaves were beginning to fall, first intimations of the year's mortality.

Rowena said, 'Imogen, there's a strange look on your face. What are you thinking?'

Imogen took a deep breath. 'My dear,' she said, 'I must tell you and Andrew what I didn't need to tell the others. Your father is dead.'

Rowena stopped in her tracks.

'He's dead? My father? How do you know? When did it happen? *How* did it happen?'

Imogen told her. When she had finished, Rowena had tears in her eyes, but didn't weep. She asked, 'What would it be *like*, to die like that?'

Imogen said, 'No one can know. But it was a hundred-foot sheer fall on to rocks. It would have killed him instantly. It wasn't a bad way to go.'

Rowena was silent for a moment. They were passing a park bench, and Andrew drew her down on to it. Imogen sat at her other side.

Rowena said, 'I'm sure you're right. He was a very sick man when I saw him last, but he would know what he was doing. And you know, Imogen, I'm not really surprised. I had a feeling he might not still be alive, and I'm glad in a way to be put out of doubt.'

Andrew put his arm round Rowena. 'Cry if you want to,' he said.

'I shan't,' Rowena said. 'I did my grieving before, at Welbourne St Mary, a lifetime ago. I shan't need to do it again.'

But she was weeping now, her head on his shoulder. Two were company; three, on this occasion, were not.

Imogen said, 'I'm so silly. I forgot, I have to see somebody, right now. I must dash.'

They didn't try to prevent her. They said their good-byes, amid promises of further meetings. Kisses were exchanged. Imogen went quickly away without looking back, walking through the dappled shadows cast by the plane trees over the path, heading for the Tube station that would take her to King's Cross, and from there to Cambridge, alone.